Seamwalker

Kingdom of Crowns series, book three
an epic sword & sorcery novel
by Paul Yoder

You can contact me at:
authorpaulyoder@gmail.com

Visit me online for launch dates and other news at:
authorpaulyoder.com
tiktok.com: @authorpaulyoder
instagram.com: author paul yoder
amazon: paul yoder
goodreads: paul yoder

ISBN: 9798334233294

D1713667

Lands of Wanderlust Novels

Paul Yoder

Lords of the Deep Hells Trilogy
Shadow of the Arisen
Lords of the Sands
Heart of the Maiden

Kingdom of Crowns Trilogy
The Rediron Warp
Firebrands
Seamwalker

LANDS
OF
WANDERLUST
By
Paul Yoder

SEAMWALKER

Kingdom of Crowns trilogy
Book Three

THE CROWNED KINGDOMS

Prologue

"What fortuitous timing for you to grow a backbone and finally decide to involve yourself. Surely Sareth has warned you of our rising dominance in the region. I'm curious, were you too scared to heed her call or too out of touch with your own god to hear her warning cries?" the prophet spat, looking down upon the once proud saren matron, now broken before him.

Shackled and locked in a pillory at the base of a giant obsidian statue, High Priestess Trensa struggled futilely in her bindings while the two saren priestesses next to her screamed in agony as they were flayed alive, ending in a disquieting gurgle of blood.

She strained in the iron clamp that held her in place, barely able to turn her head enough to see a grotesque bundle of flesh where one of her sisters in the faith had been shackled just moments ago.

"No!" the elderly saren screamed, now hearing only silence from her companions after the Seam-scarred zealot finished warping them into unrecognizable piles of gore by the supernatural powers of the enigmatic god, Umbraz.

"You held your composure through the other ninety-seven sacrifices this day. Do you only care about your saren sisters?" the prophet asked, standing over her. He lifted her head to look into her tear-streaked eyes.

"You bastard," she groaned at the old prophet, one that she had in years past, sat across from in city council meetings. She had never liked the man, but she could hardly believe what absolute depravity the prophet of Elendium had sunk to.

"Sareth will hold you accountable for those deaths, Yunus. You will be brought low for this," she seethed, struggling vainly once more at her yoke, only managing to rub her skin bloody and raw along her neck and wrists.

"She may hold me accountable, yes; but there's nothing she can do to prevent the coming of our god into this world. Even now, his body is being prepared," the prophet whispered as he looked down upon the ragged woman. He stepped aside to allow her a view of the large stone statue looming before her. "And this time, we rely not upon secrecy but of the security of strength to ensure what happened in Rosewood does not happen a second time to our blessed god's fetus."

He smiled, savoring her distress. "You will nourish him this day—our fledgling god. You will help usher him into this realm. One day, very soon, we'll no longer pray and sacrifice souls to a statue, but a living being among us—"

The Seam-scarred zealot croaked incoherently, disrupting the prophet's monologue.

The prophet looked with a judging, cruel eye at the misshapen man at his side. The mutant was once a reverend father of the church, essential in the effort that had got the church to its position of dominance in the region. Now, scars and veins of Seam light distorted his figure. He seemed hardly human at all—a mere executioner with a single function: to warp the flesh of those the prophet placed in front of him.

The prophet's demeanor reset, now ready to finish the day's quota of sacrifices. "It is apparent you will serve no other god, matron saren. You are a slave to the one you serve, much like us. No man can serve two masters—not when *absolute* resolve is required by their lord."

"Opposition will be swift and violent for the crimes you have committed this day," Trensa promised, her scowl undermined by her frazzled hair and tear-streaked face.

"Swift? My dear child…" The prophet chuckled. "We have been sacrificing the peoples of the Crowned Kingdoms for years now, and though all officials suspected as much, what have any done to stop our campaign? They've made it a point to keep their concerns to themselves for fear of retribution. What's a hundred more sacrifices going to do to change that? Even of your own people, the only saren I have seen with any amount of moxie is Reza Malay."

He looked to her, assessing her response. "As I understand it, she's but a lowly knight amongst your ranks. On top of that, I hear that she already petitioned you to involve your order in this matter. What did you or any of your leadership do with her warning cry? Nothing. And that's exactly what the rest of the Crowned Kingdoms will do after whispers of today's ceremony gets out into the public. Everyone is too worried about their own hide to risk being labeled our enemy."

Trensa was left without words. The prophet was right. Her hubris had damned not just her, but the two sisters that had come with her to the temple gates that day to openly condemn the church for taking over

Alumin. If she had only listened to Reza that rainy day weeks earlier….

"Any last words, matron Trensa?" the prophet asked.

Trensa began to tremble, the immediacy of the moment hitting her hard. "Sareth, forgive me. I have failed you."

Looking to the father, Prophet Yunus said, "Carry on," prompting the deformed reverend father to slowly limp towards the bound saren.

"Mother Sareth, save us," she cried as the father's Seam-streaked arm raised to clutch around her skull.

The searing agony of the Seam flayed her skin quickly, and the blinding light of the pearlescent Seam was the last thing the High Priestess bore witness to.

Chapter One

Expedient Withdraw

Nomad threw back his hood as he entered the front gates of West Perch. He moved with purpose, even as the gate knights made to intercept him.

"I need to speak with the sister's council immediately. Where is Kaia," he ordered more than asked.

Though the two saren knights did not appreciate Nomad's demands, the two had been ordered by Freya, their Knight Champion, to admit him. "She is with Freya now in the solarium. Come."

The knight left her companion to tend to the gate, leading Nomad through the tight pathways between buildings until they came to a large stone greenhouse with a sunroof made of filigree glass panes allowing plenty of light in to nourish the exotic blooms within. It was not simply a greenhouse, however. There was plenty of sitting space and even a round table favored by Freya, used in hosting dignitaries and informal intimate meetings when not held in the audience hall.

The fresh bouquet of floral richness hit his nose as he walked through the threshold, the warm amber light of the evening amplified by the filigree glass roof overhead.

The two saren looked up from their conversation at the round table at the center of the room.

"Nomad," Kaia greeted. "You're back early. It's only been a day since you left."

Nomad nodded and sat next to Kaia.

"What did you find?" she asked, worried by the grim look of the man.

"The White Cloaks and the Black Queen's forces are heading this way. They're moving with purpose and speed."

"How far out are they?"

"If they push, they could be here late into the night."

"Size of the force?"

"At least a regiment strong. A thousand soldiers, maybe more. The Golden Crowns calvary does not seem to be with them."

"What do you suspect of their intent?"

"They are prepared for war, that much is clear. Their target, hard to say. Alumin most likely, to support the church's effort to subjugate the people—suppression of any dissenters."

"Would we be seen as dissenters?" Kaia asked.

"I'm not sure I could answer that. But I worry from what we've seen of their actions thus far, if you aren't in strict compliance and submission to this cult, you will be eradicated."

"I wonder, could they be marching upon West Perch?" Freya asked, taking the report in.

"They could be, and their force is more than enough to give West Perch hell," Nomad answered. It was clear he had given that possibility more than a passing thought.

The air in the room was charged with tension, which only heightened as hasty footsteps approached the building. The door swung open without even the courtesy of a knock.

A saren knight appeared in the doorway, speaking to Freya even before she approached the table. "High Priestess Trensa and the others were taken by force. I slipped out before the White Cloaks could catch me, but Trensa and the rest—"

"Calm," Freya ordered, holding up a hand. "You were with Trensa's envoy, correct? You're saying the negotiations went south?"

"Very. They were hardly within the synagogue's gates when White Cloaks surrounded Trensa and the others, armed with crossbows."

"How did you escape then?"

"I was ordered to stay on watch street side. They spotted me though after they took the others inside. I was chased for a few blocks, but I outpaced them."

Freya rubbed her chin in thought, considering both Nomad's and the knight's reports.

"We need to talk to the sisterhood," she said after a few moments. "We need to rally an emergency meeting. I'll need all three of you there."

They all nodded.

"Meet me there. I'll gather the sisterhood," Freya ordered.

"I'll gather everyone else," said Kaia. "The whole coven needs to hear these developments, not just the sisterhood."

The audience hall was filled on surprisingly short notice. Kaia thought how different the energy was from anything she had seen before. The sisterhood, the eldest of their numbers and subsequently the leaders of the monastery, sat at the large table at the head of the room.

The middle seat was noticeably empty, where Trensa would usually have been.

The balconies were all filled. Even on short notice, most saren at West Perch had been hearing nothing but ill news coming from Alumin of late, and Kaia had been quick and efficient at getting the word out to the others at the monastery.

Kaia joined Nomad and the other saren knight that had been with the envoy, sitting on the benches to the side of the audience hall as Freya entered the room. Freya walked to the center and looked around at the unexpected number of sarens.

Kaia was glad to see the four other sisters were there at the table. Their voices carried the most weight, perhaps even more so than Freya's. The saren faith was an old faith, steeped in tradition and authority. The High Priestesses were the pinnacle of authority for their people.

Freya held up her hand for quiet. Though the sisterhood held the authority, Freya, as the senior knight, held everyone's respect. She had been leading West Perch's military operations for a decade now, and all knew of her skill, strength, and favor in Sareth's eyes.

"Sisters, a black day has befallen us," Freya began. "Trensa's envoy has been forcibly detained by armed members of the Valiant Synagogue, and the Mad Queen moves in force to our location. There seems to be an alliance formed between the church of Elendium, the White Cloak's cult, the Mad Queen, and now there's reports of the Golden Crowns' forces joining them. Within a short span, Alumin's judicial and enforcement arm has become a mere extension of Valiant

Synagogue's whim. They openly detain whomever they please.

"We do not have the numbers to both ward off an attack from the Mad Queen's approaching army and march on Valiant Synagogue to retrieve Trensa and her envoy. By all accounts, we wouldn't even stand a chance at holding our monastery if the Mad Queen wishes our extermination. We must come to some decisions on these matters, and fast."

"Freya, these are serious matters," one of the sisterhood said. "But before we discuss this Mad Queen speculation, I would hear more of Trensa's abduction. She only just left to speak with Prophet Yunus this morning. You are reporting that some misfortune fell upon her?"

"Indeed, abducted at weapon point. One of the knights attached to the envoy escaped. Everyone else was surrounded by White Cloak crossbowmen. Perhaps this is all a misunderstanding, but even so, threatening a High Priestess of Sareth is a matter that must be dealt with. We need to confront the church over their motives, force them to explain their actions, and insist on our people's return—immediately."

"It would be prudent to not jump to any conclusions," the elder sister said. "The church of Elendium has long been an ally to followers of Sareth. We need to see that Trensa is escorted home safely, but I will not have you leading a platoon to the synagogue's gates. Go with a small team and investigate the matter further."

Freya eyed the speaker. Kim, the envoy knight standing next to Kaia and Nomad, broke the silence.

"It was no mix-up. The White Cloaks were prodding our sisters with loaded crossbows. They were taken against their will—"

"Silence, child," the elderly woman ordered. "And simply allow the sisterhood to dismiss key reports like you did with Reza Malay? You are being warned of danger and instead of confronting the truth, you continue to ignore every sign of warning. What if the thousands of the Mad Queen's soldiers headed to West Perch don't wish to simply talk with us? When will you listen to the signs? Once West Perch is occupied by the servants of Umbraz and all our sisters enslaved to a false god?"

"I said *silence!*"

The tension in the room was underpinned by the brief silence, every saren, even the elder sisterhood, knowing some line had been crossed.

The hall's great doors opened suddenly, and the captain of the watch barged in. Looking to Freya, she announced, "A band of White Cloaks and Alumin city guard just left the city and are on the road here. They'll be at our gates within the hour."

Freya looked to the sisterhood, daring them to remain indifferent to the news.

"The sisterhood will meet them at the gates and assess their intentions from there. We will not jump to conclusions and act out of haste," the second-most senior High Priestess said. "Likely they mean to return Trensa to us and explain this misunderstanding."

"This torpid response will be the end of our people," Freya rebuked.

"What do you intend for us to do? Give orders for the knights to confront and attack our long-time ally over rumors and speculation? We don't have the numbers to even hope to win an engagement, Freya."

"Exactly, we stand no chance against such a force. We need to withdraw. If they want West Perch, they will have it. It would be better for us to remain free than chained under their order."

"West Perch has not been occupied by any other than saren-kind for five hundred years. It is our home. It will not fall under our watch, and we will rely upon Sareth to help these rising forces to see sense. If your faith is so despondent, then perhaps that champion's crown is not befitting of you."

"To lie and wait for our domination is not Sareth's wish. There is another way." Freya looked up to the host of sarens that watched the proceedings. "I will lead us out of the jaws of our enemy so that we may regroup with those who have the strength and courage to oppose Umbraz. Kaia tells me that there is a resistance afoot in the south, in Rediron. We must leave immediately. Meet up at the back pastern. We need to make our escape before both forces join and surround West Perch. Pack light. Be suited for battle."

The sisterhood attempted to temper the rising voices from the hundreds of onlooking sarens, but even their shouts for order were drowned out. The discussion of retreat would be had by the masses, regardless of whether the sisterhood wished it.

Kaia took Nomad's hand as he helped her down the cliffside, light failing them as the sun dropped below the horizon. The shadows of dusk both hindered and aided the contingent of Freya's sarens as they snuck down. Navigating the difficult terrain in the dark was the price they had to pay for concealment from the approaching hoards.

The reports had not been exaggerated. Torchlight from the Mad Queen's army clearly marked their host within the range of a thousand men, and the White Cloaks coming from Alumin had come out in no trifling numbers either. It was clear as they made distance between the two, seeing the enclosing armies on their home, that resistance would have been futile. Freya and her knights were no strangers to battle. Most could see that the best solution was to issue a retreat under such impossible odds. It hadn't made leaving their home any easier, however. They were distressed over what the approaching host would do to their sisters that had chosen to stubbornly stay, still staunch in the hope that diplomacy would prove their strongest play. They had stood no chance in resistance before more than half of the monastery had departed, but now, to resist an attack would simply be suicide.

"It feels...wrong to be leaving West Perch," a saren said. Though the comment was nothing more than a whisper, the evening countryside was calm and the remark carried to Freya at the head of the march.

Knowing she needed to address the sentiment before doubt spread, she called for a halt, seeing that they were now far from the encirclement of the monastery.

She looked around at her saren sisters. For many, the reality of leaving their home was sinking in for the first time as they looked back at the familiar structure on the mountain. Now, it was surrounded by hundreds of torches as the White Cloaks gathered outside of its walls.

She cleared her throat, thinking on words that might address the anonymous voice. In the end, they were right. It did feel wrong to leave the place they all had lived for the majority of their lives—a place that had been a safe haven for saren-kind for centuries. It was wrong that the flames surrounding the place of worship and peace would soon likely be overrun by cultists and a horde of soldiers. She could only offer one thing to the heartbroken group.

She knelt and began a prayer. Other saren knelt in solidarity as she spoke.

"Sareth, blessed mother. Hard times have fallen upon your daughters. Please, grant us that we may have a portion of thy strength as we embark upon this new pilgrimage. Bless us that we may one day return to West Perch, with allies and strength, to bring harmony back to the Crowned Kingdoms, that we may clear the blight that is Umbraz and its followers from this realm. Grant us this, mighty Sareth, and be with us this night."

Though her prayer had been short, as she opened her eyes, she could see tears in many of her fellow sarens' eyes. Perhaps it was a trick of the evening's last light, but a warm gust of wind blew through their kneeling ranks, and a soft glow graced them even as low-hanging storm clouds began to blow in and shroud the lone mountain and the torches all across its foothills.

The light illuminated their path before them as if Sareth herself were showing them the way forward through the wilderness to the south—a trail that led them to Rediron country.

Chapter Two

High Cliffs Monastery

Reza remembered the mountain path she had just turned onto, even with the blanket of snow coating the evergreens and trail. She had hunted in the foothills as a child in the Jeenyre mountain range.

Sleet pelted against her cloak, and she squinted through a bluster of wind as it pressed her from the side. It forced her to halt for a moment to brace against the sleet. She had not been expecting ill weather on her trek back to High Cliffs Monastery, but then again, she had begun to lose track of time and seasons a while ago.

She slogged ahead once more along the old path that she knew would connect her to the main road leading to the monastery.

She stopped suddenly, though this time not because of the weather. She had heard a voice calling through the storm. She looked around, then the voice called once again.

"Anyone there?"

She shivered slightly from the cold and wet as she tried to place the voice.

"Alva, is that you?" Reza called out, now seeing a figure cutting a path through the sleet towards her.

"Reza!" the saren knight exclaimed, practically leaping through the last few yards of wet snow to embrace Reza.

Alva hugged Reza tightly. "When I saw a campfire out in the northern paths last night, I admit, I was hoping it'd be you and the others returning. Had to come see for myself."

"Alva, what if it hadn't been me? Is it just you out here? You shouldn't be in the foothills during a storm."

"That applies to you, too. You're soaked through," Alva said, turning the chastisement back on her. "But I didn't come alone."

Before Reza could question her peer's remark, a taller figure made its way through the gloom of the storm towards them, slower than Alva had.

"Lanereth—" Reza breathed, seeing her matron's frail figure appear before her. Lanereth looked terribly exhausted but had a relieved smile on her face.

"Reza, my child," the High Priestess whispered, close to tears.

Detaching herself from Alva's warm hug, Reza went to embrace the older, taller saren. She sighed at the motherly embrace, but something had changed. Reza felt the age in Lanereth's frame now, even more so than a few months ago upon her departure. She had thought Lanereth's weariness had just been from her journey through the Plains of Ash, which had pushed the High Priestess far beyond her breaking point and had given her scars that she would likely never fully heal from.

"You made it back to us, thank Sareth," Lanereth said softly, out of breath.

"You'll catch your death out here," Reza said, realizing that now was not the time for a reunion. Lanereth was chilled through and through.

"Alva, help me clear out that large conifer over there," Reza ordered. She looped a supporting arm under Lanereth's arm, guiding her over to an evergreen with a low branch cover skirt, keeping its base dry.

Alva unsheathed her sword and made a few cuts to the underbrush, using the pine needle branches as bedding. Within a minute or two, she had fashioned a dry shelter for them. Helping Lanereth to duck under the branch cover, Reza placed her mentor down on the bed of dry needles.

"She was barely standing on her own, Alva. Why would you let her come out in such weather?" Reza scolded, coming back out into the storm.

"She was the one that insisted on coming to find you, Reza. She would have come looking for you if I had accompanied her or not. Though I spotted your campfire last night, Lanereth had had a vision of you recently. She was sure you were on your way home. I caught her at the gate alone. I had to demand I accompany her. Even then, she didn't consent. I'm here against her orders."

Reza considered Alva's words for a moment, trying to find the logic in Lanereth's hasty actions.

As if in answer to her thoughts, Alva continued in a hushed whisper. "Lanereth hasn't been the same since you left. Ever since she returned from the Planes of Ash, her health has gone downhill."

Reza turned back to the shelter, but the bite of sleet put a pause on her ponderings.

"Come, we'll fall ill staying out here in this weather. There's enough room for all of us in there," Reza said, holding up the needle branch for Alva to head in.

Taking one last look around, seeing that the storm was not likely to let up any time soon, Reza ducked her head and entered the shelter.

Lanereth breathed lightly, her eyes closed as she rested against the rough tree trunk. Alva had moved to one side of her, enveloping her as much as she could in her cloak to help provide her with warmth. Reza moved gently to her other side and wrapped herself around the freezing woman. The three existed in quiet for a time, listening to the constant bluster outside the green covering. They were thankful for the thickness of cover the grandfather tree was able to provide.

After a half hour, their communal body heat had warmed up the space enough for Lanereth to sluggishly open her lids and raise a hand to pat Reza and Alva on their heads in appreciation.

"You…both have grown into wonderful daughters. Sareth is pleased with you," Lanereth slurred, clearly exhausted, but now content.

"Lanereth…" Reza grumbled, for a moment falling easily into their daughter/mother role that Reza had struggled her whole life to escape from. She was about to offer complaints of the matron putting her health at such risk to come to meet her on the trail, but let the point go.

If anyone had the right to act the part of a worried mother to her, it was Lanereth. She had been Reza's first and only matron, after all. Even though Reza had insisted from youth to forge herself independently of any other helping hand, she had, over the last few years, found the importance of relying upon others. She had relied upon Lanereth's steadfast nature more than she had realized in her youth, and now that Lanereth was showing signs of impermanence, she admitted she did not know how to take it.

"We have so much to catch up on," Lanereth sighed, resting her head on Reza's.

If there was more to her thoughts, she was too weary to continue the thread. Lanereth closed her eyes, going still, slumped on Reza's shoulder.

Reza soothingly shushed her surrogate mother, rocking her slightly into a deep sleep as the storm outside continued on through the day.

It was sundown by the time Reza, Alva, and Lanereth made it back to High Cliffs watchtower. All were good and numb by the nip of the early spring mountain air. Thankfully, the sleet and snow had let up at the least.

Alva waved her torch as she heard familiar calls from the tower. She left Reza to handle supporting Lanereth as she rushed up to call for aid from whomever was on watch.

"We'll get you a warm meal and get you in bed. Hang in there," Reza encouraged, carrying more of Lanereth's weight than Lanereth was at that point.

"I won't deny, that sounds wonderful right now," she said with a weak smile, "but I need to talk with you, Reza. It's imperative. Sareth has shown me many things—"

A coughing fit forced Lanereth to halt mid-thought, and before she could recover, a booming voice called out, bringing their attention to the canyon pass that led to the monastery.

"Reza Malay, it's about time you made it back to us. I was about ready to come searching for you myself," the large man said as he rushed up to greet her.

"Cavok." Reza let out an exhausted laugh. "It feels like a lifetime ago since I heard your voice."

"Aye, that it has," Cavok agreed. His tone turned serious. "Yozo and Malagar have brought terrible news of schemes facing the peoples of the Rediron Crowns Kingdom, Reza."

"Lanereth…has had visions. She believes it goes further than Rediron," Reza admitted.

Cavok turned his attention towards Lanereth. "What has Sareth shown you, Lanereth?"

Lanereth had recovered somewhat from her coughing fit but still clung weakly to Reza for support. "She has shown me a great many things, dear. I fear some things are even out of Sareth's control at this point. We…need to discuss your findings in detail. But not here, not now." She managed to finish before another coughing fit overcame her.

Cavok came to take Lanereth from Reza, but Reza waved him away. "No, I'll take her home. Send for some hot broth and victuals. I'll see to her from there."

"As you wish," he acquiesced. "I'll let Terra, Yozo, and Mal know you're here. They'll be happy to hear the news. We'll give you some time to catch up with Lanereth before we come to check up on you."

"Thank you, Cavok," Reza said, patting him on the side as he walked beside her. "It is good to see you." The weight in her voice carried more sentiment than just her words.

Cavok saw them to the snow-covered cliffside trail that led to Lanereth's home and watched as the ragged pair slowly made their way inside the shrine-like abode.

Reza gingerly helped to disrobe Lanereth from her soaked travel garb. Grabbing a sheet and a heavy quilt, she wrapped the older saren up once she was dried off.

"Lanereth…you're scarred from head to toe."

Though Lanereth had kept silent of her ordeals in the hellish realm she had visited the previous year, the marks on her body told Reza that she had seen horrors that would have broken most anyone other than the strong-willed saren.

Reza propped her up on the plush sofa facing the unlit fireplace, making sure she was comfortable before going to grab some firewood from the back porch.

She needed to hurry with the fire. She could hear Lanereth's teeth chattering even from outside as she gathered pine logs from the standing firewood ring.

After some preparation, she lit the kindling and placed, one after another, small logs onto a growing flame, lighting the living room that Reza had spent plenty of time in throughout the years. She knew the smell of old tomes and shadowy, relic-adorned corners of that room rather well. They were not all good memories. Most, in fact, were frustrating ones. She had been a troublesome youth for Lanereth to deal with, and she had received many scoldings in the dim living room and study that she now bustled about, attempting to warm up.

She was in the middle of collecting snow in a large bucket to fill the copper tub with when there came a knock at the door.

"Who's there?" Reza called, on edge as she rushed in from the back porch.

"I'm bringing a meal, dearie. Settle your feathers," an older kitchen maid announced after Reza's defensive tone.

The elderly maid entered the space, found Lanereth, and began to talk with her in quiet tones as she shuffled about and set a side table with a steaming meal that had been packed up in a wooden box. She unstacked it and placed it in front of Lanereth to enjoy.

Seeing that Lanereth was occupied with company for a bit, Reza continued filling the tub with snow. Placing a small caldron over the fireplace iron, she boiled a pot, poured it into the tub, and watched the snowpack melt.

After dumping a few caldrons of boiling water into the tub now filled with snow melt, Reza tested its temperature and found it to be comfortably warm, but not scalding.

The front door closed, the cook having finished packing up most of the meal. Reza moved to sit next to Lanereth and asked how her meal was.

"Oh, fine," the older saren said. "I saved the tomato soup for you, Reza. I'm sure you're just as in need of a meal as I was."

Normally, Reza would refuse such an offer, but she hadn't eaten all day, and she could not deny that she really could use the energy and warmth to help sustain her through the inevitable long night ahead. She had a terrible amount of catching up to do, not just with Lanereth, but with Cavok and the rest. She accepted the wooden bowl and spoon and made quick work of the hot soup.

Lanereth was attempting to make a comment about going to grab something from the kitchen for her, but her teeth chattered so badly that Reza stopped her mid-sentence.

"Here, let's get you into the bath. It's not getting any warmer after all."

Lanereth hesitated but didn't resist the advice. She offered her hand to Reza, and the two walked over to the copper tub, Reza helping her to untangle herself from her blankets and to slip into it.

Lanereth released a comfortable sigh of approval as she slid down into the warm water, her shivering frame melting as she closed her eyes.

Lanereth looked lost in the moment. For a small space of time, the weight of the world that she had carried with her since the Arisen War a year ago was lifted from her. Reza was almost worried for her, seeing her so unwound. She waited at the side of the tub, ready to help steady the frail woman at the first sign of trouble.

It was many minutes later, when the steam began to die down a bit, that Lanereth softly spoke, sluggish at first as she was coming out of her exhausted stupor.

"I've been to hell, Reza. The Plane of Ash is a realm of endless pain and despair. I have beheld the Blood Eye, that cursed court of the damned gods. I know how horrible things can get if evil is allowed to go unchecked in our realm. This is why I insisted on you looking into this unknown threat in the Crowned Kingdoms."

Reza considered her mentor's words for a time, then placed a hand on her shoulder. "Your intuition was right. There is an evil force at work in the north. Unfortunately, I am not sure if we were able to catch it soon enough."

"Umbraz," Lanereth whispered, the words almost sounding like a spell on her lips in the quiet place. "The light in the void."

"How…did you know?"

"Sareth's sight on the subject has been expanding, and she has shared some of these insights with me. I think more and more sarens have been coming in contact with followers of Umbraz. You yourself have faced off against them—I have seen it in a vision."

"Yes—" Reza admitted, trailing off as she absently rubbed her temples, thinking back to the time in Rosewood when her mind had almost been split in two by the cultists.

"What do you know of West Perch? How do they fair? Nomad and Kaia were headed there…" Reza asked, thinking that would likely be the focus of Sareth's gaze in the region.

Lanereth was slow to answer. She washed her face and let her hair down for Reza to help her wash it. As Reza untangled her hair with a wide-toothed comb, Lanereth dolefully admitted, "West Perch has fallen upon dark days. It was in my dreams two nights ago. A dissension, a rift in the faith. Sareth weeps over her flock. I fear a pall has shrouded her sight there."

Reza sat still at the bath's edge, worry for Nomad and Kaia's wellbeing cascading down on her. If the White Cloaks had moved upon the monastery that quickly, then Umbraz's followers must have confidence enough in their strength to make an open move against such a key organization as the saren headquarters in the region. If Lanereth had seen correctly, then it would only be a matter of time before Umbraz's hand began to sweep across the land, sectioning off key threats one by one until there would not be enough remaining players to band together and confront the oppressing force.

"Umbraz has the support of the Golden Crown and the Black Steel kingdoms. Alumin has fallen under the cult's influence, so too has the church of Elendium. There are very few now in Umbraz's way that could effectively contest a complete takeover of the region."

"It does look dire," Lanereth agreed.

"Fin and I were thinking...perhaps we could enlist the aid of outside regions. Sephentho, or perhaps the Plainstate. Sultan Metus would surely come to our aid."

Reza waited for Lanereth's reply. When she did respond, it was clear Lanereth was uncomfortable. "This is not the responsibility of other nations. It would be a heavy burden upon any kingdom or state outside of the Crowned Kingdoms to support a cause that is so quickly developing and as of yet, does not concern them."

"But it likely will if we don't end Umbraz here and now," Reza argued.

"The only potential ally I see even entertaining sending aid would be Sultan Metus, and that's only due to your relationship with him. But even then, think of what you'd be asking of him. To send men to another region to pick a side in a war that he knows nothing about, based on your word. This is not his fight, Reza. I wouldn't want you to put him in a position that would compromise his integrity as a leader of a state. Such a war effort would not go over well with his subjects, surely. He is a good leader. I do not wish to see him deposed because of something like this." Lanereth let the subject sit for a moment as she rested in the tub before clarifying her point. "No, this fight is the Crowned Kingdom's alone to bear."

"Then why did you send me and my friends? We had nothing to do with that nation until you asked us to intervene, Lanereth," Reza said, almost in disbelief over what she was hearing.

"Yes, I know," Lanereth said, exhausted. "I…was not strong enough to see to it myself, or I would have. I'm sorry, Reza. This is not your responsibility. It's just…you are perfect for this sort of thing. You've shown more resilience and resourcefulness than any I've encountered. If there was anyone capable of handling the troubles of the Crowned Kingdoms, I knew it was you."

"Lanereth…" Reza sighed. "I don't like it."

Lanereth placed a hand upon Reza's, bringing it to her and kissing it as a mother would her daughter. "I know. I'm truly sorry for bringing you into this, dear. I hope that you can someday forgive me for this."

"If we are to expect no support from outside nations, then what's our next move? I came here to recruit for the cause. Am I to return empty handed? The Lost King and King Reid put faith in me to come through," Reza huffed.

Lanereth shook her head. "You will not return empty handed. Your friends will come with you. Cavok has been itching to hunt you down and help, as has Terra and Yozo. Revna, Alva, Malagar, and I will also accompany you."

"A seven-member crew when I was hoping to return with an army, in a war where we are vastly outnumbered," Reza argued.

"Reza, I feel that Sareth has given her blessing for this path. There is still strength with the peoples of the Crowned Kingdoms. They will rise to the occasion if led by the right souls, and with you there to guide them,

I'm more confident in victory than if we sent a whole army of neighboring nations to settle their problems for them. This is their war, and all they need is a bit of guidance to see the clear path to a just conclusion."

Reza got up and walked to the fireplace, thinking over the heavy subject. From the start, she had struggled to fully commit to the path Lanereth had been placing her on. The Crowned Kingdoms were not her people. That they were in desperate need of a strong leader, it was undeniable, but she had many doubts that that person could be her. Fin was more kin to the northerners than her. It was possible Lanereth was overconfident in her abilities. It was possible that Sareth overestimated her worth.

"Lanereth, I just don't know if I can be what you want me to be," Reza whispered as she looked into the hearth's fire.

Lanereth left the remark alone and struggled to get up from her bath, standing shakily in the tub. Reza pulled her eyes away from the flames and retrieved a towel for her matron. Patting her dry, she robed her and got her bundled on the sofa next to the fireplace just as another knock at the door sounded.

Opening it, Reza said in surprise, "Revna." The priestess was a few years older than her, and the two hadn't spent too much time together in their youth, but she knew her well enough to make the greeting awkward.

"Reza," the priestess said. "It is good to have you back with us, safe and sound. Lanereth has been terribly worried over you."

"Yes," Reza acknowledged. "Did you come to see her?"

Revna nodded. "I did. I heard from Alva that she could use company, but it seems she already has that."

"I…was just about to leave," Reza said, shifting to a whisper so that Lanereth couldn't hear. "Perhaps it would be good for you to visit with her for a time. Her condition is a bit worrying. Strength has left her."

Revna's somber expression alone said that she understood.

"I'll take care of her," Revna said, nodding her head gracefully, her black locks tumbling over her slender shoulders.

Reza looked back to the swaddled woman on the couch and hesitantly turned to leave. Revna placed a gentle hand on Reza's shoulder. "I hope you will find time to visit with me as well at some point, Reza. Lanereth has told me of your mission. I wish to support you if you would let me."

Reza paused, thinking on the offer. She nodded and headed down the mountain trail.

She needed some space to think everything over before agreeing to anything else.

Cavok sat upon a snow-covered log on the side of the trail, looking out over the snowy mountain scene in silence. He turned to meet Reza's eyes.

She sighed. It was clear that she would not be finding time to herself that day. She trudged over to him.

"How long do you intend to stay before returning?" Cavok asked as he made room for her on the log, sweeping some snow off beside him.

"I don't know," Reza sighed, sitting in a huff of frustration. "I should probably get headed back as soon as possible—tomorrow maybe? I was hoping for

Lanereth to send word far and wide to help recruit for the war up north."

"And *will* she be sending word?" Cavok asked.

"She thinks that it would be best to allow the North kingdoms to handle this conflict themselves," Reza said as she stared out into the snowcapped mountain range. She looked over to Cavok. "She mentioned that you and the others would likely wish to join my return."

"Yes."

"Well? Why? What's up there for you, Cavok?"

Cavok finally tore his eyes from the horizon and looked at her. "You're returning, aren't you? There's something up there that you're not done with, right?" He turned his gaze back to the Jeenyre mountains. "I'll help you finish it."

Reza let out a chuckle. Cavok turned to consider her mood.

"Just like that, eh? We'll just go up there and end a war together? You don't even know what it is I'm returning to do, Cavok."

Cavok shifted. "Doesn't matter what lies up north. If you feel you have to return, then I'm coming with you."

Reza dipped her head, hunched over on the log. She was tired—exhausted through and through. She knew that people she cared for in the Crowned Kingdoms needed her to pull through. They had trusted her to do her part.

She looked at Cavok, thinking of the laughable number of reinforcements she would return to Rediron with—a band of seven. She thought of the understandable disappointment from the kings—from Fin.

Her heart sank at the thought. She breathed deeply, focusing on the cold of the winter weather to fight back the tears building up.

Cavok's large hand rested on her hunched back. She was still for a time before giving in and resting against him. Hot tears streamed into her hair as she lay motionless against Cavok, attempting to forget about her responsibilities with everything and everyone—just for a moment.

Cavok threw his cloak over her. Reza knew that he would let her rest there as long as she needed.

The sun peeked through thick clouds and shone upon them, warming them as the morning wore on.

Chapter Three

Overview

She walked through the large chapel doors, the same that she had passed through a thousand times as a child. Following Cavok to the back of the church's studies, entering the very sitting room that Lanereth had attempted to exorcize Nomad a year prior.

Entering the room, she was taken aback with the sight of friends that she had not seen in months. Alva was there sitting beside Terra, with Yozo and Malagar on the other side of the table.

"Reza!" Terra cried out upon seeing her. She ran up and gave her a big hug.

Reza looked around at everyone as she held Terra. Warm smiles greeted her from all in the room. Despite feeling depleted, she couldn't help but be touched.

"I missed you," Terra whispered as she finally let Reza go.

"We all have," Alva agreed. "Welcome back."

Cavok motioned for her to sit as everyone waited for her to settle in and begin explaining the situation to them.

"I—assume you all have gathered to have my report of the Crowned Kingdoms?" she asked, attempting to at least sound in better spirits.

"And to share ours to you and come up with a plan together," Terra said, still wearing a big smile.

"Right, then I'll lay it out very simply. The kingdoms are upon the doorstep of war. The Black Steel

Crowns, Golden Crowns, and Alumin are allied, propping up the cult of Umbraz. Rediron is attempting to gather any resistance factions to counteract the takeover of the region. I'll be returning to help solidify alliances where I can, be it with the Silver Crowns or West Perch. There are a lot of unknowns right now. If Rediron fails to secure Silver Crowns as an ally, or worse, the cult is successful in recruiting them, it could spell certain doom to our cause."

"And Fin is sided with Rediron?" Cavok asked.

"Yes," Reza nodded. "Nomad as well. The cult's ability to do permanent harm to the Crowned Kingdoms and its people is very real if someone does not step up to stop them. Tens of thousands of innocents will suffer if the followers of Umbraz are left unopposed."

"If the three of you deem it a worthy fight, then that's good enough for me," Cavok stated.

"It's not as simple as defeating the enemy in battle, Cavok. This war has many complex details to it that, quite frankly, has made it a tough decision for even me to fully commit myself to."

"You're wrong," Cavok brushed aside. "War is always filled with complexity, but at the end of the day, it all comes down to defeating the enemy. This is what our crew does well. If it is a hopeless war, then we will at least make it less…hopeless."

"It's not hopeless, not at all," Terra said with more confidence than Reza had ever seen from the young woman. "I've seen ahead of this conflict. Elendium has shown me Umbraz's fate, and as long as we remain true to each other and to this cause, Umbraz and his worshipers will be thwarted."

Reza studied Cavok and Terra awhile, mulling over their answers. Malagar, seeing an opening, spoke. "I am acquainted with the cruelty of Umbraz's zealots. I also know of this entity of the Seam perhaps even better than the majority of his followers. I have felt his aura grow within the rift reality. He is quickly becoming a dominating presence in the fabric of the Seam dimension. I may be able to help you and your allies, Reza. I'll come with you back to the Crowned Kingdoms."

"I as well," Yozo offered after Malagar.

"Lanereth is determined to join you. She's talked with me multiple times about it. I'll accompany her on this journey," Alva added.

Reza nodded, seeing that the whole room was in accordance with coming with her. "I won't stop you from coming, nor do I believe I could even if I refused your company, but I will leave you with one final warning before you make up your mind about returning to Rediron with me. There are some fates worse than death. I have seen people get turned inside out within seconds. Umbraz is consuming his victims, both body and spirit. Their very existence is fueling him. This is a dangerous path—one that even I am frightened to walk down. I appreciate your willingness to support me and the rest of the free people of the Crowned Kingdoms, but if any part of you wishes to remain here, please do. You would be sane to heed the voice of warning."

Her appeal was fruitless. The members in the room all seemed more resolute in joining Reza's return north than before.

"It is good to see you all again," Reza said after a moment, placing a steadying hand on Cavok's arm. "Now, if you will excuse me, I need to rest before our departure tomorrow. We can speak more on the trail to Rediron."

Cavok took the cue and led her out of the room thereafter, guiding her to the guest wing dorms.

"Cavok," Reza whispered as they entered her room for the night.

He turned to her.

She dropped her eyes from his gaze. "I...don't know if all of this is worth it. I saw Fin almost die at my side in battle. That the Crowned Kingdoms needs leadership is undeniable, but..."

Cavok stood in silence for a time, waiting for Reza to meet his eyes before he responded. She gathered herself somewhat after a brief time and looked to him for his thoughts.

"If you stepped away from this fight, would you have regrets about it later?"

His tone was genuine. The simple question was a breath of fresh air to her. With the situation and her feelings on their mission so complex and muddled, Cavok's prompt had cut right through all her reasoning, and she knew the answer to his question as soon as he had posed it. If she turned back now, there was no way she'd be able to live with that choice the remainder of her life.

She now realized there was only one route ahead of her. If she had to do this, then she needed to commit to their cause completely, no room for hesitations or doubts. Her friends were invested in the defense of the good people of the Crowned Kingdoms. They would go to war even without her. If that was the case, she needed to be there fully, both in body and mind, not just for Rediron and Silver Crowns, but for her friends. Especially for her friends.

Some of the weariness left her then, a second wind bolstering her. Cavok could see the change in her countenance and patted her on the shoulder before turning to leave.

"Thank you, Cavok," she said.

"Anytime." He waved, heading back the way they had come.

Chapter Four

Reunion

Reza watched as Alva and Cavok rode off at a leisurely trot on horseback down the trail towards Canopy Glen. They were chatting easily with each other, and Reza had noticed since being on the road with them over the last few days that they had become more than acquaintances.

Good. Cavok needs a few more friends, Reza thought. Cavok had grown increasingly guarded since Yozo entered their circle of friends, perhaps even before that. He had been less willing to keep the peace within their group than anyone else. She was happy to see that Alva was keeping him company these days.

Soon, the two were out of sight of the main caravan, headed to scout ahead to ensure that they would not be caught off guard if any trouble did lie in wait for them along their trail to Rediron.

She fell back in the formation to trot alongside Yozo and Malagar, wanting to catch up with the two a bit more than time had permitted the last few days. Often, they had been the scouts for the group and not been within camp, even at night when everyone was bedded down and talking around the campfire.

They made space for her to walk along at their side as she fell in step with them.

"Yozo," Reza began, "Fin did not tell me much of your initial trip to Rediron—even if he had, he's terrible with details. Half the time I'm not sure whether to believe his stories. I was hoping to talk with you about your experience in Rediron."

"What *did* Fin tell you of our trek?" Yozo asked after a moment of awkward silence.

"That the king had gone mad and was involved in poisoning the population."

"That is correct. He was not embellishing."

Reza trotted alongside the two silent men for a bit more, trying to find a different approach to open them up to conversation.

"Malagar. He mentioned..." She paused, knowing the subject she was attempting to broach to be an extremely sensitive one. "He mentioned that you had been captured by the White Cloaks and treated harshly. Did Revna see to your wound since then? Sarens can heal almost any condition, and we have two very competent healers in our company."

Malagar did not meet her eyes. He was looking blankly down the trail as he echoed her words in almost a whisper. "*Almost* any condition."

She hung her head, shamed by her clunky approach. She had never been skillful like Fin was with connecting with others on sensitive matters.

She fell out of step with the two and rode up alongside Terra, Revna, and Lanereth. Revna didn't even notice Reza's approach. The saren priestess' whole focus was on Lanereth, who seemed hardly fit to ride horseback. The day's journey had taxed the matron saren heavily, it was clear to see.

"The boys not talkative?" Terra asked Reza.

Reza shook her head.

"Well that just gives me more time with you then," Terra remarked, giving Reza an infectious smile that reminded her faintly of Kaia.

She mused that the two girls would get along swimmingly if they ever happened to meet.

"You're rather upbeat," Reza remarked, happy for the beacon of positivity amongst an otherwise gloomy group.

"That I am."

"Why?"

"Shouldn't I be?"

"*War* is no joyous occasion, Terra," Reza said with a sigh. "And by the looks of it, the one ahead looks to be a damn bloody one."

"I suppose that is one way to see things," Terra allowed. "But the Crowned Kingdoms is my home. I've seen injustice there all through my upbringing. It is because of persecution that me, my mother, and Bede left for the Plainstate. The last year of strife in the kingdoms comes as no surprise to me, but from the sounds of it, and from what Elendium has shown to me through visions, things are changing. Those who have suffered under the oppressive hand of the old-guard of the kingdoms might soon have reprieve, if we perform our duty well enough, and that is a positive notion—the chance to make a positive change for my homeland."

Reza let the explanation sit with her as she looked ahead to the rest of the members in their troop, thinking over everyone's reasons for taking up the call of duty in the conflict.

"You don't approve of my motive, Reza?" Terra asked.

Reza shook herself from her thoughts. "Does it matter if I approve? You have your view of it all and seem to be quite happy with your direction. That's more than most have."

Reza looked over to see that her comment had stolen some of the wind from the young woman's sails. "I'm sorry, I really am glad you're heading into this conflict in a positive mindset, Terra. I just worry that things will soon get ugly. I worry about our position in this fight. It's an uphill battle by the numbers, and unless some god decides to grant us a miracle or two…things do not look to be in our favor."

"I…have hope that a god or two will grant us strength and guidance through this conflict. I know resolution will not come easy, but I believe good will prevail, and many will appreciate the sacrifices we will soon be asked to make."

Reza offered the weakest of smiles. Try as she did, Reza still struggled with the subject of hope.

"A large force ahead. They move eastwards through Canopy Glen," Cavok called to Reza as he and Alva returned from up the trail.

"Their colors?" Reza asked, riding up to meet the two.

"Red and gray banners, though there was another black and gold flag flying amongst a smaller section of the troop."

"Rediron then, likely joined by the Lost Kingsmen. Exactly how large is their force?"

"From what we could see, the host is split into three bodies, a large battalion and two smaller companies. In all, perhaps a couple thousand."

"Not a small showing by any means. Wherever they are headed, they must deem critical, otherwise they would not leave their castle so vulnerable."

Reza turned to the rest in their group who had gathered to hear the report. "We need to connect with the Rediron force before they pass through Canopy Glen. There's only two places they could be headed: to Silver Crowns or Alumin. I have a feeling it is to Alumin. Only the capitol poses enough of a threat to warrant coming out in force like this. We'll search out Fin, King Reid, or one of the Waldocks, get caught up to speed, and from there determine how and where we can offer our support. Is that clear?"

Revna spoke up. "Reza, are you the one to be giving the orders? Lanereth is with us now. She is our superior. She alone should have the final say on our direction."

Reza answered firmly. "It was not an order that she gave to involve myself in this conflict, it was a request. This is *my* mission. I assume that all of you here are here to support and aid me in this effort. If that is not the case, detach from my camp and find your own path in how you wish to fight this war."

Revna was not pleased with Reza's directness but held her tongue. Reza reiterated, "If you stay with me here and now, you *will* follow my orders."

"We are with you, Reza," Lanereth offered.

Reza eyed Revna one more time to see if there would be any further comment on the matter. Hearing no further objection, she turned her horse towards Canopy Glen and waved a hand forward.

"To canter," she called, pulling ahead to lead the group onwards towards the small woodland village that lay just over the next rise.

Reza's small group of eight had been spotted and intercepted by Rediron troops before entering the town's boundaries. Reza explained her credentials and asked to be brought to Fin or King Reid. Two of the soldiers took to escorting the group to the head of the line. They brought Reza within sight of Fin deep in conversation with King Reid and a few of what she assumed to be his upper-ranked officers.

Fin spotted her before she could get close enough to call his name. He smiled and waved to her, abruptly dropping his conversation with King Reid to rush over to greet her.

"Thank the gods. You made it back just in time," he said, pulling her in for a brief embrace.

The rest of the group caught up, and Fin's smile widened. "Well look who you brought with you. Yozo, Mal, and the big guy himself."

"Nice duds. That sword in particular looks especially costly. Who'd you pick it off of?" Cavok grunted.

"That's…a tale best left for another time," Fin grumbled, glancing at Yozo and Malagar, who knew the story all too well.

"Another time, then," Cavok agreed.

"It's good to see you all," Fin said, lingering on Cavok's gaze before returning his attention to Reza. "How did you fare in your recruiting efforts?"

"This is the support we can expect from the southlands," she offered.

For a moment, she could see the disappointment in Fin's countenance, but he recovered quickly. "If I were to have my pick of any in all the Southern Sands, it would be this lot. Job well done, Reza. Thank you."

Though she genuinely knew Fin meant what he said, the only thing she was focused on now was the brief moment when Fin's mask had slipped. She felt ashamed of the results of her efforts. She expected more of herself—and others.

"What's the situation?" she asked. "By the looks of it, it seems as though Rediron is making a move upon Alumin."

"Not exactly. We don't intend to approach Alumin itself. We've received reports of the fall of West Perch. There's a detachment of saren knights that made it out of there before the fort was surrounded. Golden Knights are chasing them southward through Salen Greenwood, and we're moving to intercept them."

"Kaia and Nomad?" Reza asked, wondering if they had left with the detachment or remained.

"Let's hope they're with the sarens heading south," Fin said, that same worry weighing on him since they had received the report the previous night. "There's a break in the trees a mile or so east of Canopy Glen." He pointed up the road. "We're headed there before moving north through the forest. It won't be easy navigating an army through Greenwood, but that's likely why the sarens would choose that route, to slow the Golden Knights down and to not be caught out on the open road."

"How large is the force pursuing them?" she asked.

"All our reports were able to say is that it's a large force of some cavalry, foot soldiers, and some White Cloaks."

Reza shook her head. "Not having good numbers on an enemy force before engaging them is a fool's game."

"I understand that, but both King Reid and King Waldock agree that not taking the risk to defend the saren troop and their borders would be even more unfavorable."

"Starting out a war already playing a trump card is not promising."

"It's the play we've got. We'll make it work. Both the Rediron and Black Steel soldiers are hardy. They've had good training and leadership. We're not fighting this battle with a rag-tag militia. Besides, they both know Salen Greenwood better than the Golden Crowns do. We have some points in our favor."

"Very well. Where do you need us?"

King Reid and Johnathan, Warchief of the Lost Kingsmen, approached the group as if in answer to Reza's question. The two were in step with each other, and the air was filled with the tension and anticipation of the battle soon to come amongst the leaders that flocked around the two commanders.

"Reza," Reid greeted. "Good to see you've returned safely from Jeenyre. What news do you bring?"

"The only aid I could procure from the southlands is standing here with me." She motioned to her group of comrades.

Neither Reid nor Johnathan hid their dissatisfaction with the report. Reza pressed past the point. "Though we're few in numbers, each of my comrades here have seen their fair share of war. Without them, the Southern Sands would be a gateway to the seven hells under the arisen hand of Sha'oul. They are experts in warfare among many other subjects. I would place my life in any of their hands with all confidence. Though I did not come back with an army, I have returned with leaders that will help in any way they can. Do not underestimate their usefulness. Utilize us well and consider them for key positions in your strategies ahead."

"We do not have the leisure to assess your troops' expertise and where they may fit within our military structure. Saren refugees from West Perch are marching this way with Golden Crowns on their heels. We mean to intercept the Golden force with all haste," Reid answered. "I know Fin best. He trusts you explicitly. I've been briefed on you and your clan's deeds in the Arisen War. It's clear you and your crew know your way around the battlefield. What I could do is hand over a troop for you to command, Reza, with Fin as your second in command, along with your comrades as your close guard."

"What troop are you considering?" she asked.

"Frontline scouts. I trust my leading officer without reservation…but you are a saren, after all. It might be appropriate for the retreating sarens to see you first. Trent, my lead scout, will remain at your side, but I'll let him know you are in charge. If we're lucky, and this mission is a success, we can discuss appropriate posts for all your crew in further detail."

"I accept those conditions. Is everyone in agreement with the plan?" Reza asked, looking around to Fin and her comrades.

"This is a key point to be shuffling command of one of your most pivotal troops," Johnathan warned Reid.

Reid nodded but countered, "Fin has shown impeccable foresight in regard to strategy. I will trust him and Reza this once." He then turned to Reza and Fin. "Do not let me or my scouts down. We win or lose depending on how the frontline initiates contact with the enemy."

Fin stood in solidarity with Reza. Reza nodded her understanding of the dire stakes. "We'll handle first contact. Show me to your scouts."

Eying her, Reid snapped a finger to his right-hand man. "Morgan will see you there. Once you are acquainted, and I've had a few moments with King Waldock and Warchief Johnathan, we'll be marching into the Greenwood. I don't expect to halt our march until we intercept the sarens and Golden Crowns army. When I call for the order to head out, you lead. Colter, Captain of the Scouts division, will be your guide once in the forest. He knows those woods better than anyone. Keep him close. He'll be an invaluable asset."

"Will do," Reza agreed, then waved to her crew to follow as Morgan moved to find the scout's division.

"That man thinks highly of you, Fin," Reza whispered as they made their way through formations.

"I don't know why. I've been a constant problem for him since the day we met."

"That's probably why. He doesn't seem to be the kind of man to tolerate problems in the least—and yet, from what I gather, you've gotten your way with him every time. He must think you capable if you've come out on top every encounter."

"Besting a king a few times over—that does make me sound quite capable, doesn't it?"

"I didn't say that you are...just that he *thinks* you are," Reza corrected. Fin shot a sly grin at her.

She allowed herself a small smirk as they walked up to the leader of the scout division. It was probably going to be the last glimpse of levity either of them would see that day. The number of deaths and atrocities they were about to bear witness to...and participate in...was no longer just a possibility.

Chapter Five

Onwards

"Forward march!" Reza shouted and heard Cavok and Fin echo the order to their respective platoons.

Setting the pace, she led the formation of seventy or so soldiers across the fields, heading towards the treeline of the Salen Greenwood. The rest of the army, which consisted of mostly King Reid's men, held back, still reforming before following off trail. King Waldock's riders were at ready, just waiting for the scouts to advance far enough ahead so as to effectively survey as vanguards to send essential intel back to the main body ahead of detection.

Reza knew the importance of the troop she led. They would set the pace of the upcoming battle, and this first meaningful engagement between armies would then set the stage for the entire war. It was also the first motion of trust Reid had placed in her. In many ways, this was her introduction to the peoples of the Crowned Kingdoms. She needed to make a good first impression. Lives were at stake if she faltered now.

"Wedge formation as we enter the forest. Stay loose," she called back. Cavok and Fin reiterated her orders to their scouts.

She had told Colter, the scout leader, to operate as the go-between for the scouts and the rest of the army. She'd need the signal and direction to be delivered quickly once they intercepted the enemy, and she had been told that Colter was fast. The other leaders knew him as well. She needed succinct and direct orders to be relayed, and though Colter did not like King Reid's orders to give up his post to an outsider, he had obeyed and agreed to be the signalman as Reza had ordered.

She had split up the platoon into two smaller groups, roughly twenty and forty. She had given the bulk of the scouts to Cavok, and the twenty sharpshooters in the platoon to Fin. Regardless of gear or specialty, all sixty of them were deathly quiet as they made their way through the forest. So silent was their march that more than once she turned to make sure the troop was still following her, only to see figures well blended with the forest hues stalking after her.

She waved Lanereth, Revna, and Alva to her and began speaking in a low voice as they marched. "How shall we handle the Saren refugees if we happen upon them first?" Reza asked.

"Let me handle talks with our sisters," Lanereth said. Reza heard more strength in her voice than she had in many months, almost as though Sareth herself was supporting her. "I'm known to a good number of sisters at West Perch. We might convince them to turn and fight with us, if Sareth is willing."

"Good. Revna, Alva, support Lanereth. With luck, those are saren *knights* heading our way. We could use some saren muscle in this war."

They agreed, and Reza moved to Terra, Malagar, and Yozo. She patted Terra on the shoulder as she announced, "I have something in mind for you three if you're willing."

"You name it, Reza," Terra answered for the others.

"I need auxiliary command in the event a commander is incapacitated or needs additional support.

I need you to remain with me and help run information between platoons and to fill in and cover any gaps that open up along the chain of command."

"We can do that," Yozo offered. Malagar and Terra nodded their acceptance.

The march proceeded, mostly in silence. The scouts were as stealthy as the Shadow Company that she had worked with in Sultan Metus' army. She could tell that this was their favored environment. Though woodland terrain wasn't necessarily hers, she at least attempted to keep her tread light and her eyes vigilant, scanning the woods before them as she thought through all the various scenarios that could be just ahead of them.

Colter suggested sending a scout back to report from time to time, to ensure each company had updated locations of each other, which she approved, and after a slowed pace for water and ration consumption, they were back to trailblazing their way northwards as the afternoon wore on.

Fin approached her and announced in a quiet voice, "A rise up ahead."

"Fin, Cavok, call for a halt," Reza ordered.

Moving to Malagar's side, she discreetly whispered, "Haltia are known for their exceptional eyesight. How is yours?"

"It is not as it was before the asylum," he admitted, then murmured, "Nothing is as before the asylum."

She sympathized with him. Rediron had left a traumatic mark upon his soul, but she had no time for gentleness now. "Would you come with me to the rise as a second pair of eyes? Perhaps your sight is still better than any of ours."

"I will," he said with a slight hint of sorrow which had lined most of the interactions she had had with the haltia.

"Colter, come with us," she requested. The three moved towards the knoll that Fin had pointed out to her for a vantagepoint of the area.

Coming to the edge of the sloping cliffside, Reza held up her hand to her brow as the late afternoon sun shone upon them through the break in the treeline. A rich gust of chill forest air rushed across the trio as they looked out over the canopy and landscape of the Salen Greenwood wilderness.

They overlooked a valley, mostly covered by woods, but there were a few meadows and openings in the stretch of land that broke up the monotony of green.

"There's a cabin down there," Malagar said after a moment of taking in the grand vista.

Reza and Colter looked to where Malagar was focusing and saw the small hovel a mile or so down in the valley, nestled along a small stream and between a set of steep, rocky rises.

"Surely enough, there is," Reza said. She turned to Colter. "What do you know about this location?"

Colter scratched his stubble. "It's backwoods after this. Thick underbrush. As for that cabin, that could be any squatter. Plenty of recluses in the Greenwood. Only one I know about in these areas is Reg. Haven't seen him in over a year in town, though—ever since the warp sickness took hold. May or may not be his place."

"Something else," Malagar cut in. "Two or three miles out, cresting the rise on the other side of the valley."

Reza and Colter paid close attention, attempting to spot what Malagar was seeing.

"Where exactly, Malagar? I don't see it," Reza admitted.

He pointed. "A formation. I'd say soldiers of some kind. Their armor glints through the trees. They're moving quickly."

"I…believe I see the glints you're talking about. It's a bit far." Colter squinted, holding a hand up to shield out the sun's rays.

"Could be the saren troop, or the Golden Knights," Reza mused. "Can you make out if the armor is silver or gold?"

"Most certainly silver," Malagar said, adding with less confidence, "Perhaps white and red tabards or sashes."

"Those are saren colors," Reza said with a sigh of relief. "We will move to intercept them posthaste. What direction are they headed?"

"They are moving towards us, into the valley. That cabin is roughly halfway between us both." He slowed as he concentrated further north of the sarens' location. "Wait, another troop, much larger, cresting the ridgeline." Reza and Colter held their questions as Malagar concentrated on what they could not see far across the valley. "They wear gold armor."

His words hung in the air like a funeral bell.

Reza bit her lip. "How close are they to the sarens?"

"Close. They'll overtake them before they make it to us."

"We need to move to intercept, now," Reza said, taking in the lay of the land one last time, attempting to determine the plan of engagement with not only the saren troop, but also the Golden Crowns' army.

She turned and rushed back to the scouts. "Fin, Cavok, gather your troops."

They did so. Most had already gathered, but the few that had fanned out to check the area were quick to return at the command.

Reza held up a hand. "Both the saren and Golden Crown armies are crossing the valley before us. We will move with all haste to connect with the sarens first at the valley floor. There's a small canyon between us.

"Fin, I need your sharpshooters to set up in positions of elevation—hidden, of course. This is imperative; if any among the enemy troop are wearing white cloaks, aim for them. They're your priority.

"Cavok, I need the rest of the scouts to position on either side of the canyon so that we can funnel and flank the enemy if they enter the valley.

"Lanereth, Revna, Alva. We may be able to contact the sarens before the enemy is upon them. Once we meet, inform them to hold their ground at the far side of the canyon to bait the enemy into the valley. The scouts will flank once the enemy arrives in sufficient number."

She looked around to ensure all were on the same page. With no objections or questions, she moved on. "Remember, it is not our job to win this battle, or even hold out for very long. It is our job to initiate first contact with the saren unit and the enemy force. Let's make sure that first contact comes with such an impact that it will knock the fight out of the enemy. Once backup arrives, their frontline will already be shaken. If we can take the wind from their sails, then King Reid will handle the rest.

"Fight with ferocity, listen to your commanding officers, and move like shadows in the woods. Scouts— may your aim be true. Fight like the wolves you are!"

Though the scouts did not call out a battle cry, Reza's words had been effective in rallying their spirits. Gripping their bows and the hilt of their sidearms, they were itching for the command to charge down the hill to take their designated positions.

"Colter, it's time to report to the king. We'll see you down there," she said, clapping him on the arm to send him off back through the woods and connect with the main host.

"Move out," she called to their company and began a quick jog down the sloped hill leading to the cabin at the bottom of the valley.

Chapter Six

Battle of the Greenwood

Her boot was the first of many that disrupted the serene woodland stream. Reza was across the knee-high brook within moments, crossing the hermit's property just as a haggard man burst out of the cabin along the cliff-face on the other side of the valley.

Before the unkempt man could make heads or tails of the seventy-man force that had appeared at his doorstep, Reza asked, "Are you Reg?"

The man could tell Reza was in no mood for hesitation or deceptions. He stood no chance at defending his home against such a force, thus deciding it best to comply outright.

"Aye."

"The Golden Crown army is about to descend from that ridge. We'll be basing an ambush here for them. Leave these woods now if you value your life."

The man wasted no time, taking his bow and a quiver of arrows and was off running eastwards before the majority of the scouts had crossed the stream.

Reza waved over her three saren sisters as Lanereth finished trudging through the stream, out of breath from the charge. As she waited for her matron to make it to her, Reza looked for Fin and Cavok. Fin and his sharpshooters were already headed up ledges mainly along two ridges that overlooked the valley, while Cavok was ordering his men to station along the blindside of the canyon wall and to ready their bows and sidearms.

"I saw the saren headed this way before we came down into the valley. They'll be arriving here any moment," Reza called to Lanereth as she approached her in the yard.

"I'll be ready to receive them," Lanereth said, winded but determined not to let her condition affect her duty.

Making her way to the only slope down into the valley from the north side, Lanereth heaved once more, steading herself, and took out a small cylinder. She released it, and it grew in the blink of an eye into a six-foot staff with a glass rod along the head which began to glow a bright white almost at once.

A few muted whispers into the evening sky and a glowing image, a symbol of their faith, washed into the air above them, like a shining banner of Sareth.

As if summoned to the glow sigil, the gleaming purified silver armor of her fellow sisters broke through the shadow of the treeline above, rushing down the steep slope to slow as they approached Lanereth and the sign of their faith.

Though they were sarens of differing regions, upon meeting, both knew they were kin, without the help of the symbol of faith or even a word between them.

—●◎●—

Holding up a hand, Lanereth made to address the approaching saren troop who were quickly filing in from the ridge. "Your sisters from High Cliffs Monastery as well as the Rediron kingdom stand with you against your enemy this day. Who speaks for your troop?"

"I do," voiced a platinum-haired woman, out of breath and flushed from the endless run the sarens had been enduring.

Their leader made her way to the front of the line and Lanereth wasted no time addressing her. "I'm High Priestess Lanereth."

Lanereth could see by the saren's armor, emblems, and crown, that she was a Knight Champion, one of the highest ranks in the military wing of their faith.

The Knight Champion still fought for breath, but proceeded with introductions as best she could. "Freya— leader of this detachment. Golden Knights will be upon us within moments. Whether your arrival is fortuitous or intentional, we must make a stand here or be cut down in flight."

By then, even though the sarens were clearly exhausted from the run, they were beginning to spot the numerous scouts hidden in the shadows along the cliffside and in the brambles up above overlooking the valley. A knight next to the speaker whispered in her ear.

Lanereth confirmed their suspicions. "We have Rediron scouts planted in the area and a large host rushing here now. Call your knights to the far side of the valley, across the stream. Goad the Golden Knights into the valley and hold your ground. We'll take care of the rest."

"We can't run another mile even if our lives depended on it," Freya shamelessly admitted. "We will hold at the stream for as long as we can."

"Sareth will see your strength returned to you," Lanereth said in a softer tone, whispering a prayer into the sky while holding up her staff.

The glass along its tip began to glow radiantly, and the light that shone across the gathering saren troop brought with it a rush of cool air, enlivening the exhausted knights being filled with power from their heavenly mother. The once ragged troop breathed a collective sigh of relief, no longer struggling to catch their breath.

Freya reached out, placing a hand upon Lanereth's shoulder. "Thank you, sister."

The peaceful moment was short-lived as a clamor along the ridge denoted the approaching hoard. Lanereth looked to the shadows of the woods, not able to make out Reza or even one of her scouts. Knowing they were there within earshot, she called out. "Reza. Ready your scouts. The battle is upon us. The knights are in position, and I hear the enemy approaching."

The Golden Knights' war chants bellowed down through the wooded slope now, loud and clear. A deep bass belted out a guttural ancient hymn of war as gold armor gleamed on the last rays of sun that touched the crest of the canyon.

The Golden Knights barreled down the hill, the saren troop now clearly in sight and consolidated across the stream.

"Form a line," Freya ordered, and her knights immediately rushed to create a formation. Fifty knights pushed forward to create a frontline at the stream's edge, all other saren lining up behind them.

The first Golden Knights rushed onto level ground, charging headlong across the hermit's yard towards the stream, ready to tear into the saren line. The tremendous cacophony of the charging army thrummed and shook the very ground, hundreds of knights pressing at full tilt at the enemy.

The sight and sound of such a mighty force before them would have been enough to make anyone tremble and despair, but Sareth's presence had been bestowed upon Freya, Lanereth, and all sarens awaiting the first of the Golden Knights to forge the stream, which had barely slowed the bloodlusting frontrunners as they thrashed their way at the unmoving line of sarens.

The first Golden Knights crashed into the wall of saren shields and swords but were quickly dispatched as the Golden Knights became surrounded by a tightly knit defensive line. The crash of steel and death screams began to sound louder as more of the main bulk of the Golden army began to catch up with the frontrunners. The saren line was quickly being stressed by the press of troops.

Lanereth waited until the last moment, just before the front line seemed to be buckling, to raise her staff high, sending out a blinding flash of light over the heads of the sarens, searing the eyes of all those rushing the outnumbered saren troop. The flash allowed the frontline of sarens to strike and go on the offensive as the Golden front's charge wavered for a moment.

Freya yelled for her women to press the attack, and the blinded Golden Knights' frontline buckled for a few moments before the hoard behind them pressed into their comrades, shoving them forward even as they were trampled or impaled by the advancing sarens. The blinding advantage was quickly eaten up by the sheer number of Golden Knights that absorbed the swath of casualties the move had allowed for.

"Now, Reza!" Lanereth shouted in vain, hoping to Sareth that Reza could hear her, but knowing full well it to be a fool's hope that orders could be given through the overwhelming din of battle.

Whether Reza had heard the command or not, it was apparent that the Golden Knights were sufficiently invested in the position. A good portion of their troops were rushing the valley now with no awareness of the numbers of lurking scouts waiting to loose a volley upon their backs.

She gave the sign, and both Fin and Cavok silently signaled their men. Arrows bit into the middle mass of Golden Knights that were pressing against their comrades' back, and after the first volley of arrows peppered the enemy host, a hesitation shook the group that was in the valley, knowing something to be wrong as knocks battered their armor and felled others around them even though they were still rows back from the front line.

"*Carry on.*" An unnaturally clear order sounded from a White Cloak stationed on a knoll to the side of the slope. The piercing command rang through the valley.

A fresh flow of Golden Knights marched onwards, filling the gaps of those that had fallen from the volley, ever pressing forward towards the small saren troop.

The second volley fired, and this time, the Golden troops were keen to the direction of the arrows. Though there was nothing to be done about the archers on the cliffs above, they began to spread out in the valley, beginning a hunt for the scouts hiding in the shadows of the trees and in the foliage.

Lanereth shot forth another blinding ray at the oncoming troops, but the sheer number of soldiers entering the valley was quickly exposing the futility of the fight before them. They would be overrun within minutes at that rate.

A saren knight along the front line had just finished a killing blow, retracting her sword point from the Golden Knight's visor, when she held up her hand and screamed in pain from a phantom strike. The two beside the frontline saren also ceased their attack, hunching over in writhing and crippling agony before all three began to slowly erupt in their armor. Flesh split and tore outwards, blooming and expanding, cutting their cries short. Within moments, all three were twitching piles of gore at the stream's edge. The Golden Knights rushed into the gap in the sarens' defensive wall, opening the formation up like a wedge hammering in through wood.

Freya jumped ahead of Lanereth, her mace bright with blood, her countenance fiercer and more vibrant than any Lanereth had seen in battle, and she had been in countless. She bounded into the Golden Knights that had broken the sarens' line, smashing the back of the leadman's helmet with her mace, crumpling it in, dropping him instantly. She swung the mace high, connecting with another knight and rushed into a third before any could retaliate. Emboldened by their leader's display, those saren close by shouted a battle cry and drove in to support Freya, attempting to regain a defensive line.

The push was valiant, but Lanereth could already see that the surge would not last for very long. Freya and her sisters were thrashing beasts, somehow overcoming the ever-growing tide of Golden Knights, but even as they rallied, the mass of bodies forced their line to bow inward, even as they slew the enemy with blinding speed.

The ground rumbled and Lanereth could hear the approach of hooves coming down from behind them followed by the battle cries and orders barked out chaotically as they drew near. She was grabbed from behind, one of the sarens pulling her forcefully to the side as the whole troop began to split in two. As she looked behind, she could see why they were giving up their hard-earned line.

Johnathan, the Warchief, led the charge of hundreds of riders, barreling down the slope, meaning to pierce directly into the Golden Crowns' main host. The sarens split rank just in time as the Kingsmen charged past and plowed into the Golden Knights' front line.

With the Kingsmen forcing their way into the packed valley, the sarens beginning to find footing in pressing the Golden hoard back, and the constant rain of arrows from above and behind, the enemy force was quickly becoming aware of the danger they were in trying to take the valley. They had been funneled, and even though their numbers still remained far greater than what resistance they were facing from the sarens and Kingsmen, they were being forced to slowly trickle in the bulk of their force through the one entry point along the slope into the valley.

Panic began to arise amidst the enemy, none more so than those at the front who were forced to face ferocious saren or trampling horsemen.

The flow of Golden Knights into the valley stemmed as the commanding officers at the top of the hill sent orders to withdraw and consolidate at the top of the hill.

The four hundred Golden Knights that had shoved their way into the valley now were being battered on every side and falling fast now with the majority of the rearguard turning about, retreating back up the hill they had so fearlessly charged down as the order of retreat made it through the chaos of battle.

Seeing that they had the momentum in the battle within the valley, Johnathan pressed the charge as the Golden Knights turned in force and were now in full retreat.

It was utter chaos on the battlefield as bolts began to fall from the sky, thudding into the riders and their mounts. At first, the Kingsmen weren't sure whether the stray missiles were friendly fire from the scouts firing too close, but as another hail of bolts rained down from ahead of them, they could see that the Golden troop had established a line of crossbowmen and were giving their beaten and battered returning knights covering fire.

Both Cavok and Reza's troop had pincered the scattering Golden Knights, and Johnathan's riders drove them into the gauntlet of harriers, thinning their numbers so effectively that by the time the last of the knights had made it out of the deathtrap valley, the size of their front guard had dwindled down to a quarter of what it was upon entering the vail.

Johnathan held up a hand, calling a halt as they reached the incline. Though his men had fared well in the charge, the bulk of the Golden army stood atop the canyon ridge up above, and by the size of what he could see, their numbers were overwhelming, even with the win over the frontline.

Only two volleys had peppered them. Johnathan looked for their crossbowmen and noticed their attention elsewhere to their flanks. Sounds of battle along the hills to the east and west began to grow louder.

"King Reid presses the attack!" the Warchief yelled, spurring his horse up the hill, leading his men up the steep slope towards the rear of the Golden Knights and quickly coming upon the battered front guard only to be ran upon brutally once more.

The riders had ripped up the slope and out of the valley within moments, leaving behind a wake of destruction, a golden carpet littering the valley floor. Scouts were already sweeping across the battlefield, short swords out, kicking off helmets and slitting throats of the wounded Golden Knights struggling to get to their feet.

"Keep some for questioning," Cavok ordered his crew as he worked on hauling wounded scouts to a central location by the house.

Reza wiped blood clean from her blade and sheathed it as she looked up the slope. The fight was still within earshot, and she could see pockets of skirmishes along the hillside, but it was clear the Golden army was in retreat. The battle was beyond them at that point—her scouts had done their jobs well. The rest was in the hands of King Reid.

"Reza, we need healers for our men. Can you spare any saren?" Cavok called, breaking her from her thoughts.

She turned to Malagar and Yozo who had stayed by her side throughout the short but devastating skirmish, and asked them to help Cavok gather the wounded. Terra had not needed the prompt, already speaking with Fin who was calling all snipers back into formation from the trees and cliffside to take a headcount.

"I'll go see," she called to Cavok above the distant battle and the moans of the wounded all about their feet. Hundreds of Golden Knights were either dead or dying, littering the grounds she had to cross to connect up with Lanereth and the saren troop.

"Reza!" Lanereth called out, relief in her voice. "Thank Sareth, child, you're safe. I saw that knights overran your position. I worried for you and your scouts."

"The knights didn't have time to scour the overgrowth to find us. As far as I'm aware, our casualties were relatively few. It was your line of saren that I worried about. You took the full brunt of the initial attack," she said, looking towards Freya, who was giving orders and tending to her troops.

"She...is an exceptional knight and leader. She showed no weakness on the battlefield," Lanereth almost reverently acknowledged.

"Some of the scouts need healing," Reza said. "Can any priestesses be spared?"

"Freya's troop is mostly all knights, but I'm sure there's some that can perform a healing. If not, Revna and I will do what we can."

Freya finished up with one of her knights and came over to them. She sized Reza up before holding out an arm in friendship. Reza clasped arms in the traditional manner.

"You the leader of those archers?" Freya asked, her fair, strong features juxtaposed by her flush skin and bloody specks across her brow and neck.

"Yes, I am. Reza Malay, of High Cliffs Monastery."

"Reza Malay..." Freya mused, thinking back to the hearing many weeks ago that had resulted in Reza's expulsion from the saren grounds. "Freya, Knight Champion of West Perch." She pointed to the rangers across the stream. "I saw your troops providing suppressive fire. Thank you. No doubt without your rangers harrying the enemy's flanks and rear, we would have had little chance in holding that line as we did."

Reza bowed her head. "This battle would have been doomed without the valiant stand of your sisters. On behalf of King Reid, King Waldock, and High Cliffs, thank you for standing firm."

"We had no choice. We could outrun them no longer. Do the horsemen stand a chance though? I do not know how many Golden Knights there were, but I know they vastly outnumbered the number of horsemen I saw pass through here."

"King Reid split his two thousand in half and charged the flanks of the Golden Knights' main force once they were focused on the valley. King Waldock's men were not pushing the enemy back alone." Reza pointed along the ridgelines in the direction of each of the ally groups' paths.

"Very well-orchestrated. There's little chance that you just happened upon us then. How did you come to know of our plight?"

"That's a longer story than we have time for. I hate to burden you with this request, but are there any saren healers you can spare to help those scouts that are on death's door?"

"My sisters are mostly knights, though some have rudimentary skill with the healer's touch. I will gather who I can spare." Freya waved to some of the knights behind her. "Livia, Flora, Ceres, and Minor. Do what you can to help some of the wounded scouts across the stream. Reza here will direct you to them."

As the knights approached Reza, Freya called out, "Reza, Lanereth! Once we've gathered our strength and tended to our wounded, we'll need to discuss next steps. We retreated south to find help and refuge—it seems we've found it. Perhaps there is some mutual ground we can meet on. By the sounds of it, you know our situation rather well. I might have some information that could be relevant to your war leaders. I also have word of Kaia and a man called Nomad that will surely interest you, Reza. The way they spoke of you, it is clear you three have close ties."

"Kaia and Nomad? How are they? *Where* are they?" Reza asked urgently.

"As you said, it's too long of a story to get into at the moment, but last I saw them, they were fine. We'll talk more after tending to our people and discussing what comes next."

Reza nodded in agreement and waved for Freya's knights to follow her over to the injured scouts. With the mention of Kaia and Nomad, her mind was now split, half on tending to her injured, and half on her missing loved ones.

Distractedly, she stepped over a Golden Knight only to freeze in place as a hand slapped onto her boot and gripped her ankle. She looked down and met eyes with a dying man, blood staining his golden chainmail where a spear had skewered through to his gut.

She stiffly jerked free of his grasp, his eyes pleading for help, or a swift death. She gave him neither.

Chapter Seven

Recovery and a New Heading

An hour had passed in the valley and with the help of the sarens, those who had been fatally injured amongst the sarens and scouts had been healed.

There had been casualties, especially among the saren. Twenty-four saren had fallen during the short but overwhelming assault by the Golden Knights. Only eight scouts would not be returning to their families back in Rediron.

The two units had done their job well, and by the looks of it, both King Reid and King Waldock were making good on the follow up.

"My scouts say that the Golden army is in full retreat," Fin said to Reza, delivering a report from a few of his scouts that had been sent to keep an eye on the two armies. "They took a good beating, but their force still numbers well into two thousand or more. Whether our forces will harry them all the way back to Alumin is yet to be seen."

"Good," she acknowledged. "Keep me informed of any new developments."

Fin nodded and headed back to connect with Cavok and oversee their troops.

"Reza," Freya called as she made her way across the bloody battlefield, mumbling under her breath something about pitying the hermit whose land this was.

Reza waved her over and pointed to meet up at the end of the yard towards the streambank, not wanting to spend any more time than necessary in the field of bodies. They linked up at the edge of camp, walking upstream to find a waist-high pocket that Reza submerged herself into, rinsing off sweat, blood, and dirt. Coming up out of the chill waters refreshed her and helped clear her head.

Slicking her hair back and wiping her face dry, she got out of the stream for Freya to wash next.

"Last I heard from Lanereth, the count was twenty-four dead on your side," Reza said as Freya waded in the stream.

The saren champion looked blankly down at the water's reflection for a moment. "Twenty-four lost," she confirmed. "So quickly were they gone from us."

"Sareth will see to them now," Reza offered. Freya seemed to appreciate the sentiment.

She submerged herself, staying under a bit longer than Reza had. Coming up, she let out an invigorated breath.

She wrung out her hair and said, "Lanereth had updated me on your situation. Some of it was simply confirmation of what Kaia discussed with me days ago. It seems that your alliance is the Crowned Kingdom's only hope of staving off the cult of Umbraz's influence. As we clearly saw, Golden Crowns are firmly on their side, as is Black Steels' and Alumin's military. They have many powerful allies. When they moved on West Perch, they were silent and swift. We who made it out barely escaped, even with advance warning."

Reza made room for Freya to sit next to her as they talked. She helped her to adjust her pauldron, seeing that she had taken a hit to her arm that bent metal and mangled leather straps.

"Umbraz's influence has corrupted a great deal of the land," Reza grunted as she worked to loose the pinch of leather that was binding Freya's left arm. She took the spine of her camp knife and wedged up the lip of metal on Freya's pauldron strap, freeing it up.

Freya moved her arm around, testing it.

"Weeks ago, I came to West Perch to partition for aid in facing this dark threat. I was rejected then," Reza started with a sigh. "The offer is still on the table, Freya. We need your help. Sareth was with your knights this day; I could see her light clearly upon your sisters."

"Our path is out before us, and our allies and enemies are plain to see. Sareth has placed you directly in our path to aid us when our strength was about to fail. It is clear Sareth is with you and Lanereth. We will join this resistance to help bring back stability to the Crowned Kingdoms."

Reza lowered her head, breathing a sigh of relief. Allies were hard to come by, and she knew the backing of a devout troop of saren knights would prove to be a great asset to their cause.

Freya, unlike most sarens she had dealt with over the years, was one she instantly had felt akin to. She spoke simply and had a resolution that thankfully aligned with Reza's. It was obvious that she knew how to take command on the battlefield, and by Lanereth's word, was an incredible warrior of valor and ferocity. Reza had no doubt that she could become very attached to such an incredible sister-in-arms.

"That…is a relief to hear," Reza said. "Only together do the people of the Crowned Kingdoms stand a chance at combating the corrupting influence of Umbraz."

Freya's wet golden hair dripped and plinked upon her armor. She reached up and wrung water out of her locks.

"Now, I must ask—what news of Kaia and Nomad?" Reza asked

"Kaia had come to me after being rejected an audience before Trensa and the leading sisterhood," she said as she began to take off her boots to pour water from them. "Being in command of the knights, I was the only other saren in a position to do anything about the threats. I did listen to both her and Nomad and worried that West Perch was not prepared for the upcoming storm that she foretold. We made preparations and sent spies to monitor the Golden Crowns' army and the unrest in Alumin. We retreated when we saw that they meant to march on West Perch. We would have stood no chance at defending our home against such numbers. Though they came with us in the initial retreat, it was soon apparent that the Golden Crowns' army was pursuing us. I sent Kaia and Nomad east before the Golden Crowns caught up to us."

"Why?" Reza asked. It was dangerous to send the two away with no support.

"You saw the size of force that pursued us. We would have surely perished—I did not think it necessary for them to die with us," Freya explained, sliding her boots back on and adjusting them.

"Why east?"

"Their mission was to deliver news to the Silver Crowns. Last I heard, they're still neutral to all of this. They need to know what happened in Alumin and how much a threat the Umbraz cult is to all of the Crowned Kingdoms."

"I see. So, they're off to Lancasteal."

"With luck, they're arriving in the Silver Crown's borders by midnight."

"Thank you, Freya." Leaving Freya to finish rinsing off, Reza headed back to camp, finding her crew already huddled, communing with each other.

Fin and Cavok were in a lively back and forth with Lanereth over whether they should give chase with the rest of the armies to see if Reid might need them in the mobile battle while Yozo, Malagar, and Terra kept silent, hearing out the two arguments.

"With the saren's help, we could help King Reid deal a crippling blow to the Golden Crowns' military if we move to catch up now," Fin argued, but Lanereth was shaking her head before Fin had finished his statement.

"We already have, and the battle has already moved well past us. Freya's knights have been hoofing it for days now. They need rest. We risk overextending ourselves. Go with your scouts if you must, but we performed our task in this battle. The rest is up to the king's men," Lanereth protested.

"I agree with Lanereth, Fin," Reza cut in. "Perhaps it wouldn't hurt for the scouts to pursue and aid in the ongoing battle where possible, but the saren troop is tapped out. Many of them just performed healings. They're going to be wiped out for days after all that they just went through. We need to allow them rest."

Fin didn't seem to approve of Reza's input, but he held his peace. Reza moved on from the subject, knowing they were short on time for what she had planned.

"I have requests of you all," she started. "Freya parted ways with Kaia and Nomad a few days ago. She sent them to the Silver Crowns kingdom as a contingency plan to warn other kingdoms of the cult's moves against West Perch in case Freya and her troop were not able to make it to Rediron. They should be at the border of the Silver Crowns by now. I'd like to catch up with them and support their mission. At this point, the Silver Crowns joining us or Umbraz could decide the fate of the war."

"Who would you have go with you on this mission?" Cavok asked.

"I don't think many need to chase after Kaia and Nomad. This would be a diplomatic mission, not a military operation. Fin, Cavok, I'd like for you two to stay with the scouts and report to King Reid upon his return—that, or give chase if you think you can still provide aid in their fight this night. You would have to make your decision on that front with all haste."

"And the sarens?" Lanereth asked.

Reza folded her arms in thought. "I think you and Freya are the most qualified to decide their orders. I talked with Freya, and she indicated that she wishes to join our alliance. In what capacity they will work with King Reid is to be seen. Which leaves you three." She looked to Yozo, Malagar, and Terra. "I was hoping that you'd accompany me to find Nomad and Kaia. With the four of us, even if the road comes with some surprises, we should be able to handle ourselves. I don't suspect Umbraz has invaded that highway as of yet, but…we must be ready for anything."

"Whatever you decide, my sword and I will accompany you," Yozo said. Malagar nodded the same sentiment.

"I don't know this Kaia, but if Nomad could use our help, I would gladly look for him," Terra chipped in.

"If we're lucky," Reza started slowly, "General Seldrin has already reported most of this himself to Silver Crown's ruling council. I doubt they would have received word of the attack on West Perch, though. We'll do what we can to convince their government to make a stand to oppose Alumin."

"You'll want to get mounted if you wish to catch up with Nomad and Kaia." Fin waved over one of his sharpshooters he had been working closely with. The marksman was sent off after a quick order to search for a few horses.

"Seems the hermit owned a horse," Fin explained as the scout returned, leading an old workhorse. "Noticed it around back in a small corral when we were setting up for the fight."

"Well it's not going to be able to carry all four of us, but thank you. It'll at least make the road a bit easier on two of us," Reza said and accepted the reins from the scout.

Fin snapped his fingers, grabbing the scout's attention. "Burl, could you and your men track down another horse? A few of King Waldock's riders fell in battle. There's got to be a few riderless horses in the surrounding area. Grab one—two or three if you're able."

The scout whistled to his crew, and within moments, four scouts were bounding off, two eastwards, two westwards in the canyon.

"Thanks, Fin." Reza smiled gratefully. "Gather anything you might need for the road," she said to Yozo, Malagar, and Kaia. "Perhaps there might be some trail food in Reg's cabin. It'll be a few days before we arrive at Lancasteal and are able to resupply."

Without a word, Yozo and Malagar vanished in the dark of the cabin's doorway to rummage for salvageable rations.

"Fin, if you will, please provide King Reid with a full report on all of this for me. He may not like my sudden departure, but I feel strongly that our success may depend on connection with Nomad, Kaia, and the Silver Crowns."

"You've got it," Fin agreed, extending an arm.

She clasped it and threw an arm over him to hug him. Holding his head to hers, she whispered, "Sareth watch over you. You always needed her eye on you more than I did."

Fin let out a chuckle. "If we make it through all this in one piece, I think I'll owe it to *some* god to attend a sermon or two."

She smiled warmly. The thought of Fin and her attending church together humored her more than a little.

Chapter Eight
A Change of Plans

"Hold tight," Reza said to Terra as she spurred the hermit's workhorse onto the bridge crossing the river that separated the Rediron and Silver Crowns borders.

Terra cinched her arms around Reza's waist. The horse was fearful of the bridge, likely treading over few structures like it in its secluded life in the woods. The last bridge near Canopy Glen they had crossed had been sturdier than this one, but the horse had crossed it with a bit of coaxing. Reza had driven the beast rather hard, and though Yozo and Malagar's mount was faring well, theirs was not.

"We may need to switch steeds after the bridge," Reza suggested. "Malagar is the lightest among us, next to you. We should give this one a break."

The horse nickered and pranced nervously, testing the bridge before Reza spurred it on forcefully. The horse obeyed a bit too well, kicking up into a gallop.

"Woah!" Reza shouted, trying to get control of the frightened beast. She pulled up on the reins, but it was determined to bolt to the other side of the bridge.

Within moments, the horse was on the other side of the river, bolting off the trail, bucking wildly. Reza clenched her thighs to the saddle and held on through the bout of bucking, but Terra was not so fortunate. On the third kick, she was launched off to the side and landed in a shrub to the side of the trail.

"Terra!" Reza called out, finally reining in the panicked horse.

As she moved to dismount and tie up the horse to a thick tree branch, Malagar and Yozo galloped up.

"Take the reins," Malagar called to Yozo, handing off his horse as he went to recover Terra from the twiggy brush just as Reza arrived to assist. The two froze as Terra suddenly let out a startled scream and practically leapt from the clump of bushes along the bridge side, right into Reza's arms.

"What in Sareth's name...?" Instead of an answer, Malagar entered the brush and returned carrying a body. He laid the dead man out on the ground for all to see.

"A fresh kill it seems. He does not yet reek of death," he said, nudging the head to the side to show a deep gash into the corpse's shoulder.

Yozo hitched the horses close to Reza's, then joined the others.

Turning her attention from the corpse, Reza turned Terra around in her arms. "Are you hurt? That was quite the throw."

"I'm...fine—I think. But what is a dead man doing discarded by the roadside?"

"Here," Yozo spoke for the first time that day, grabbing everyone's attention. "Signs of a scuffle."

Reza was no tracker, but even for her, it was clear the ground had been trodden upon recently.

"What do you make of it?" Reza asked.

Yozo remained silent, but was pacing the area thoughtfully, pointing to a spot of grass smattered with blood.

"This is where that man's life was ended. Here's where he landed, and here's where he was dragged over to those bushes."

"This does not bode well. A killing so closely timed to our crossing…few use these roads. Most use the highway north running by the Silver Streams Mountain pass," Reza mused aloud. "General Seldrin did mention reports of bandits in the area last time we were through here. Perhaps this is their doing."

"We have yet to come across Nomad and Kaia. If they came this way like you were told, do you think they had anything to do with this?" Malagar asked, looking to Reza, though it was Yozo that answered instead.

"Nomad favors a downwards cut. In training in our youth, he broke my shoulder twice from a move much like the one that man wears. Luckily for me, we practiced mostly with wooden swords."

"If…Nomad did this…" Reza started but held her tongue. She wasn't sure what exactly it was, but something about the whole scene felt off to her. It wasn't like Nomad to toss a body in some bushes along a road.

"There had to have been more than one assailant," she said, "if this is Nomad we're talking about. He would have simply disarmed or disabled a highwayman if that was the case. Yozo, can you make out how many were here?"

"Two here, our dead man here," he said, focused on the ground once more. He pointed to the sets of tracks in the dirt.

"More over here," Malagar pointed to a trodden section of trail back roadside. He stooped and plucked up a bristly brown split feather. "Yozo, take a look."

Yozo confirmed Malagar's suspicions immediately. "A bolt fletching."

"There was a crude chopper in the bushes, but I saw no crossbow on that man," Malagar offered.

The group considered the ominous connotations of the scene before them.

Yozo expanded his gaze, hounding a trodden path through the grass on the other side of the road. Looking across the waist-high grassy meadow, he announced, "Whomever did this left southwards across those hills."

Reza looked south, considering the vastness of the open wild in that direction. She knew the territory slightly—the Verdant Expanse. It was so named because it was a wilderness, untamed and rarely trailblazed due to the number of folktales and sightings of fey spirits said to walk the region. It was considered to be a land lorded over by Farenlome, the Green Lord, one of the seven lords of the heavens.

She looked back down the trail they had been heading along. "Are you certain that cut was made by Nomad?"

"No. It's just a cut. I am no diviner," Yozo admitted flatly. "That's his strongest angle, though."

Aside from the river's peaceful rumble, her travel companions were quiet, looking to her for guidance. Ultimately, she could see that it would be her choice on whether to investigate the trail southwards or continue on with their initial destination and attempt to sway Silver Crowns to their cause.

"Nomad and Kaia could be mixed up in all of this," Reza said, eyeing the serene grasslands to the south. "We need to look into this before we continue on to Lancasteal."

"Agreed," Terra said. Yozo and Malagar nodded their acceptance of the detour.

Reza turned towards the roadside, waving everyone along. "Let's retrieve our horses. By the looks of it, whomever ran south were on foot. With luck, we'll catch up with them quickly."

Chapter Nine

Finding the Camp

They had lost the trail a few times that day. There had not been many signs of disturbance to guide them. The grass was tall and concealing, but Yozo had proven a competent tracker and picked it up each time. For the better half of the afternoon, they had crossed grassland and navigated around a marsh, and in the end, the trail had led into the forest.

"Their camp is there, maybe a few hundred yards into the woods." Malagar pointed as they neared the treeline.

Yozo seemed to understand his confidence in the statement, but Reza and Terra's questioning looks prompted a further explanation. "See the traces of smoke rising above the canopy?"

Reza squinted, studying the area Malagar indicated, but remained silent.

"It's a small fire, and whatever they're burning, burns clean," Malagar explained.

"It is as he says," Yozo confirmed. "Perhaps it would be wise for me and Malagar to scout the camp before continuing."

Reza nodded. "Terra and I can stay with the horses." She looked up and down the treeline, searching for a spot to hitch the horses. "Half a mile that way along the forest's edge," she said. "Terra and I will ride the horses there. You two gather intel on the camp. I want numbers and to know if Nomad and Kaia have anything to do with this group. Rendezvous with us after. We'll make plans together at that point."

"Understood," Malagar agreed.

The two dismounted and handed over their horses to the women, then were off through the tall grass field, headed towards the forest.

Terra rode Malagar's horse while Reza led Yozo's alongside her until they reached the location she had indicated. They hitched all three horses up to a tree, preparing to wait quietly for the two scouts' return.

The evening air was chill, and with the last sunlight of the day disappearing the last remnants of warmth also left, leaving the two women shivering and searching through their packs for their heavy winter cloaks.

Nibbling on what vittles they had borrowed from the hermit's home, they sat with backs against the horse-hitch tree, swaddled in their furs, watching in the direction of the camp.

It was all but dark by the time they heard movement in the woods. Though there was a sliver of moonlight that would have helped illuminate who approached, the cloak of shadows the trees cast made it impossible to make out who it was until Yozo's voice whispered to them.

"They hold a number of prisoners, including Nomad."

"Have they harmed him?" Reza whispered back.

"Not that we could see."

"Who are they and how many of them?"

It was Malagar who answered this time. "I counted twenty or so. They're ruffians, it is clear. I overheard some of their conversation. Talk of highway robbery, drugs, their latest jobs. They're holding some kind of dignitary of the Silver Crowns kingdom. Also spoke of the foreign man, Nomad, and his female acquaintance—I'd assume that'd be Kaia. They were discussing what they were going to do with them tonight after the duties of the day were completed."

"I assume something deplorable."

"Yes. It would be in their best interest if we intend to intervene, to come to their rescue sooner than later."

"There were also a few White Cloaks in camp," Yozo said.

"Bandits in league with White Cloaks. Why wouldn't they be? The White Cloaks are recruiting everyone they can right now," Reza mused. "Twenty armed thugs are more than I wish to risk an outright conflict with. Could we release the prisoners discreetly?"

After a moment of thought, Yozo answered, "Possibly. They're on the perimeter of camp lashed to log posts, but it's in the open and there are two guards diligent in their watch. We'd need to take them out first and retrieve the three prisoners. But as I said, there's no cover. If anyone in camp looks too closely in that direction, we will be spotted. Our only saving grace is that it is a very dark night. The campfire's light doesn't quite illuminate that section of camp."

Reza thought through the risks. "That might be our best bet. We don't have the numbers to confront them. I'll take Terra and the horses and ride up to the edge of the trees. You and Malagar move in, handle the guards, release Nomad and the others, and then we'll double up on horses and ride back to the road. Does that sound like a plan?"

Yozo readily agreed, but Malagar thought to ask, "Killing the two guards will be the easiest way to 'take care' of them. Are you sanctioning deadly force, or do you want us to attempt to put them unconscious?"

Reza could feel Terra's eyes on her. Out of everyone, she knew Terra would have the hardest time hearing what she was about to say. "It sounds like they are in league with the enemy. We don't have the time or margin for error to mess this extraction up. Deadly force is necessary."

"Understood," Malagar acknowledged. "We should be able to handle the guards and free the prisoners without raising the alarm."

"If killing is not necessary when the time arises, then please, don't," Terra said.

Though Yozo looked cross, Malagar seemed to understand Terra's reticence. "That…is not a decision one can waffle on. Either we move in with the intent to kill, or we don't. Hesitation in the moment, even for a split second, can mean the difference between *our* life or *theirs*."

"The order remains," Reza concluded.

Though she knew she was not winning any points with the more tender youth, Reza knew the full truth of Malagar's words. The stakes were too high to treat the bandit camp with kid gloves. The fate of the kingdom, as well their captive friends, relied on them making with all haste to Lancasteal.

"Let's move. We've no time to dally," Reza concluded, refusing to meet Terra's eyes.

Yozo and Malagar were off the next moment, back the way they had come. Reza moved to retrieve the horses. Terra, however, didn't budge.

"Those guards might not be as guilty of crime as the ones Malagar reported on. They might—"

"Even have families?" Reza finished for her. "I guarantee those Golden Knights we killed had families too. War is messy, Terra. Have you forgotten that since the Arisen War in the Southern Sands? Speak no more of this. Our full attention is on getting Nomad and the others safely back to us."

"I had protests in that war as well," Terra murmured.

"Where were your protests when your god torched all those White Cloaks in Brigganden?"

Reza knew as soon as the words had left her mouth that she would regret them. She looked away and breathed deeply, collecting herself.

She turned back to Terra. "I'm sorry, that was too far."

Terra had no reply. Seeing that Reza was not going to budge on the subject, she snatched one of the horse's reins and mounted up.

The silence between them would at any other time have been downright painful for Reza, especially since she and Terra had had very few fights, but with so much riding on her focus now, Terra's disapproval was the last thing on her mind. As they rode back out into the grasslands under the faint moonlight, her only thoughts were on finding the best spot to lie in wait for Malagar and Yozo to return with the others.

Chapter Ten

Extraction

Malagar followed behind Yozo as the two skulked up to the perimeter of the camp. With the majority of the bandit camp finishing up supper and cracking open a keg, their approach had gone undetected.

In Malagar's assessment, even if the ruffians had been on high alert, he still doubted any in the camp would have spotted them. He couldn't help but wonder at Yozo's adept movements. It was clear he was an expert stalker. He too was skilled at scouting. Matt had trained him in reconnaissance, more so than any of his former crew. He had to dig back into his past training now and hope that it would be adequate for tonight's mission.

Yozo halted for a moment, grabbing Malagar's attention. He pointed to him and then to one of the bandits all but snoozing at his post on the perimeter of the prisoner circle. Malagar nodded his understanding and began to move around the foliage to get as close to his target as possible, then waited for Yozo's move.

The other guard was very much at attention. He was having his fun ahead of the rest of the bandit crew's allotted time with the poor souls that had been picked up roadside.

A swift kick to the groin sent General Seldrin slack, held up by the hemp ropes tying him to the tall stake in the ground. The guard cackled to see the high status haltia crumple under the pain. He backhanded Nomad as his chuckles died off, then staggered over to the young saren and eyed her wantonly. His lusts were on full display. Grabbing her jaw roughly, opening her mouth forcefully, he reached down to undo his grease-stained trousers.

Malagar was just about to rush in, forgetting all about his target, when the man went rigid. It was only a moment later that Malagar noticed Yozo letting the man down softly to the ground, gloved hand covering the guard's mouth and a deep red slit across his neck.

Malagar leapt into action, covering the ground between him and his target. Gripping his knife tight, he clapped a hand over his guard's snoring mouth and ran his blade from one side of the guard's neck to the other, opening up arteries. The man was dead within moments with little struggle.

By the time Malagar had put down the body, Yozo had already cut the bindings of the three prisoners, all rubbing their wrists, which were red and bleeding from the rough treatment that evening. General Seldrin looked the worse for wear out of all of them. It was clear he'd been held there the longest and his condition was worrisome.

Malagar didn't see any signs that anyone in the main camp had noticed their scuffle. Most were too busy fighting over who got the last dregs of the keg to concern themselves with anything else.

He moved over and joined up with the group, helping Nomad and Kaia while Yozo shouldered Seldrin's weight. The group left the camp without a sound, the inky black forest shadows enveloping them within yards of leaving the prisoner's circle.

The first words spoken were not of thanks. "I need to retrieve my sword," Nomad whispered, looking Yozo in the eye.

"Reza is waiting for us with horses at the edge of the forest, there's too many of them to worry about retrieving your belongings," Malagar replied.

"Go then. I'll retrieve it and meet up with you back at the road," Nomad stated.

"Nomad, we don't have time for this—" Malagar started, but Nomad cut him off.

"That is the last thing I have of my heritage. It's blessed by Bede and the light of Elendium. It's worth more to me than my very life. I will not leave it here with that scum."

To Malagar's surprise, Yozo spoke. "Take these two and return to Reza and Terra. I will see that Nomad retrieves his sword. If the highwaymen come out of that forest instead of us, ride hard and fast to Lancasteal. Don't come back for us."

Yozo handed off Seldrin to Malagar and placed a hand on the hilt of his sword, ready to turn back to camp once Nomad had taken a moment to recover his strength.

Malagar chuffed in frustration and disbelief, watching their well-executed plan needlessly unravel.

"Nomad," Kaia whispered, "be careful."

He met her eyes and nodded before attempting to get back to his feet. Yozo waited, watching Nomad struggle to stand upright, clutching his side. The two turned back towards camp and disappeared in the shadows of the night.

"Damned fools. All for a sword," Malagar murmured. Hefting Seldrin, he called quietly to Kaia. "Come, with luck, they'll return to us. If they do or don't—perhaps *especially* if they don't—we need to be ready to bolt."

Chapter Eleven

Return

"His what?" Reza whispered.

"His sword," Malagar explained. "He refused to leave without it."

"I suppose I can understand that," she said softly, though deep down, she could appreciate Malagar's exasperation. Without context, she would have been just as upset with his decision to stay and look for his sword.

"I don't see why. That camp will find the guards' dead bodies any moment now. I'm surprised they haven't already!" Malagar hissed.

"That sword saved more than just his life through the years." She was about to say more but knew that now was not the time.

Looking back into the dark forest, she considered their next move. Kaia and Terra were whispering in soft tones to each other as she and Malagar discussed the plan. She was glad to see Kaia safe. Now was not the time for catching up, however, and she needed to make a hard choice that would split them up once more.

"Malagar. You take Terra, Kaia, and General Seldrin on two horses and ride to Lancasteal. Our message needs to be delivered to Silver Crown officials, with or without me. I'll head to camp and make sure Yozo and Nomad make it out of there safely. We'll take the other two horses and meet you in Lancasteal."

"You, alone? I cannot allow you to—"

"Yes you can. I need to know General Seldrin and the others make it to Lancasteal. That objective is more important than anyone else's safety. The fate of the war may rely upon it, and Seldrin isn't fit to lead that journey in his current state," she said, a hint of sorrow in her voice as she looked upon a worn-down man that she had only hitherto seen as proud and strong. "This is an order. Nomad and Yozo are competent warriors, so am I. We'll be fine."

Though Malagar looked cross with Reza's decision, he did not refute it. He turned and helped Seldrin to his feet and called to Terra and Kaia to get mounted on one of the horses. Reza released a sigh of relief, seeing Malagar rounding up the group quickly. Within a minute, the four were heading north into the night, leaving her alone with the other two horses hitched along the treeline.

She breathed deeply. The whirl of the last few days had exhausted her. She did not wish to search for the bandits' camp. She wanted to lie down in the grassy meadow and gaze at the sliver of moon that illuminated the quiet countryside.

It was a fool's dream, she knew. Letting out a heavy breath, she placed a tired hand along her sword hilt and started into the shadows of the forest to look for her companions.

———•◎•———

Nomad nodded silently, indicating that this was the tent where they had placed his, Kaia's, and Seldrin's things.

The two moved in closer, crouching low and listening to count how many were in the tent.

There were low murmurs within, nothing discernible, but both Nomad and Yozo could tell that there was a small group inside. There would be no way for them to discreetly retrieve the sword.

A shout on the other side of camp caused all within the tent to go quiet. More voices rang out, and both Yozo and Nomad knew that the direction the yelling was coming from was the prisoner circle where they had left the dead guards slumped against the stakes. They had been found.

The tent flap flew open and multiple White Cloaks rushed out and ran towards the commotion.

Nomad and Yozo listened for signs of any stragglers within, but all they could hear were commands being shouted from the main camp.

Yozo signaled for Nomad to follow him in. The two skulked around to the front, slipping in through the draped tent flap.

Nomad followed Yozo as he leapt inside. Yozo was quick to handle the situation. He held a White Cloak by the wrist, sword to the bald man's throat.

Nomad was waiting for Yozo to execute the White Cloak but was surprised when he gave the order for Nomad to retrieve his things, even while Yozo brought the White Cloak in front of him to hold him better.

To ask if Yozo intended on killing him would affect the White Cloak's next move, and so Nomad carried out Yozo's orders silently, quickly finding their stash of gear in a corner of the tent.

Consolidating a few of Seldrin and Kaia's items in one bag, he threw the pack on and secured his sword at his side.

The tent was eerily quiet as Nomad finished up. He nodded to Yozo.

The bald man was trembling now, seeing that whatever their business was with him, it was now concluding.

"The saren and that haltia with you—you're all dead you know. Umbraz's followers know you by *name* and *face* now. There will be no place to hide in the kingdoms."

Nomad considered his words, the chaos in camp underscoring the direness of the moment. The White Cloaks had extracted information from General Seldrin somehow before they had been brought into camp, and he had readily given the zealots information on him and Kaia upon their arrival. This man knew much of their aims.

Nomad cautiously opposed the point. "If the Silver Crowns join our cause, then Umbraz will be hard pressed to contend against the free peoples of the Crowned Kingdoms."

"It doesn't matter if they join the fight or not, either on his side or against him. Umbraz doesn't need armies to claim this realm. Soon, he will be the *only* reality. It's only a matter of time before he fully manifests. And when he does, all who oppose him will be annihilated in a blink—"

Footsteps were quickly approaching. Nomad drew his sword, ready for whomever was unfortunate enough to open the tent flap.

With a swift smack of Yozo's sword butt to the back of the zealot's head, the White Cloak fell forward, collapsing on the ground, just as the tent flap was hastily thrown open. Nomad halted his thrust just in time as Reza appeared before them, startled.

"Time to leave," Reza whispered, leading Yozo and Nomad out of the tent and into the dark woods.

Chapter Twelve

Coming to Terms

"You retrieved my book?" Kaia asked Nomad as he fished through his pack.

"Here." He handed the thick scripture over to her as he approached the other half of the group.

They had waited for the three roadside, against Reza's orders. Though Reza was not pleased with the decision, she let the matter go without further remarks other than a disgruntled stern eye.

"I grabbed what I could," Nomad offered, unstringing a sword from the side of the pack. "General. Here's your blade."

General Seldrin stared at the weapon.

"Take it," Nomad said.

"I…don't deserve to carry that blade. Not after breaking to the enemy," he mumbled, looking away.

"White Cloaks can be…convincing," Yozo said. Everyone but Malagar looked at the soft-spoken man. "There is no shame upon you from whatever happened in that camp. Be kind to yourself, at least till all this is over. We all will have plenty of time to punish ourselves for our mistakes in this war after Umbraz is no longer a threat. But for now, we each need to have a steady hand, even if it's just an outwardly act."

Seldrin was left speechless by Yozo's words, as well as everyone else. Yozo's eyes drilled the general as he pointed to the sword. "Now take your sword and lead like a general of the Silver Crowns."

Reza was genuinely surprised at the drastic change in Seldrin. He had been so proud, so resolute and strong in the time that she had known him. Now, he was utterly withdrawn.

He made an effort and unceremoniously took the saber from Nomad, allowing everyone in the circle to breathe a bit easier.

Nomad turned to Reza. "The White Cloaks in camp. We spoke to one of them briefly. I don't know if his words are important, but he did not seem to think that Umbraz needs an army to conquer the realm. He said that it is only a matter of time before he manifests, and that once he arrives in our realm, all who oppose him will be annihilated in a blink."

Reza looked concerned by the threat but had no response

"That makes sense," Kaia mumbled to herself, flipping through the scripture Nomad had handed over to her.

"Explain," Reza demanded.

"Well, ever since Rosewood, I've been reading through this scripture I recovered from the pulpit there. It's a compendium of their doctrine. It's a record of visions and sermon notes from the father of the faith there at Rosewood. Most of it is, quite honestly, the hard to follow ravings of a madman." Kaia turned to a page in the book. "There are multiple references to the end and the beginning. An intersection in time when all that was *ends*, and all that follows is *new*. The point of no return. Once Umbraz enters our realm and becomes conscious."

"Does this scripture tell of *how* Umbraz will manifest?" Reza asked.

"I...think so. It is unclear, but from what I can discern, a monument built of flesh and soul will be the catalyst for opening up the gateway between the Seam and our realm," Kaia replied.

"A monument," Reza whispered. "Perhaps a statue?"

Kaia thought on the suggestion. "I suppose something like that."

"Like the statue in the basement of Rosewood," Nomad said.

Reza nodded. "I saw that statue shatter. Even if it had not been destroyed, I doubt they would have kept it there after our uncovering it. The only thing Rosewood had going for it was seclusion and secrecy."

"Well, if they needed to constitute another statue to summon Umbraz, and you don't believe that they would construct it in Rosewood again, where would they build it next?" Kaia asked.

"They have effectively taken over Alumin. That is likely their stronghold—there or the Black Steels or Golden Crowns, but since the church is the head of this cult, I would think they would want to maintain their base in a location where they have full possession and autonomy," Reza reasoned.

"There is a lot of guesswork in these assumptions," Malagar prodded.

"Indeed. Kaia, when there's time, please review that scripture with Terra. Terra has insight on this religion that may prove essential to understanding this father's ravings. I want additional eyes on that text. Make sure to report anything significant either of you find."

"Gladly," Kaia agreed, shuffling closer to Terra to whisper with her over the tome.

Reza turned to the rest of the group. "As for what's next, we need to get General Seldrin to Lancasteal immediately to explain the situation."

"They took my crown. I've been beaten and humiliated. The judges won't look kindly upon me disobeying orders and coming back home a failure."

"You have a duty to your people, to the Crowned Kingdoms, and to us. You will testify before your government of Umbraz's actions."

Though Seldrin did not reply, Reza could see he had no grounds to refute her command.

"One last thing," she added. "Yozo and Malagar. If for whatever reason the Silver Crowns officials move against us once in Lancasteal, see that you two escape so that you can report to King Reid. There is always the possibility that we're too late and they've already allied with the White Cloaks. Remain ready to give the slip at any moment."

"Understood. We'll remain as detached as possible," Malagar answered for them both.

"Alright. That's the plan as it stands," Reza concluded. "We don't know what we'll be riding into, so keep sharp. Let's mount up."

A chill breeze rushed through the huddle, forcing everyone to clutch at their winter cloaks as they sluggishly made it to their horses. With everyone double mounted, the only consolation was that they would at least have another warm body to press against on the long ride ahead.

As they started at a slow clip down the highway, the open road before them, all remained quiet, save for Kaia and Terra softly conversing over the scripture.

The trail would offer them long hours in solitude with their thoughts. A fact that none found comfort in.

Chapter Thirteen
Addressing the Council

"I'm sorry, General Seldrin, but the judges gave strict orders that there were to be no interruptions during this conference," said the haltia behind the desk in the court building. "They're surely to be soon finished and you can speak with them after they return from the high court room on their way out."

Seldrin had already been held up once by guards at the building's entrance. He was losing his patience with the spectacled man that stood between them and an audience with the high judges. "I need to speak with them, now, while they're all together in session. The fate of the kingdom is at risk."

"The fate of the kingdom has been at risk since you left last month, General," the desk clerk sighed.

"Remous. I need to get into that room," Seldrin pressed, his tone softening.

The clerk eyed the general hard, testing Seldrin's determination. It was clear the general was not going to step down from his demands. Looking back at the four guards at the entrance of the hallway to the high court, Remous sighed, exasperated, and waved his hands for the guards to allow Seldrin and his crew to pass.

"But only you and two others. I can't allow your whole group to barge in on the judges. I'd surely be fired if I allowed that to happen."

"Reza and Kaia then," General Seldrin said. "After all, the high judges already know you."

Remous waved the three along. He was flustered at the General's presence and wanted him to quickly conclude his business in the court building as soon as possible.

Two of the guards escorted the three down the long hallway, taking them past a sweeping view of the city. It was overcast outside, fittingly so, casting a dour mood on the group as they entered the courtroom lined with lower circuit judges as well as the high judges. Seldrin could tell, whatever the meeting was about, it was important. He had only seen such a showing of officials in times of war.

"Where in damnations have you been, General? Your attachment came back without you and without any explanation of why," the youngest judge, High Judge Astrin scolded, silencing the debate as all judges turned their attention to the newcomers.

"I…was delayed. Actually, I was taken prisoner by a group of White Cloaks. Reza and her crew rescued me."

"You were supposed to have delivered those two to the church in Alumin a month ago. How could they have rescued you? And why did Jake and Neri return without their general?" Astrin argued.

"A lot has happened since we last left Lancasteal." Seldrin held a hand up. "The church and the White Cloaks are the same. They've allied with the Golden Crowns and the Black Steels. They are moving in force upon the Rediron kingdom and will soon set their sights on overthrowing Silver Crowns. We need to mobilize our army and move to support Rediron. This is our only hope of protecting our kingdom from Umbraz's force. They will move upon us soon, if they haven't already."

The room went silent. Seldrin didn't know if that meant they were considering what to do about the grave news, or what to do with him.

Judge Astrin rubbed his eyes. "For three days the Black Steels have been marching upon our lands. Silver Streams Mountain and Thurn have been overrun. Neither resisted the invasion. From our reports, it seems no harm has come to them as of yet, but their force is dividing and marching. If they reach Lancasteal, we will have no choice but to defend our city borders."

"*If* they reach Lancasteal?" Seldrin said. "The towns of this kingdom have been invaded, and this council now waits for our enemy to surround us and squander our ability to retaliate? At the sign of the first border crossing, there should have been an aggressive response."

"And where was our general to lead that response?" Astrin retorted. "This is not a council of tacticians, Seldrin. Their numbers are great, and they have the full backing of Alumin and the church. They know the size of our army. We don't have the force needed to contest them."

"We always have the capability to defend our country, our people, and way of life. The Rediron kingdom even now is fighting Umbraz and his armies. We are not alone in this war. We need to repel the Black Steel Crowns from our lands and ally ourselves with Rediron at once, we don't have a day to spare."

"And how are you so sure that they will come to our aid?" Astrin asked.

"I am here on their behalf," Reza said, stepping up to answer. "Though, I do not know how much aid they will be able to offer. They are hard pressed with defending against the Golden Crowns' main force right now."

"This offers us no solace. What good is an alliance if we receive no support if a war is to come."

"The war has come already! Just because you haven't officially declared it to be means nothing to Umbraz. He will have all of Silver Crowns if we do not act now."

"Both Rediron and Silver Crowns are in a rough spot, but not confronting the enemy together will all but ensure both kingdoms' demise. Unifying our efforts is our only path through this," Seldrin added, his voice strained for patience.

The mood among the judges was dark. Judge Astrin spoke his mind. "Both the Golden Crowns and the Black Steels are well versed in warfare. Already, the odds are not in Rediron or our favor, but with Alumin and this cult of White Cloaks…victory is all but impossible."

"Not all of Black Steel Crowns or Alumin fell in with Umbraz," Reza replied. "The saren at West Perch have retreated to the South and now fight alongside Rediron. The Lost King and his band of resistance soldiers also found a place with King Reid. Some even came from Jeenyre Monastery to join the cause. There's more hope in an insurgency than you make it out to be. There is a chance to win this war—if we act now and all stand together against Umbraz."

"Please, council," Seldrin said, humbling himself in a final attempt to reason with the judges. "I have served as the general of the Silver Crowns for many years and have devoted my life to protect it. Allow me to make the call now to go to war. Believe me when I say, from what I've seen and heard out there in the kingdoms the last few weeks, that this may be our only window to stand and make a difference. If the Silver Crowns yield now to our enemy, our people have no future."

The young judge sighed and looked around the room to his colleagues. "We will call for a vote."

Seldrin nodded his approval and Judge Astrin raised a hand to make an announcement.

"All those in favor of *declaring war* with the faction of kingdoms and entities which are namely: Black Steel kingdom, the Golden Crowns kingdom, Alumin, and the war cult of Umbraz, formerly known as the church of Elendium, say *yea*."

Each fellow judge in the room voiced *yea*, one after another.

"Those against, *nay*"

All was quiet.

"Let the record so reflect that the vote to declare war was unanimous by the ring of high judges. Gentlemen, we are at war. General, gather your leaders. Make preparations to defend our city and regain our lands if it is feasible and prudent. We will attend war councils when you see necessary."

The moment came with impact. None dared break the silence until Astrin's final decree was issued.

"General Seldrin, you have executive command of our kingdom until this war's conclusion."

Chapter Fourteen

A Path Forward

"You've brought the remaining sacks of white spice and the shipment of foodstuffs?" Reid asked of his right-hand man, Morgan.

The quiet man nodded.

"Have the substance mixed in with anything that won't look suspicious: grains, bread, dried meats, wine. We'll leave a small force along the highway with it. If Alumin sends a force south along the highway, have the men leave the supplies and retreat to the fallback point at the bridge with the main force."

"Aye," Morgan grunted and snapped his horse's reins. He headed down to the camp to set the plan in motion.

King Reid turned his attention from his men's encampment along the highway to his leaders behind him. Trotting up, he addressed them.

"Yesterday's victory was a testament to each of you as leaders of your people. Lanereth and Freya, we are in your debt for the healings you have performed. Beyond that, you have proven yourselves fearless in the face of unbeatable odds. We are honored by your presence and participation in the free-people's alliance in this war against Umbraz and his followers."

Freya held up a hand. "It is you who should be thanked. Without your intervention, it would have been a massacre. Facing the enemy with courage or not, my saren would have ended there and then."

"By helping each other, we help ourselves," King Waldock said. The others muttered their agreements. He continued. "Johnathan, your men were fierce and swift in their assault upon the Golden Crowns' rearguard. I dare say it was your contingent that forced the full-on retreat of their host, not my army's presence. You have trained your soldiers well, it is apparent."

Johnathan bowed his head, accepting the compliment.

"Fin and Cavok, you two should also be commended in your performance in yesterday's battle. Without your experienced eyes and quick actions, initial contact of both the saren force could have gone very differently."

Fin waved away the compliment. "It's the scouts that deserve the credit. They're expertly skilled both with aim and stalking. True huntsmen, all of them."

"I would like to include Reza in this acknowledgement," Reid said with some exasperation lining his voice. "However, it's reported that she left for the Silver Crowns kingdom soon after the Golden Crowns' retreat."

"It was essential that she left with all haste," Fin was quick to explain. "Nomad and Kaia were last known headed for Lancasteal to tell Silver Crowns news of the war. She knows the Silver Crowns general and believes she may be able to convince the governing body there to join our cause. If she can accomplish this, we would have a strong ally in this war."

"Yes…" Reid allowed after a moment. "That was the plan we had discussed, though moving ahead of schedule has the potential to complicate things. I had others in mind for seeking diplomacy with the haltia."

Reid turned and looked over the army once more. Redironers, King Waldock's clan, the sarens, all mingled, tending to duties and helping where they could with each other's wounded. They had just had their first major battle with a still relatively obscure enemy banner that was Umbraz. Black Steels and Golden Crowns had always been warfaring nations. Alumin had been the glue holding all four kingdoms together for so long. Now with its dissolution, all pretenses of civility had been cast off. A month ago, none of this would have seemed real to any of them.

"We need to form a line at Jaren's Crossing. That bridge is essential if Reza is successful in securing a Silver Crowns alliance," Reid said, his breath mist in the cold morning air. "We also need to protect our western flank. The Mad Queen may seek to take advantage of our eastern-heavy presence. If she pressed with a force along our western borders, Leniefoot and Norburry Abbey will fall swiftly. They are small establishments and have few defenses against an armed and trained force of any considerable size. If those locations fall, it's only a matter of time before Castle Sauvignon is threatened. Without Castle Sauvignon, our alliance has no home, and we'd be cut off from supplies and multiple strategic essentials—our resistance would be fatally compromised."

He took out a thin cigar and struck a match. He counted out the alliance's numbers in his head, thinking through the possible positions of each. All waited patiently for him to consider their next move. Somewhere in the last few days, it had become clear that King Reid had inherited the unspoken title of commander of the gathering resistance movement. None had contested his orders in the last battle, and with its unquestionable success, even against unfavorable odds, his lead had been cemented amongst his peers.

He pointed with embered cigar in hand to the highway leading to Alumin. "Warchief Waldock, we shall leave your cavalry unit on the highway here with a supplies shipment I've prepared. When Alumin comes to attack, you'll retreat to Jaren's Crossing where half of my army and Freya's knights will be waiting. There is favorable terrain for us to hold there. The hills and forests offer natural choke points which we can set up. My men are adept at guerilla warfare. If Alumin really wants a fight, we can give them more than they can chew."

"Why leave the supplies?" King Waldock cut in.

"We've poisoned them," Reid said. "They may see it for the ruse that it is, but it's worth a try. Make sure not to retreat too soon, Johnathan. We'll need to sell the illusion that we don't want to part with those supplies.

"If all goes according to plan, that may just weaken the Golden Crowns' main force enough for us to press them all the way back to Alumin, though that plan does take time to set in. The poison we're using is White Spice. A poison Redironers' know the effects of all too well. Those affected with the Warp sickness don't have a speedy recovery. We're not sure one can recover from it at all. Once the damage is done, we'll not be expecting those troops to return to their posts anytime soon."

"And if they don't take the bait?" Johnathan asked.

"Then we have established a strong fallback point. We keep the Golden Crowns from advancing and hope that Reza comes through with an alliance with Silver Crowns," Reid answered.

"And your army's other half?"

"I'll send supporting contingents to shore up Leniefoot, Dunnmur, and Norburry Abbey to ensure our western front is not defenseless."

Johnathan's father spoke up. "What of Castle Sauvignon, what sort of numbers do you have there? What if Black Steels' army overcomes your defenses?"

Reid took a quick puff of smoke. "Well, I left all castle guardsmen and reserves stationed at Castle Sauvignon—maybe two hundred trained soldiers with another three hundred militia, minimal training. That should be enough to withstand an assault on the castle proper for us to receive word and return to give fight."

As Reid spoke, Morgan rode back up to the leadership gathering and waited for Reid's acknowledgement, which he readily gave upon noticing him.

"The White Spice is being administered to the supplies, as ordered," he reported. Reid nodded his approval. Morgan turned in his saddle and waved over a group of soldiers marching three White Cloak zealots their way.

"Among the prisoners of war were three White Cloaks. The rest of their brethren all took their lives before we could even begin to reason with them. We have a number of Golden Knights detained, but I suspect you'll want to be interrogating these White Cloaks first," Morgan surmised.

"Yes, that is a wise assumption. That they value their life more than their devotion to Umbraz gives us leverage to work with," Reid mused as the demoralized zealots shuffled to the spot.

Reid looked down at the three White Cloaks before him. "You will be given a chance to make recompense. If you cooperate with my man here and answer his questions truthfully, you will be allowed to live. This is the only choice you will be given. Cooperation, or death."

Waving them away, he held Morgan back and whispered orders of the details he wished him to extract from the men if possible, then turned back to the leaders' circle and addressed them.

"Yesterday was ours—our victory. Today, we collect ourselves, see to our people, our wounded, and our plans. All save for King Waldock's cavalry will move out by nightfall. A march through the night will see us to Jaren's Crossing by morning. We'll reconvene to discuss the following days at that time. Are we in agreement?"

Some hope had been allowed the leadership after the fresh victory, but each was experienced enough in warfare to know that the road ahead was fraught with peril. It was the first battle of many to come in the war that they had entered. Reid could feel their nervousness of the odds that were stacked against them.

He toked on his cigar as the leadership mulled over their situation privately for a moment before concluding. "Spend time with your people till nightfall. They need assurance. This war came on quicker than any expected. They need your guidance now. They need your strength."

Chapter Fifteen
In the Study

They had not had much trouble with settling into their rooms; they were traveling light after all and there was hardly anything to unpack. Kaia had stayed in that very room weeks earlier, not as a guest, but as a prisoner. The view of Lancasteal seemed different to her now, however. Perhaps it was the cloud cover that did not look to be letting up anytime that day, but the city looked in a dour mood. War was at its doorstep, and she could feel the dread just by looking over the city itself.

"This is interesting," Terra said after spending minutes reading the scripture. "*The gray ships of time pass onwards at a steady pace as they ever have, but now, another ship sets sail—a destroyer. One that shall conquer the seas and plunge the gray ships to the depths—relics of a soon forgotten era.*"

"Such ravings," Kaia whispered, still looking out the window upon the gloomy city.

"Perhaps not," Terra mused. "The gray ships of time is common symbolism used in my faith. Elendium often refers to existence as a great and endless body of water. All living things ride upon these gray ships, going ever forward to the sunset. Perhaps…they are mixing doctrine here."

Kaia thought of the verse's meaning with more interest. "I would assume that the destroyer is Umbraz."

"Yes. Are they saying time itself will cease upon Umbraz's coming?"

Kaia sighed, taking one last look at the city before coming to sit at the table with Terra. "If that's the case, we had better make sure that his ship doesn't leave port. We need to learn more about his prophesied inception. Maybe there's a way to interrupt or stop his arrival into our realm."

"Do you know anything about his summoning ritual?" Terra asked, skimming through the tome.

"Well, the text is rather cryptic, or at least I don't understand most of what the father was trying to say. There is a section discussing the monument of Umbraz, though, same as I mentioned on the trail yesterday." She scooted up next to Kaia. "This likely refers to the statue Reza and Nomad saw in Rosewood."

They read through the section together, lingering on the crude illustrations depicting Umbraz upon a throne, as well as a rune-like code neither could interpret.

Terra began to read aloud: "*A great number of souls must feed the Seam dimension and an equal portion of flesh must be transmuted in our dimension in order for our god to properly be admitted into our realm. This stability, this balance of soul and flesh, matter and antimatter, must remain constant in the early stages of his holy inception…*"

They sat in silence for a while, thinking on the grave passage. Kaia spoke up first. "This cult has been harvesting people for some time now. I wonder how close they are to bringing him into this world."

"Unless we ask the clergy in the faith itself, I doubt we'll discover the answer on our own," Terra answered.

Kaia muttered, "I despise the prospect of interrogating one of those zealots."

"Whether we despise the idea or not, we might need to do it if the chance arises. At least now we have an idea of what to ask. We need to know where they keep the monument and how close they are to welcoming in Umbraz to our dimension."

"Reza seems to think they're housing it in Alumin, perhaps in the Elendium synagogue," Kaia offered.

"They very well could be holding it there, performing the sacrificial rites in the synagogue, but before we make firm plans centered around that key piece of information, we need to confirm it somehow."

Kaia shrugged. "Well, I agree with you, but who we really need to convince is Reza. She's the one that makes the calls."

"Yes, she does tend to force herself into positions where she's able to call the shots," Terra said. Kaia could hear the irritation in her voice.

"Is that a bad thing?"

"Not usually, no." Terra sighed. "I suppose if she wasn't so bull-headed, then, well, she wouldn't be Reza, now, would she? That trait does tend to help her accomplish her goals."

"You wish she would ease up a bit?"

"Maybe," Terra admitted. "Would it kill her to rely upon others every now and then, or trust in someone else's opinion over hers for once? Sometimes I don't feel she's listening to others, or if she is, she isn't taking their opinions into consideration."

Kaia put a comforting hand on Terra's thigh. "I haven't known her for long, but even since I first met her, I have seen a change in her. She is working on herself, Terra. I think she is realizing that it's okay to allow herself to open up and show a little vulnerability to her friends."

Terra sighed again. "I sure hope so. She can be so closed off and self-assured sometimes."

"As a fellow saren, I can understand why," Kaia said.

Terra looked questioningly at Kaia, waiting for an explanation. Kaia slowly stood up and moved to the window, once again looking out into the city's cloudy vista.

"We don't really have families like most cultures do. We're not born into this world through natural means. Sareth is our mother. We're placed here as youths with very little memory of how we got here. We find our way to other sarens, drawn to them inextricably like hatchling tortoises drawn to the sea. Once there, we are assigned a matron. Matrons essentially function as surrogate mothers in Sareth's physical absence, but…I won't lie, I have seen the bonds of other family units in Alumin and part of me does envy what they have. I think sarens tend to lack closeness with others because of this method of rearing. Reza is no exception. She struggles to connect, even with those that are considered extremely close to her, and to me, that's understandable."

"I know I just met you, but…you don't seem to be like most sarens I've met. Why aren't you more rigid like your sisters? Were you raised differently than most sarens?"

"No. I've had a traditional saren upbringing."

"Then what's different?"

"I…don't know. It's true, I do feel somewhat out of place at West Perch. Never really felt like I belonged there. Perhaps that's why when Reza showed up, I practically forced myself into her company. I knew I needed to leave."

Terra walked over to stand next to her at the window. "Well it's been lovely to have you along. Perhaps someday, when the fate of the world is not hanging in the balance, we'll all be able to enjoy some rest together and have some proper time to get to know each other."

Terra held her hand out and Kaia accepted it with a smile.

The moment didn't last long as a sudden knock came at their door.

Opening the door, they welcomed Yozo and Malagar into the room.

They laid two full packs on the ground, opened both up, and began dividing the rations and gear into six equal portions, one pile for each in their group.

"How'd the afternoon go?" Terra asked.

Yozo kept organizing, but Malagar stopped and answered. "Fine enough. We secured everything we'll need for a week or two on the road, minus water, which we'll have to stop for. But there's plenty of streams in this region. Shouldn't be an issue."

There was an awkward silence. "And the horses? Were you able to get one for everyone?"

"Yes," Malagar replied. "Though we had to sell the hermit's horse…it was much too cumbersome to deal with."

"We'll need to repay him when we get a chance," Kaia chipped in.

"I highly doubt there will be a chance," Malagar shot down, beginning to help Yozo sort the gear. The disappointment of the two young women got to him, even though his back was to them. He slowed after a few moments. "But…if there is time after the war—then yes—we should do that. He is owed reparations for more than just the horse."

Yozo handed both Kaia and Terra a bundle of supplies. "That should last you at least a week on the road."

Malagar scooped up the other supply bundles and placed them back in the packs to hand one off to Yozo. Without another word, the two departed, leaving the two women alone and at a loss for words.

Both placed the supply bundles down on the bed and returned to the scripture at the table, picking up where they had left off.

"Where were we before all of that?" Terra mumbled, looking through the page of vague summoning incantations.

"We need a cooperative White Cloak to question," Kaia answered in a forlorn voice. "Without one, I doubt we'll be able to fully unlock this text."

Chapter Sixteen
Moving Out

Reza had been briefed the night before with the rest of the crew. After having spent all day in meetings with Seldrin and the haltia military and government, she and Nomad had returned late that night and instructed the crew to be ready to move out and to meet up at the city gate at sunrise.

The morning fog was heavy, hanging low to the ground, penetrating through even their heavy winter coats, chilling them to the bone as they waited shivering in the dawn's first rays of sunlight just outside of Lancasteal's city walls.

Kaia lifted a shivering arm to wave to Reza and Nomad as they approached the gate. They were being escorted out of town by a large troop of haltia soldiers, prompting questions to Kaia and the others about why an armed escort was necessary. Both Yozo and Malagar were on edge over the militaristic show and looked ready to bolt. Terra and Kaia approached Reza, calling to her through the gate now opening for them.

"What's with the armed escort?" Terra asked as they met at the gate.

The gate had been raised. Reza turned and called for the long line of mounted haltia soldiers to move forward to begin their long march towards Rediron.

She waved Terra and the others off to the side of the highway as the cavalry unit moved on past.

"Are you...in command of this troop? What happened in your meetings yesterday?" Malagar asked. "Mount up, Nomad will explain on the way back to Rediron. We'll have plenty of time to go over the details of the situation," she answered as she and Nomad took the two extra horses.

The six were riding to catch up to take the lead of the hundred soldier unit soon thereafter, settling in at the head of the line, setting a comfortable trot along the road westwards.

"Nomad. Drive ahead with the others for a bit. Report back once they've been briefed or if you spot anything out of the ordinary along the road," Reza ordered. The crew could tell that she expected complete compliance.

Trotting ahead a few hundred yards, Nomad eventually slowed their pace and turned to address Terra, Kaia, Malagar, and Yozo.

"Apologies for keeping you all in the dark about all of this, there was simply not enough time granted us to connect with you until now.

"General Seldrin was granted executive power over the Silver Crowns military without needing the court's approval on movements. Seldrin and Reza were in war councils all yesterday, attempting to construct a plan of action against Umbraz's forces. Reza has been petitioning to send some of the Silver Crown's troops to help support the Rediron effort, but it seems as it stands, even with their full force focused on defending their lands, they still will have a tough fight simply in repelling the Black Steels from their borders. He was advised by all his council to use every last haltia in their control to fight their own war and not to lend any support to Rediron. Reza was persistent, though, and General Seldrin is sympathetic to the Rediron plight. In the end, he allowed a hundred cavalry units to return with us back to Rediron."

"What's the total number of their military?" Malagar asked.

"Six thousand two hundred forty. One thousand seven hundred forty are being held in reserve to defend Lancasteal itself. One thousand are headed east to take back Thurn, and the main force of three thousand five hundred are headed to Silver Streams and will connect with the one thousand force at the crossroads if all goes according to plan. From there, they will secure their borders and the highways and will move in on Rosewood Cloister and raze the location.

"Seldrin did ask me to relay his apologies for not being able to entrust more troops to our cause, and that he couldn't continue with us, but he is needed to lead the war effort for his people. They feel that the situation they face is dire and will require their full focus. They wish us luck on our side of the border and encourage us to keep open communications if at all possible as the war wages on."

Nomad could tell the news was less than the group had hoped for, but at length, Yozo offered, "*At the least* the Silver Crowns are dedicating themselves to confront the Black Steel Crown's main force, that alone is cause for relief for Rediron."

"That does give this resistance effort a chance," Nomad agreed. "I know we were hoping for more from Seldrin's people, but this will have to do. I can't blame them. In the end, the safety of their own kingdom should come first, and from what I heard yesterday, Seldrin seems to have a good head on his shoulders when it comes to war stratagem."

"What's our next move?" Kaia asked.

"First, we'll revisit the bandit camp and clear it out. They could cause trouble for carriers which will be essential during this war in order to keep both kingdoms informed. After that, we'll head back to Rediron and connect up with King Reid and the others and assist in any way we can."

Nomad let the subject sit for a time, and with no follow up questions, he glanced back to Reza who was busy leading the haltia troop.

"How's Reza holding up with all this?" Terra asked, knowing Nomad well enough to recognize the lines of worry on his brow for what they were.

"She's tired," he said softly.

Terra looked back down the trail at the saren she had grown so close to over the years. Turning her horse around, she said, "Then let's make sure she knows we're by her side."

Chapter Seventeen
Return to Camp

Yozo and Malagar signaled to their respective detachments to move into the forest hundreds of yards in either direction from Reza and the remaining haltia force. Though over a hundred riders were now marching to surround the bandit camp, the riders moved with hardly a sound to indicate otherwise.

Yozo and Malagar had been impeccable with guiding them back to the bandit camp. Even Reza had been somewhat doubtful they had the right patch of trees after the long gallop through the grass fields, but now she began to see the familiar structures through the trees as they rode.

All riders converged and rushed into encampment, spears leading the way—but there was nothing to bury their points in. The place was vacant. Lifting up tent flaps with their spear points, the force confirmed that the bandit base had packed up and deserted the location some time ago.

The group began to dismount to further investigate. Reza dismounted at the firepit. Poking at the coals and ash, she surmised it had been lit somewhat recently, perhaps the night before. Someone had recently been here.

"Captain Malay," the haltia soldier called to Reza.

She made her way past the gathering troops around the largest tent where the summons had come from.

She walked past the haltia holding the tent flap open and found two of her soldiers detaining a dirty, rough-looking man. He made no move to escape, but simply eyed Reza.

Nomad pressed his way past the haltia soldiers to stand beside Reza as they looked upon the bald man adorned in pelt garb. He looked like a trapper or bandit, but Nomad knew this man. When he had seen him last, he had been wearing White Cloak robes.

Nomad spoke first. "You've shed your White Cloak mantle."

The man, sitting hunched on the edge of the cot looked up at Nomad with distaste in his eyes, then turned to the rest of the crowd and spat on the ground.

"Nomad, you know this man?" Reza asked, seeing that it would be easier to gather information from her companion than from the wretch that sat before them.

"He was the White Cloak Yozo and I interrogated here at camp days ago. We knocked him unconscious in this very tent."

"A mercy that I didn't ask for. You should have ended me that night," the prisoner murmured. "Umbraz no longer visits me in dreams. He has forsaken me. I am fallen…"

Yozo had silently appeared behind Nomad. "Don't be so dramatic. Your god never intended to reward you in the first place. You were fallen since the day you joined his cursed cult."

"Little do you simpletons know." He laughed brokenly.

"What don't we know?" Reza prompted.

"There is no other god that will soon matter in all the many realms of Wanderlust. Our whole universe is soon to be his. *Umbraz* will be our reality. The end of everything we knew will come to an end…and I am no longer in his favor. Allowing you and your miscreants to escape was my doom. Now…even if I were to die, I still would not be able to escape his strings. Even the material of a soul is his property to do with what he will. His reach is endless—boundless. You have no comprehension of what power he is to inherit."

"Teach us," Terra interjected, slipping in through the line of guards with Kaia. She held the scripture. "We wish to learn."

The man sneered at the request, then sighed in defeat, slumped over, head in hands.

Reza whispered for the haltia to leave the tent, seeing that the crowd would only serve to close him up further. She hoped a more intimate setting would help the former White Cloak to open up more.

He glanced at the two women, and his eyes caught on the scripture.

"Is that…the father's sermon book?" he asked.

"I found it on a pulpit in Rosewood," Kaia confessed.

The White Cloak almost looked hopeful, as though a memory of the book held some importance, but then it was gone, and he retreated to his destitute self once more.

Terra took a cautious step forward. "You say that Umbraz will soon be our own reality—that is to say, he has not come to power *yet*. Is his rise to power fated or still uncertain?"

He shook his head. "None are in a position to halt his birth. Alumin is all but locked down and defended by not just the parish, but by the military might of two kingdoms and the capital itself. We have laid the groundwork necessary to eliminate any meaningful opposition."

"So his birth place is to be Alumin? That is where the end of this reality as we know it will take place?"

"Yes. Poetically, that is where Umbraz's inception in the first place began, in the synagogue that shall eventually birth him. A womb of unknowing in the cosmic fabric of Wanderlust. There, his image shall turn from inanimate, to animate—unreality, to reality, and vice versa. What we are, shall end, and what he is, shall begin."

"His image," Terra whispered. "Is this *womb* or *image*—is this the obsidian statue?"

"I have spent many an hour gazing into its cold, dark eyes. I have seen his coming. It will be like nothing that has come before it, not even the gods and devils realize yet what his birth will mean for their existence. They think themselves eternal…they are not. One comes, even now, that has the power to render them as mortal as the very mortals that have worshiped them since the beginning. Not even prophecy is powerful enough to have predicted this cataclysm. Nothing will be the same—the *same* won't even have existed in the first place. And I…I have fallen from his grace at the very hour of his coming—"

"They have moved the obsidian statue to the Valiant synagogue." Kaia leaned in and whispered in Reza's ear. "That is the *womb* that Umbraz is using to enter our reality. It is essential we find a way to destroy it before he is fully realized."

Terra asked, "When and how will Umbraz enter our realm?"

"In many ways, he already has, but a complete transference of his self to Wanderlust must wait until there is enough substance collected and consecrated to form an adequate bridge from the Seam to our realm. His reality must be laid in our realm, stone by stone, thought by thought. Even our talking of him helps to solidify his existence here. Every conversation and reflection of him is like a thread, knitting the fabric that will tie him to us," the White Cloak admitted.

Malagar had remained silent throughout his ramblings, but with talk of the Seam entering the conversation, he stepped up. "This is why you've been collecting Seam residue, isn't it?"

"We've done more than collect Seam residue; we've created it. With the Breath of Life pearl, Torchbearers are given direct connection to the webways of the Seam. I've touched countless souls with my pearl," he said proudly. "But now, I've been robbed even of that. My brethren must have taken me for dead after you knocked me out here, lying on the floor. They took my pearl and left me for dead."

Reza unclipped the leather pouch at her hip and pulled out a tangle of corded pearls. She held them aloft before him.

"Where did you…" he gasped, a flame of hope sparking in his eyes.

The air was suddenly charged, and all could feel instantly that the man was unhinged at the sight of the beads.

He lunged for them, almost ravenous. Malagar was quick to trip and shove him to the ground before he made it to Reza. Nomad stepped between Reza and the crazed White Cloak, but he hardly noticed Nomad with hand on sword hilt.

He scrambled to his feet and rushed towards the beads once more. This time, it wasn't a harmless trip that knocked him to the ground, but the butt of Nomad's sword, crushing directly into the side of his head.

The White Cloak lay sprawled on the tent's dirt floor, not moving.

"Put those pearls away," Malagar calmly requested, then stepped over the zealot and cautiously turned him over. The man's breath was shallow; he did not appear conscious. Checking his skull where Nomad had struck him, all could see a caved-in section of his temple.

"Not good," Malagar said. "I doubt he's waking up from that one."

"I hate to ask, but would a healing be appropriate?" Terra asked. "He has the information that we've been looking for."

"A healing in his condition…would not be wise," Reza answered.

The tent was quiet as Malagar held two fingers to the White Cloak's neck, feeling the weakening pulse fade for a minute, and then die off.

"Well, that is that," he sighed, confirming to all in the tent that he had succumbed to his wound.

"We got what we could from him," Reza said. She patted Nomad on the shoulder and left the tent to give orders for a grave to be dug.

Coming back into the still quiet tent, she broke the silence. "We should talk about all of this tonight when we break for camp."

Her suggestion was met with nods of agreement.

"Until then, we need to press on. We've got what we came back here for. Let's leave this place."

Behind her, she heard Malagar murmur, "And pray that we never need to return."

Chapter Eighteen
Alignment

"Soon, soon, soon," Reid sighed as he entered the command tent. "That's all they say. I'm starting to think they don't even know when their god will show his ugly head."

Fin had also taken a crack at obtaining some answers from the White Cloak prisoners—and he shared Reid's sentiments. "One thing's for sure, they believe their god is about to arrive in the Crowned Kingdoms, and when he does, it'll be in style."

Reid grabbed a bottle of spirits and poured a healthy splash into a glass. He took a seat next to Fin, and the two sat with their thoughts for a moment, listening to the wind beating upon the tent's thick walls and the sound of the army in the camp below.

"Who knows what it all means," Reid mused aloud, taking another sip of the fiery drink. "If it's all the rantings of an insane, deluded cult, or if there really is danger to this Umbraz making a move on our world—it's anyone's guess at this point."

"I do think we've gotten what we're going to get from the White Cloak prisoners, little though that seems to be. What do you want done with them?" Fin asked.

"Keep them with the rest of the prisoners of war and ship them back to Castle Sauvignon for trial after this war is concluded."

"As you command."

"King Reid," came a female voice from outside the tent.

He beckoned her to enter.

Lanereth ducked her head to enter the tent and graciously took a seat as Reid offered one.

"You holding up alright?" Reid asked.

She looked down at her thin hands, studying them for a moment. "The last few years have taken their toll on me, unfortunately. Keeping up with a warband on the campaign trail may prove to be too rigorous a task for this old saren."

Though Reid didn't have a deep understanding of the woman's character, Fin felt like he did—at least more than most. He knew that she was a proud woman, rightfully so. For her to admit such a statement worried him. She was probably more spent than she was letting on.

"How will this affect your ability to act as a mediator with the saren troop?" Reid asked with some degree of tenderness in his voice.

"That's what I came here to speak with you about," Lanereth answered. "I've been talking with Freya. She's on board with your cause. She's willing to work with you to fight in this war. Perhaps it would be best for her to report directly to you. I…may need to retire soon to Canopy Glen to recover my strength."

"Will she be willing to obey my orders?"

"Depends on the order," Lanereth was quick to answer. "That will be up to you to prove a good sense of leadership and competency. She has served under strong and exceptional leaders in the past. She is well-known among sarens for being a war hero, even among distant parishes like mine. She will be a valuable ally if you can win her over."

Reid sipped on his drink, thinking over the change in the chain of command.

"Is she available to talk?" he asked.

"Yes, she's in camp with her sisters."

He set the glass aside. "I'll go see her now then. We may not get a better chance to talk later. Waldock's men should be arriving at any moment, and who knows what they're going to bring home with them."

He was about to stand when a thought came to him. "My apologies. I almost forgot to ask. Do you require any assistance with your return to Canopy Glen? I can spare a small detachment to escort you there if needed."

"No need. I have Alva to care for me. We'll be packing up and heading out soon though." She looked to Fin. "I wanted to be here for Reza. I need you to tell her that I'm sorry I couldn't help more than I did. Please let her know, if you see her before I do, how proud I am of her. Sareth watches over that one. She is special, to both Sareth and to me."

"I will," Fin answered. He helped the older saren to her feet and gave her a short embrace. "I'll make sure the gang comes and visits you as soon as we can. We'll stay in touch, lady Lanereth. Don't leave too soon though, I'd like to say goodbye to Alva as well before you head off."

"Will do, Fin," she said, a rare smile gracing her countenance. "I'll show you to Freya, if you're ready, King Reid."

He indicated for her to lead the way, and the two departed the command tent.

Morgan, the king's right-hand man standing watch outside the tent, took up pace with them as they made their way to the far side of the encampment where the sarens had pitched camp.

The three arrived just as Freya was sending off her leading officers on various tasks. Lanereth released her grip on the king's steady arm as Freya motioned for them to sit at the now vacant officer's chairs around the low-burning campfire. The chairs were little more than well-cut logs, but for Lanereth, it was better than standing for any amount of time, so the two readily took the invitation with Morgan remaining back, surveying the area quietly.

"Welcome, High Priestess Lanereth, King Reid, and—" Freya asked, looking at the man standing behind the two.

"That's my man, Morgan. He goes everywhere with me," Reid answered. "Lanereth tells me that she's talked to you about working together more closely in this war effort as she may be retiring from the campaign soon."

"Yes. We have talked at length about the situation. I am more than happy to help fight against those that stormed our home and displaced us. Our motives seem to be well enough in line with each other."

"So it seems." Reid rolled an unlit thin cigar between his fingers, thinking on how he should frame the next line of questions. He could tell, just by the comfortable way she handled herself and her troops, that she was a strong leader. How would she feel about him asking her to obey his orders on the battlefield?

"We are extremely grateful for the healing your sisters have provided to our people," he started. He'd heard that some of the wounded scouts would not be alive in camp if it were not for the saren's blessing at the last battle. "My people—this land—means more to me than my own life. I doubt we're dissimilar in that regard. What can I do to return the favor? What do you need? I'll do my best to see that it is done."

Freya was taken aback. "That's very gracious of you to offer. My home, West Perch, is often on my mind, as it is with all of my sisters. I know it might not be prudent to return there at this moment, but I do wish to return in force and liberate it as soon as possible. I understand Alumin must first be won for us to truly have a chance at reclaiming the fort, but if you wish to offer your aid in any way, I would ask that you not forget my people's plight."

Reid bowed his head in agreement. "As soon as it's strategically sensible, we will storm Alumin, and from there, West Perch. The capital is a key location in this war, it is our top priority. Once we've driven out the invaders from your people's land, we'll both be well served. Having such strong allies centrally located should prove advantageous to both parties."

"That sounds fair to me. I look forward to fighting at your side, King Reid."

The two shook hands to seal the alliance, happy that their goals and aims were so well suited for each other—it was one less thing to fret over.

Reid dipped the tip of the cigar he had been fidgeting with into the campfire's low burning flame, then brought it to his lips to draw in the first thin lines of smoke.

"King Reid," Morgan's quiet voice sounded as he stepped up to place a hand on the king's shoulder. "Looks like the Waldocks have arrived back in camp."

Taking one more draw, Reid stood and tipped his brimmed hat to Freya. "I'd best be off. Call on me whenever you need me. I'll do the same."

Reid turned to Lanereth. He placed a comforting hand on her back and whispered, "If time permits, come see me one last time before you head out of camp, lady Lanereth. I enjoy our talks."

She gave a smile and nodded, but it was clear the matron was worn down from the last few days' excitement.

"Lead the way," Reid said to Morgan.

Riders were entering the east side of camp, and it wasn't long before Reid and Morgan began to hear shouts from the lead riders barking orders to speak with the king.

They navigated through the crowd with Morgan making way for them to press through to the riders. Reid came upon both Waldocks shouting over the din with Fin. He approached the group, raising a hand to order some quiet, at least from those in the surrounding area.

Fin, King Waldock, and Johnathan all turned to Reid and Morgan as they broke through the circle of Kingsguard that surrounded them.

"Good to see you both," Reid said as he took one final drag on his cigar nub and flicked it to the dirt as the men in the surrounding area quieted down to let the kings talk. "How did the plan go?"

Johnathan dismounted and handed his horse off to one of his men. "Golden Crowns are in pursuit. They've committed a great deal of their force to press the attack.

They're moving much slower than us, but in greater numbers. If they push the march, they may reach us by tomorrow."

Reid stroked his stubbled chin. "How large is their army? We dealt them a devastating blow in the Greenwood."

"Their main force has been bolstered since last we ran them back to Alumin," Johnathan answered. "Upwards of three thousand units—maybe even four thousand—our numbers varied with reports somewhat. That includes calvary, infantry, and crossbowmen. I hope this is the remainder of their military because if it isn't, we have little hope of outlasting them if there are even more reinforcements on their way."

Reid held the king's horse as the king dismounted. "That is a considerable force. Even with the high ground and use of fortifiable positions here. This will be a tough fight, no matter how you slice it. But, if no further reinforcements are on their way, the odds should still favor us. I can send a rider to gather the militia from Canopy Glen. I gave the word days ago for them to be at the ready. If they march at first light, they'll be here within time. That's another two hundred archers. They're experts with the bow, though not much training with the sword or spear. Maybe they won't need more than a good aim."

King Waldock could hold his peace no longer. "Two hundred archers is something, but what of the rest of our numbers? Do we even break three thousand in total at this chokepoint? That does not sound like favorable odds to me."

Reid was not deterred by the statement. "We have range, we have cover, we understand the lay of the land.

We have elevation, and we have time to prepare for their arrival. If they come at us on the road, they're going to have hell brought down upon them making their way up those muddy slopes and getting past our barricades. If they reroute through the Greenwood, they'll be in even worse straits. Our people know these woods and have hunted in them for generations. We are in a good location to receive such a force, and I believe our numbers are sufficient to warrant a stand here—even if they outnumber us."

King Waldock remained unconvinced. "Even with those strategic advantages, they still number well over a thousand men more than us. I am no stranger to war. The casualties we're likely to suffer, even if we win, will still be crippling. We quite possibly won't have much of an army left after this battle to push the front line if we fully commit to winning."

"Then what's our move, King Waldock? Retreat to where? Canopy Glen? Tarrolaine? *They're* worse defensible positions than *here*. The only place more favorable to stand against the Golden Crowns would be all the way back at Castle Sauvignon, but what would be the point of holding out there? They have all our lands and could slowly starve us out within our castle walls. They would have effectively won the war," Reid replied. "We likely will take heavy casualties in this battle, I understand, but we have very few alternatives. This is our best shot at hobbling the Golden Crowns' main force. With them out of the war, we can then focus on just the Black Steels and Alumin. With any luck, the Silver Crowns can step in to carry our cause to the end."

There was a hush amongst the group as Reid argued the point. Seeing no objections, he proceeded with a slightly more understanding tone. "Now, I know there is a lot of hope and luck in all of this, but the fact is, we are outmatched, and the enemy has the advantage on the first few moves. They've been preparing for this war behind the scenes for years—but we still have a chance at turning it around, for the whole kingdom, for all of our people, *even though* it will likely come at great cost."

The king thought over Reid's words for a moment, the dreary sky turning more into a light drizzle than a foggy bank. At length, he turned to his son. "Johnathan, what do you make of it?"

Johnathan answered without hesitation. "I would agree with King Reid, Father. This location was not easy to traverse these last few miles—even with horses. The rains may hold, and we may see the enemy force bogged down in mud which would give our archers time to thin their ranks considerably."

The king turned to Fin. "Sir Fin?"

Fin stroked his chin, considering his words carefully. "King Reid has not failed us thus far. I am no strategist as you three are, but I *have* fought in my fair share of battles. The woods to either side of the road offer plenty of perches for the bowmen, and I have seen their aim and range first hand. You couldn't ask for a better setup. If we are to make a stand, I would be comfortable in saying that if they come at us from the north along the road, this is probably as good as we'll get."

King Waldock nodded, hearing both men out fully before addressing Reid once more. "My people, those still with me, are the reason Johnathan and I still live. For years they have fought for me and died for me, even though it was not required of them to follow me into exile. They did so of their own accord. If my people are wasted…if we are signing up for a doomed cause, I will not forget this."

Reid gave his fellow king a hard look. "I don't waste lives, King Waldock. We have a chance at this, and it's a good one, I believe."

"So be it, we will sign to this battle," King Waldock said just as a sheet of light rain swept through the camp.

Reid wasted no time now that the matter was settled. The council broke and Reid and Morgan were off to see that his men made haste to batten down camp, seeing to it that their supplies were well covered under tarp or in a tent.

The Waldock riders had just finished moving out when one of Reid's scouts rode up, catching the king just as he was about to retire to a tent himself.

His horse was heaving from the hard ride. The scout wasted no time in delivering his report to his king. "A small troop led by White Cloaks headed this way across the bridge, my lord. Not sure if they saw me or the scouts, but they're sure to see our warband if they turn left once across the bridge instead of right."

"Numbers?" Reid asked.

"Twenty or so."

"On foot, or on horse?"

"On foot."

King Reid pointed up the hill deep in camp. "Find Fin; he's likely at the command tent. Tell him to gather an attachment of thirty scouts, mount up, and run the White Cloaks' troop down tonight, with all haste. We don't need them connecting with the Golden Crowns army if possible. It'll only make tomorrow's battle that much tougher. Tell him to engage the White Cloaks at range and when the enemy is out in the open. We don't want to risk unnecessary harm to our men."

"Yes, my lord. Right away," the scout issued. He rode off through camp towards the command tent.

Reid looked around. All but a few stalwart sentries had retreated to the cover and warmth of their tents. Except for his head which was covered by his brimmed hat, he was soaked through and through.

"What I wouldn't give to be back in my den with a glass of brandy and smoke right now," he grumbled.

Giving the idle murmurings a second thought, he banished the daydream. If they didn't give their all in this war, there would be no home to return to—Umbraz and his followers would see to that.

__Chapter Nineteen__

Regroup

The gloomy evening had faded to a foggy night, and though the rain had died down, the air hung thick with humidity, threatening to start up again at any moment. The moon was behind the clouds, and as Fin and his scouting party made their way across the bridge at the start of night, they had to trot their horses carefully along the slippery cobblestone.

Fin called a halt, and all thirty scouts formed up behind him, waiting for orders.

He could hear movement somewhere up ahead. He motioned a signal for silence from his men, listening for what was ahead. It could very well be the White Cloaks they had been dispatched to eradicate, but…he thought he heard the clop of hooves. Had their reports been wrong? Were the White Cloaks mounted?

The fog was too thick to get a visual. Holding up a hand, he ordered the troop to remain where they were. He waved two leading scouts to investigate the area.

They approached slowly, careful to make as little noise as they could. They were barely out of view of their troop when they heard a voice cut through the fog.

"What banner do you ride under? Speak now or be dropped where you stand."

The warning voice was not far off, but enough so that he still could not make out who spoke or how many were with them. He was at a disadvantage. Rather than risk him and his men being shot by concealed assailants, he offered up his allegiance.

"Fin, riding under the King of Rediron."

He readied to bolt, and his two scouts did the same, making themselves as small a target as possible. They were in a bad spot, but…something told him to wait and see. He doubted White Cloaks would have given a warning call.

"Friend Fin, the Silver Crowns are here to provide their support," the fair voice issued as a figure rode closer, cutting through the fog to expose a Silver Crowns bowman riding horseback, flanked by four others coming to greet them.

"God damn. Reza pulled through." Fin smiled in relief. He sent one of the scouts back to gather the troop and turned back to the lead haltia. "Is Reza with you?"

"Yes," the bowman answered. "She leads this company. I'll take you to her."

Fin turned to make sure that the scouts were in tow. As he began to pick up pace with the bowman, he asked, "How did you spot us through the fog? I knew haltias could see further than most, but through fog?"

The bowman sent the other haltia on ahead to give Reza and the others a warning of the approaching ally force so as not to cause undue alarm. "Haltia eyes can discern more spectrums than any other people. Our sight is one of our most prized gifts."

Fin nodded, taking note of the fact he hadn't known before then. On a night such as this, he wondered how they might utilize that sight to their advantage.

The bowman interrupted Fin's thoughts. "We've just finished up with the last of the bandit crew. Just giving you a warning before we come upon the first of the dead bodies."

"Were there any White Cloaks among their numbers?"

"Yes. A small number of them were followers of Umbraz," the bowman replied, his horse maneuvering a bandit face down with two arrows sticking out of his back. "Luckily, we were able to take them down at range. There was little retaliation even attempted, we neutralized them before they could gain cover.

"Did our job for us," Fin spoke loud enough for his lead scout to hear.

"You were sent to handle that group?"

"Yes." A large group of mounted haltia came into view. He wondered just how large the cavalry unit was. "They were likely to connect up with the Golden Crowns army headed this way."

Through the fog came a familiar voice. "Well they won't be now, not unless *some god* on the other side owes them favors."

"I only know one mortal that *even the gods themselves* owe those kinds of favors to, and that'd be you, Reza Malay."

Reza trotted up to Fin with a knowing smirk. Fin was glad to see Malagar, Yozo, and Terra leisurely coming up behind, but he was especially relieved to see Nomad and Kaia amongst the group.

"It seems your venture was a success." Fin clapped. "Not only did you find Nomad and Kaia, but the Silver Crowns have heard your call to arms. Well done ol' girl."

Reza's countenance was reason to pause the early celebration. He could tell she was dissatisfied. She didn't leave him guessing long.

"The Silver Crowns have agreed to join the war, *but* they will be spending most of their focus on defending their homelands. Seldrin did allow for one hundred of his finest to come with me to help Rediron as I see fit, but that is likely the only aid we can expect to come to Rediron."

Fin was quick to dismiss her concerns. "That they're engaged with the enemy is help enough. Umbraz will have to split up his efforts which will take some heat off us. And I saw those ruffian corpses, this troop are fine aims. They got you and the others back to Rediron country safe and sound. I'd say that's a success."

"How's Cavok and Lanereth?" Reza asked.

"They're…fine," Fin said, but Reza could tell from his tone that there was more to the statement.

"There's more I think we both would like to catch up with each other over, but we have a bit of a situation," Fin explained. "The Golden Crowns army is headed this way. I was sent to take out this White Cloak group so that they didn't have the chance to join up with the main force but was told to come right back as soon as that was done so as not to get cut off past the bridge."

"How close are they? Where are we returning to?".

"After the battle in Greenwood—after you left— King Reid pursued the Golden army northwards a ways, then exited the forest and made it back to the highway. We traveled south and established a base camp close to here. It's a choke point along the highway, very defensible. He figured that was our best location to confront the Goldens head on. Last our scouts reported, they're coming for us, could be here anywhere between now and tomorrow. That's why we need to move—now.

We don't want to get caught between them longer than we need to be."

Reza circled an arm in the air, signaling for the band to gather and be ready to move out. She called to the bowman that had first spotted Fin and ordered him to scout ahead with eyes to the north and to report at the first sign of the approaching army. He disappeared in the fog within moments.

Fin nodded, following Reza's lead to round his men up.

Reza was about to call to move out, but Kaia and Terra trotted up to speak with her. The young women could tell Reza was not in the mood for small talk.

Kaia spoke up. "We should collect the prayer beads from the fallen White Cloaks before we leave. We think they're important."

Reza exhaled, her breath vaporous in the chill air. "Gather them—quickly."

The two did not dally. They turned over the zealots that lay face down in the mud and snatched the pearls from the dead quickly as they could. Reza eyed them impatiently through the whole process.

With pearls recovered, they returned to their horses. As soon as they were mounted, Reza called for the troop to move out, and Fin echoed the march for his troops.

Before long, they had returned to the bridge and were about to begin the crossing when the haltia bowman that had been sent ahead to scout the other side of the bridge, came racing back.

"Sander, what is it?" Reza asked as he reined in his steed beside her. She could tell she wasn't going to like his report.

"Horsemen approaching from the north. Golden armor. They'll be to the bridge before long," the haltia blurted out.

"Can we get ahead of them before they reach the bridge?"

He looked back, thinking for a moment, then shook his head. "This bridge is a long one. Likely will be there by the time we race across it."

All eyes were on Reza and Sander, waiting for orders.

"Damn it," Reza grumbled.

In the end, she decided that to risk a charge to try and get ahead of the Golden army's cavalry could end disastrously.

She called to the haltia close to her. "I need a few of the best eyes keeping a watch on activity across the bridge. Keep well out of sight. I want constant reports of the army's movement. Pack up and head back immediately if it looks like the army intends to cross this bridge."

"Reza, this is a large army—probably the full force of the Golden Crowns' military. Waldock's scouts estimate there's four thousand heads on the other side of that river. If we let them pass ahead of us, we may be here a while," Fin warned.

Reza nodded. "Then we had better hope that if their attention does turn this way, our horses are faster than theirs. We wouldn't stand a chance at stopping them from crossing the bridge if they truly committed to it."

She looked around. All haltia as well as the Rediron scouts were glued to her, waiting.

"Fin, may I?" she asked, wanting to address the group as a whole—man and haltia alike.

He nodded his approval.

She spoke up with as much volume as she thought reasonable so as not to allow her voice to carry across the river. "Spread the word amongst the troops. There will be no lights—no torches this night. We wait for the Golden army to pass, and when it does, we'll follow behind and start our attack then. We'll keep at range. I want no hand-to-hand combat unless absolutely necessary—they're far too large a force to consider a charge."

She paused, looking around at the many faces that she realized she didn't know. She had not fought alongside most of this crew. She had no way of knowing how prepared they were to face such a large force. She slowed down and tried to calm the many worried looks. She figured that she'd be worried too, following a stranger into an unfavorable battle.

"I don't know who here has witnessed an army of four thousand—it is a sight to behold. We are not here to single-handedly win this battle. Stick to your commanding officers, obey your orders. We will attempt to obtain clear visuals on our enemy's back, and we'll shower them with arrows from as far a distance as effective.

"With luck, the enemy's foremost attention will be ahead on the battlefield, and Sareth willing, King Reid and the others will give them enough hell that their commanding officers will have their hands full up front. May your aims be true this night. Have courage and keep your wits about you."

To her relief, her words seemed to calm the soldiers.

She looked to Fin and called him. He came readily to her side. By the reported size of the enemy army, she figured that they would have plenty of time to get caught up on everything that had happened in Rediron while she had been away as the enemy passed them by.

Chapter Twenty
The Chaos of War

"And the riders are still there?" Reza asked the latest scout to report on the enemy's movements.

"They are. Looks like they've posted ten riders to watch the bridge as the rest of the army is moving past it on to Canopy Glen," the haltia scout spoke softly back.

"Let's hope they move out with the rearguard once the army has moved through," Reza murmured.

The scout bowed and moved silently off on foot into the fog back to his post at the midpoint of the bridge. Reza tapped a finger to her chin in thought, considering their move if the army did choose to leave behind sentries at the bridge pass.

"You're wondering how good a shot our archers are, aren't you?" Fin asked.

"Surely that's one thought I'm mulling over."

"And the other thought?"

"What our move will be if their sentries happen to get away to alert their command."

Fin shook his head. "King Reid has placed his men well. They'll be more than a fight for the Golden Crown army. I think, even if a scout gets away and alerts the rear guard, they might still have more pressing matters to worry over."

"How can you be so sure? Their back half might find it a good use of time to turn and deal with us if all they're doing is waiting for their front half to call for support," Reza countered.

"Treelines cover the hills along the highway, and our archers line most of those woods for the better half of a mile before the barricade. I'm thinking the Golden Crowns, their whole force, will be peppered with arrow rain for the majority of this battle. I doubt the rear guard is going to be as idle as you're suspecting," Fin explained. Chills ran through his body from the frigid night air.

Reza's horse pranced in place. She soothed it with a pat along its neck. "Regardless, we'll be better off if no word of our presence reaches their command until after we've positioned ourselves and are ready to issue the first hail of arrows."

"None can argue that." Fin shrugged. "We'll have to wait and see. They may not even leave their sentries at the bridge."

Reza didn't have a reply for Fin, and the two were quiet, looking ahead to the ramp of the bridge, waiting for a haltia scout to return and report. They could hear movement across the river. The Golden Crowns army was large; simply the march of their troops was enough to sound a constant thumping drone across the countryside.

Reza rubbed her arms to keep warm as the night wore on. The fog was beginning to penetrate her layers. The dampness of the air was not likely to let up any time soon—she suspected she'd be soaked through and frozen by morning. It was a dreadful thought at best, potentially debilitating at worst.

She thought of all those men and women who were soon to be gravely injured on the battlefield that night—perhaps within the hour. How many would succumb to hypothermia after having lost a worrying amount of blood from battle wounds? She looked around her, connecting eyes with her soldiers, and wondered how many would be dead by the morning.

"You ready for this, Fin?" she asked softly, her breath steaming in the dark of the night.

"Of course," he said, pulling his eyes from the bridge in the fog to consider her.

"Are *your men* ready for this?"

He looked harder at her. "Are *yours*?"

From the fogbank along the river, the haltia scout came running back towards Reza.

"We'll soon find out," Reza darkly murmured.

"Captain," the scout called. "The army has finally passed. It does appear Sir Fin's estimates were correct on the army's size. It's a large force, and their troops have not only a sizable amount of mounted riders and crossbowmen, but infantry armed with spears, shields, and various sidearms. They're well fitted."

"And the sentries at the far side of the bridge? Are they still on guard?" she asked.

"Yes, all ten of them."

"Sander," she called. He trotted up the next moment. "Pick ten of your best shots to dismount and make their way to the halfway point on the bridge. See if they can take these riders down in one volley. Once the first shot is fired, call for a charge. I'll have everyone else mounted and ready to rush over the bridge to see if we catch up to any that might survive."

"Right away," Sander said and headed off into the group to find his best shots.

"Everyone, be ready to charge as soon as the order is given at the bridge. Our first task is to take out the enemy's bridge sentries. Open fire if you see them after we cross. Our next task is to place the rearguard in our sight. Wait for the signal to open fire upon the rearguard."

Horses pranced in place, the animals sensing their masters' tension mounting. The beasts didn't need to pace for long. A shout came from the bridge, signaling that arrows had been loosed.

Reza rushed ahead of the group, her mount's hooves clopping angrily as it moved across the bridge. She passed by the archers on foot who were keeping well to the sides of the railings so as not to get trampled by the hundred plus riders racing across.

Making it to the other side, she stuck to the muddy path leading to the highway and passed six of the ten sentries lying down in the mud. *Where were the other four?*

She could hear the stampede of riders behind her. She couldn't see any sign of the four sentries up ahead, she only hoped the haltia at her side could.

Her horse almost tripped as they reached the main highway. The road had been trampled by four thousand soldiers, and the muddy path had practically turned into a bog by that point. She slowed her horse's pace considerably to lower the risk of it breaking a leg in the deep mud.

Her haltia riders followed her lead and a few along the front line began opening fire up the road. She could hear whinnies from up ahead now—then came shouts. She pressed forward steadily.

She could see a blurry mass ahead on the road. The haltia next to her loosed two arrows into the figure and it went still. A few more silhouettes came into view; she counted three more Golden sentries down in the mud.

"Do you see the last one?" she asked the haltia closest to her. He shook his head, desperately trying to make sense of the shapes in the fog.

She could hear a droning noise ahead—a great tumult muted by the thickness of the air. The haltia next to her aimed and shot. A scream sounded out, then another. They passed two bodies on the road, then four, then eight. They were coming up on the stragglers of the army. Their chance to catch the last sentry was likely past—not that it probably mattered at that point. They had inadvertently engaged the enemy already; the word of their presence was imminent at that point.

"Fire at will!" Reza shouted, breaking the relative quiet along their frontline.

Only a few took aim at first, but after a few minutes of steady advancement, they began to creep up on the main back line of the rear guard. Word had made it to them that there were bowmen coming up on their back. A number of large shields were up along the back line and overhead to ward off easy shots into the main body of troops.

Reza fell back a line, riding up to Malagar, Nomad, and Yozo.

She shouted to Malagar, "What's the terrain look like to the right of the highway? Think we could keep up with the army if we ride along the ridge?"

"Those slopes might be difficult to manage if they're as wet as these roads," he called back. "Might make it hard for the archers to concentrate on their aim—but we're dealing with that anyways here in this mud."

She snapped her horse's reins and charged ahead of the group once more. She called out loud and clear to her and Fin's troop. "Up the hill, follow me!"

The successive distinctive clang of crossbows firing sent a jolt of dread into her. A split second later, she heard cries from both horse and rider alike to her left.

"Fire at their crossbowmen!" she yelled back and hoped that the order had been heard.

A second volley of bolts shot into her troop, dropping more than a few riders into the thick mud. Through the first two volleys, her archers kept focused, and now that the line of crossbowmen had made their shot came the tedious gap of cranking to reset their crossbows' tensions. In the mud and with their defensive wall of shields slowly advancing forward, leaving them behind and exposed, it would prove to be disastrous for the line of sacrificial crossbowmen.

"Decimate their line before they reload!" Reza shouted, still trying to make her way to the right of the road, finally getting out of the worst of the mud of the highway.

She called for a charge up the hill, risking a bit more speed as her horse cleared the muddy road, and charged on ahead along the grassy rise. The rise had been slight, but even so, she noticed the fog lightened up a degree as she made her way up close to the treeline.

She knew that they had created a great deal of panic amongst the Golden army's rear unit. A few hundred were likely already lying face down in the mud, but she worried how many she had lost from the two volleys that had been loosed upon them. There at least hadn't been a third or a fourth volley of bolts, which was a good sign. Her archers handling the crossbowmen was meant to act as a deterrent to their harassment.

A bolt whistled towards her and thudded deep into her horse's shoulder. It bucked violently. She held on, but as the beast pitched over, she attempted to throw herself as far from the tumbling animal as she could. She rolled several yards downhill before coming to a stop.

She sat up, getting her bearings a moment before attempting to get to her feet. She was lucky that she paused to stop her head from spinning as a bolt shot right over her. She sprung to her feet and scrambled up the hill, attempting to get out of sight of the Golden crossbowman.

A hand reached down and grabbed her arm. She looked up to find Nomad helping her onto his mount. She struggled onto the saddle and settled in behind him as he worked on urging his mount up the steep part of the hill.

The haltia, along with Fin's scouts, were close behind, charging up the grassy hill towards the treeline.

Reza could hear the roar of battle far up the Golden Crowns' line. She wondered fleetingly how the Redironers were faring, but more bolts whistling at her troop brought her attention back to the Golden army's rear guard, who appeared to be organizing their troops to respond to Reza's bowmen.

Another detachment of crossbowmen were lining up along the unit's flank, and shield bearers were shoving their way through the footmen's ranks to get out in front of the crossbowmen and provide them cover as they fired and reloaded.

"Another couple of volleys, then get into the trees!" Reza yelled above the screams of haltia, men, and horses being pelted by thick bolts, bringing them to the ground in pain and death.

The rain of arrows had torn up the rear guard, effectively scattering and disorganizing the soldiers. She gave the scene one last look before telling Nomad to retreat to the woods with everyone else. At a glance, they had felled three times their own numbers. It had come at a cost though. They needed to regroup and assess their next move.

"Behind the trees, keep moving west. We need to get out of range!" Reza heard Fin yell far up the line, now leading the charge for both groups since she had fallen behind.

"Have you seen Kaia and Terra?" Reza called ahead to Nomad as she held on tight to him, their steed jostling them as it was having a difficult time navigating the uneven floor of the dark woods.

"Mal and Yozo led them up into the treeline early. They're probably ahead up there, maybe close to Fin," Nomad yelled back.

She hoped that was the truth of it. The four didn't have bows, so there had been no reason for them to join them in the initial strafing run. She was glad one of them had taken the initiative to get the others to cover as soon as possible.

They had managed some ground westwards through the forest's border, and they had left the rain of bolts a ways back. She doubted that the crossbowmen had a clear line of sight on them when they had skirted the treeline, let alone once they were through it. They were likely a safe distance away from the ranged unit of the rear guard. They needed to begin planning their re-engagement strategy.

"We need to get to the front," Reza urged Nomad. He was attempting to comply, but the whole troop was in a charge, following Fin's lead through the forest.

They started to pass several haltia bowmen, and Reza noted that they were slowing down purposefully.

Peeking around Nomad's shoulder, she saw a halt had been called.

Nomad slowed; there was a commotion ahead. Finding Fin, he made his way up to the front line. They both could see why Fin had called for a stop—Rediron rangers were conversing tersely with Fin.

"Dismount!" Fin shouted to all haltia and his scouts. "Tie your horses up here, we'll go on foot a ways and bunker down at the treeline. We'll be supporting the Rediron rangers as they hit the enemy's middle company. We'll come back for the horses when we're ready to move out."

Reza went along with Fin's orders and was one of the first to dismount. Others were more reluctant, not wanting to lose their mobility; if a cavalry unit rushed them, they'd be left vulnerable.

Reza knew it was a bold choice to dismount, but it was the move she would have chosen as well. Firing from horseback was difficult, and even with expert bowmen, it would be easier to hit what they were aiming at if they were stationary. Aside from that, they could establish cover behind trees along the edge of the woods. With owning the ridge, they'd be a terrible disruption to the bogged-down army making their way to the barricade up ahead. They would be whittled down by the time they made it to the actual battle.

Tying up her horse, Reza spotted Malagar and the others. She waved them over to her location.

"How many rangers are there?" she asked as she reached Fin.

"Two hundred and fifty last I heard before I left camp," he answered quickly, shouting out orders to scouts between answers.

"They have some serious fire power. We should not waste our initial attack. We need to ensure all archers hold their fire until given the word—and that once the order is given, to loose as many arrows as they possibly can. I have a feeling they're going to respond to us swiftly."

"I'll make sure the scouts and rangers understand," Fin agreed and ran off to call upon leaders of both groups.

"How can we help?" Terra asked.

"Stay close to me. I have a feeling it may come to blows later this evening. We'll need both blade and magic in due time," Reza said to her friends as she marched up the forest rise to get a vantage point over the Golden army below.

Reza looked back. All haltia eyes were on her, waiting for her orders. The group had noticeably thinned. She only hoped stragglers were still on their way to their location after losing their mounts or getting separated from the main unit.

Looking over to Fin and the ranger team, she saw that they were quickly getting into position behind thick tree trunks at the edge of the woods, both Fin and the ranger leader were looking to her for the command to open fire.

"Cock feather proud," she called back in a low, steady tone. "Aim…"

Her soldiers were ready, and she held up a hand in anticipation as she looked down upon the massive block of Golden warriors double timing through the thick muck along the highway.

The barricade was lit up in flames, and the glow coming from half a mile up the highway cast an eerie umber glow upon the scene. Reza trembled. She was about to end hundreds of lives with a single downwards movement of her hand.

She shook off the thought and thrust her hand down. "Fire!"

The thrum of bows hummed through the trees like a thousand birds taking flight at once.

The Golden army heard the dreaded sound for what it was, though from which direction the volley was coming from, most could not anticipate. A number of shields went up, but plenty others were caught unawares, looking skywards just as the arrows began to thump into them.

Screams burst from the middle company as waves of soldiers fell to the mud. Panic erupted to secure a shield overhead as the next volley was already on its way, arcing through the air towards the troops.

Crossbowmen made their way to the side of the formation, carrying heavy pavis shields to deflect the incoming arrows. A long line formed, and the crossbowmen thrust their spiked pavises down into the soft ground in front of them.

Crossbows were raised. Though Reza could not hear the commands of the Golden Crowns, she knew when a volley was imminent.

"Take cover!" she yelled both ways down their archer line, just as the thump of crossbows firing started to sound from down the hill.

The bark blew off of the tree she and Nomad had hunkered down next to, and more bolts whizzed past them as the crossbowmen finished their first volley.

"Continue fire!" she yelled, hoping that their shooters would win out with accuracy over the sheer numbers of the enemy ranged units.

Reza looked over to where Terra and Kaia had hunkered down. They had good cover; the low boughs of the tree provided enough protection for them to weather any number of volleys. Yozo and Malagar had less protection, their tree much leaner, but from what she could see through the dark of the night, everyone had managed to avoid the first wave of bolts.

Something caught her attention as she looked over her friends. Even through the dark of the night, she perceived shouts and movement towards the end of their line of haltia archers.

Another volley of bolts flew past them. She drew her sword, as did Nomad. After the last few bolts whistled through the woods, she got up, running to the back of the line.

"Stay," she said to Terra and Kaia.

Malagar and Yozo fell in behind them as they passed by.

They ran past haltia bowmen focused wholly on their targets down the hill before another hail of bolts forced them to seek cover along a felled tree along the ridge.

The brief pause gave Reza time to get a better look at what was approaching. Haltia bowmen were running their way, even through incoming volleys. Something was chasing them, but it was too distant for her to see in the dark.

"Foot soldiers," one of the retreating haltia shouted as they ran up to Reza, hunkering down next to her. "Lots of them too. They're back at the horses."

"Shit," Reza spat, his last statement instantly nulling her plan to mount up and reposition. "Fall back!" She waved the haltia on past her. Those archers that had been focused on the Golden army down the hill on the road ceased fire and made to follow her order. Everyone was packing up and moving up towards Fin and his scouts and the Rediron rangers.

Reza looked back at her group of friends. "Malagar. Take Terra and Kaia and get them out of danger's way. They've no place in this melee."

With a nod of understanding, Malagar waved to the women to follow him and were off running.

"Nomad, Yozo. Stick with me. I'll need your swords soon," she ordered.

The bolts had thinned, either because of the loss of crossbowmen down below, or because they had been informed of the foot soldiers' flanking maneuver. Whichever it was, Reza took advantage of the reprieve and ran back up the line, shouting at haltia the whole way to follow her and form a line once they reached the Redironers.

Fin had been informed well before she made her way through to him. He had already sent most of his men further into the woods in hopes of hitting the advancing foot soldiers at an angle from the side. The brush was thick deeper in, and he knew it would not be worth the Golden Crowns' effort to get at the scouts once they were set up deep in the thick brush.

"The rangers will bolster your about-face," he assured her, pointing to the rangers' leader, who was running up to get in on the impromptu battlefield assessment. "Do you know how many infantry are coming our way?"

"I don't. I was told *many*. All I know is that our horses are behind their line by now. Mounting up is out of the option currently."

"Yozo, Nomad, stay with her," Fin ordered. He knew the real fight, for them at least, was about to begin.

The two men nodded in unison.

"My scouts will be stationed over there," Fin said, pointing deeper in the woods. "We'll hit them from the side. Good luck, Reza."

With that, Fin skipped off into the woods to join his already concealed troop of scouts, each finding a position behind shrubs and trees out of sight.

"I want two lines, here and twenty yards back up on that knoll." Reza shouted her order, her voice going hoarse from a long night of use. "Front line, ready yourself—once the enemy is in sight, fire at will. Fall back when they get close."

She then addressed the bowmen further back. "Second line, shoot if you can get a shot, but be ready to provide covering fire when the first line falls back."

Just before her closing orders, the twang of a longbowman along the forming front line sounded. Reza could not see what the haltia shot at in the dark, but others readied their arrows. The enemy was already within the frontline's sight.

"Spears and shields!" Sander called out to Reza, a warning she did not want to hear. "Heavy infantry! Well armored and well-armed!"

She didn't hesitate and adjusted her orders. "Both lines—arrows down range! I want that unit well and peppered before they get here!"

The thrum of bows began sounding in unison. She knew she risked wearing her own troop's arms down with every early opening shot, but she also knew she was going to have to risk more than she'd prefer the remainder of that night. She just hoped their strength would last through the inevitable skirmish.

She looked over to where Fin's scouts should be. She could not see a single cloaked figure in the woods.

The surreal ceiling of arrows constantly cutting the air over her made it hard to concentrate. The moon-stained gleam of a shield in the distance brought her back to the moment as the first foot soldier came into view, followed by many others.

She could see the gleam of chainmail and plate armor wherever their golden-black gambesons did not cover. Their helmets were not overly ornate, but well-functioning all the same. Their kite shields were well shaped to allow for ease of use for the partisan spear they all held in the other hand. They were going to be a formidable opponent.

Luckily, she did see her bowmen's work yielding results. As the footmen advanced, a considerable number were staggering or outright dropping upon impact.

"Flamberge swordsmen in the second line, more spears in the third!" Sander called out, warning Reza and his men of the formation approaching.

Reza drew her sword, getting ready to call for the haltia frontline to fall back to the much larger Rediron ranger's group. The first of the spearmen were clearly visible to her now; it would only be a matter of seconds before they would be within striking distance, but those seconds meant one or two more volleys of arrows from her and Fin's bowmen.

The lead spearman fell, tumbling to a stop, a spear length from Reza. "Fall back!" she shouted, other spearmen getting a second wind of confidence from the order, yelling and whooping as they charged through the forest.

The haltia were quick to obey, and quicker yet on their feet, picking up and bounding off after Reza, headed the hundred yards back to the rangers' wedge formation along a rise of hill in the forest.

Reza could see the advantages of elevation from both her haltias' second line of bowmen as well as the rangers' base location. They'd have the advantage of a sound viewpoint of the approaching enemy. The Golden Crowns unit would surely take heavy losses in choosing to pursue them—her only worry was she didn't know how many had been sent after them. The strategic advantages she might have over the heavy infantry unit could still pale in comparison to their sheer commitment of numbers.

"Fall in with the second line!" she yelled. Nomad had to repeat the order as Reza's voice fell out.

"Be ready to drop your bows and switch to sidearms!" Sander ordered as the two groups linked up, the haltia fallback point only a stone's throw away from the formidable rangers' wedge to their flank.

Most of the front row of spearmen had been thoroughly spent, falling to the incredible amount of arrow fire through the long charge. The second line of swordsmen had gaps in it as well but were filled by the following line of spearmen. Reza could see their pattern: spearmen layered with long swordsmen, layered with more spearmen. Their depth continued for as far as she could see into the gloom of the night...

The last organized volley of arrows let fly, many finding their way into the gaps of the approaching soldiers' defenses. Haltia along the frontline were dropping their bows now, drawing their troops standard issue haltia scimitar, ready to attempt to deflect the leading spearpoints.

Most spear tips were batted expertly downwards harmlessly into the soil—some were not and found purchase in their targets. There was an explosive clash of sword and shield. The impact of the colliding charge changed the scene of battle suddenly, dizzying those not quite ready for the flurry of violence that surrounded them.

Nomad and Yozo stepped up on either side of Reza, their curved swords batting aside the far-reaching flamberges that chopped down and thrusted in at them. Nomad kicked the soldier lunging at Reza off balance. Yozo's blade jabbed in at their foe as he struggled to regain his footing. The Golden swordsmen never made it back to his feet. It was a small gain, however, as a rush of the man's compatriots trampled over him to get at Reza, Nomad, and Yozo.

The haltia to both sides of them saw the push and attempted to support them, cracking down on the helms and slicing through the sides of the swordsmen as they rushed Reza.

"Back! Reza, back!" Sander shouted, pushing his way up to her. "You're a target. I'll command the front line, you handle the support—"

Sander was cut off as a horseman came crashing through the melee and dug a spear tip deep in through his neck and down through his chest, plowing him into the ground.

The horseman was about to draw his sidearm when Yozo's sword point thrust into the man's face, pitching him backwards and off the horse.

More riders were crashing into the haltia front line, and Reza noted the horses were their own that they had left hitched to trees further back. They were now being used against them in the charge.

Nomad deflected another spear intended for Reza's head, and Yozo followed up, thrusting under a Golden's sallet and through his jaw to send him back into the crowd. Two more Golden soldiers took his place.

Arrows flew in just overhead, most clanking off armor and shields—some finding purchase. Chaos was all around her, and she swung and thrust at the mass of golden tabored men that managed to press through the haltia front line that had closed in around her.

She tried to shout to the back line of archers to draw swords and engage, but her voice was gone; any pathetic attempt at a command was drowned out by the roar of battle all about her.

Haltia were falling fast, the armored soldiers were performing to their strengths now that they had closed the gap. The only thing that had kept them from completely ripping through their line was the continued archery fire thinning out their men behind the line of skirmish.

A Golden swordsman fell past Nomad and Yozo. He collapsed at Reza's feet and struggled to regain his footing. She kicked at his head hard, and he jolted to the side, but remained conscious. Still gripping his sword tightly, he attempted to get it around to defend himself, but the long flamberge snagged on the bodies of the fallen around him. Reza took a jab downwards at his head, rendering his face a bloody mess as he sluggishly gave up his struggle.

She was knocked backwards, tumbling over the man she had just killed, and a flood of soldiers came recklessly over their defensive line. Boots obliviously kicked and stomped over her until something struck her head with enough force to knock the sense out of her.

Her hearing and vision were leaving her fast. Her every thought was slipping through her fingers like smoke in the wind.

A fresh wave of men was being slaughtered overhead. The last thing she recalled was a breastplate slamming into her face.

Chapter Twenty-One

The Day After

She groaned awake and clutched at her stinging face. A rush of commotion flooded in. She could hear a great number of others moving around about her: urgent voices calling for aid, cries of pain, wails of the wounded.

She winced and chanced opening her eyes. Blood seeped in, forcing her to close them once more.

"Hold on," Nomad soothed.

He helped her to sit up and she rested on him as he poured water from his waterskin onto a scrap of cloth and set to work rubbing off the blood from her eyes and forehead.

"How...bad?" she squeaked out, her voice stripped raw. She winced painfully, her head throbbing as he cleaned her face.

He paused for a moment to assess her. "Your forehead opened up a bit."

She didn't like the worry she heard in his tone. He waved someone over, seeing that the head wound had reopened, and fresh blood flowed down her face. She could feel hot blood in her eyes again even though he had just wiped it clean.

"A healing," he said to the person that approached.

She felt the cold touch of a woman's soft hand upon her cheek. The chill turned quickly into a comfortable warmth as a saren began to perform a healing, only enough to rebind the gash along her forehead to stop the bleeding.

"There," a familiar voice said. "I'm sorry, Reza, that's all I can give you."

Nomad wiped her face clean again and allowed Reza to open her eyes once more just as Kaia leaned down to hug her.

"Kaia," Reza whispered, still dazed.

"Can you stand?" Nomad asked. He held her as she tried to get to her feet.

She stood, shakily but well enough that after a few moments, Nomad allowed her to stand on her own and handed her discarded sword.

Sheathing her sword clumsily, Reza began to look around, trying to catch up on what had happened while she had been out.

The battle had come to an end, at least for them in the forest. Hundreds of Golden Crowns soldiers lay dead or dying in every direction she could see. Up the hillside lay a good number of her own haltia soldiers, dead beside their Rediron allies. The survivors were tending to the wounded, though some were fleeing out of the woods, rushing to the sound of battle down along the road.

In the distance, she could still hear combat: screams, metal clanging against metal, wood, and flesh. To some degree, the fight was not yet over.

She began to head towards the forest's edge, but Nomad stopped her. "They can handle the rest. We've all but won the battle at this point."

She watched more archers pick up discarded quivers and head to the treeline. Nomad could see her hesitancy. "The enemy is in full retreat. Don't worry. You do not need to rejoin."

She gave up struggling with him and turned back to the scene of destruction before her.

"They were not able to withstand our firepower. Soon after the initial charge, their numbers waned. We finished them off soon after you fell, thankfully."

"Has there been a count yet—" she coughed, trying to get through her sentence without her voice breaking up "—of our people?"

"Not as far as I know. I was focused on finding you. But Fin is looking over the battlefield now. He may have rough numbers," Nomad said, pointing in Fin's direction. "Are you okay?" He held her shoulders.

"I'm…fine," she said. She was not sure if the statement was true, but she didn't want him worrying over her.

She shook him off and headed towards Fin, taking it slow, as she still could feel weakness in her legs.

Fin saw her coming his way. He finished talking with a scout and carefully stepped over bodies to meet Reza in a small clearing instead of amongst the dead and dying.

"Sareth truly is with you, Reza Malay. I didn't give myself room to hope that you, Nomad, or Yozo would have survived at the front line of that charge."

"How bad was it?" she asked, clearing her throat before attempting to explain, "I was knocked unconscious shortly after the initial melee."

"Their first impact was intense. Their troops were better armored, better equipped for close combat. They did a lot of damage very quickly." He sighed regretfully. "But neither the scouts nor the rangers let up for a second with thinning their numbers. After the haltia withstood the first wave's fury, the main body of their infantry unit had lost most of its bite. We cleaned them up proper after that."

Movement amongst the dead alerted them to a bloodied Golden soldier flopping over on his back, gasping for air.

They watched for a moment to see if he was a serious threat or not. Reza plucked a nearby spear from the ground and leveled the point at him. Both Fin and the Golden soldier froze.

"We'll send him off with the rest of the prisoners," Fin said softly.

"We're taking prisoners?" she asked flatly.

"Of course," Fin said, taken aback for a moment. He called another scout over to handle detaining the soldier.

Fin put an arm around Reza and turned her away, walking off to the rest of the haltia troop so they could reconnect with her.

"Reza, I can't speak for the White Cloaks, perhaps the majority of them are truly rotten to the core, but an army like the Golden Crowns is not made up of zealots. Most likely have no choice but to serve their king and fight his wars. There's plenty of honest enough men that died on the other side of this confrontation tonight."

Reza huffed at the thought but said nothing and tried to clear her stubborn throat once more.

Fin continued his thought. "I'm sure there's an equal amount of repugnant curs that are only here for the plunder rights they're promised on the warpath—but that's what the war courts are for. I don't want you becoming too comfortable in the role of judge and executioner."

"You think they would be so thoughtful of us if the roles were reversed?" Reza rasped.

Fin shook his head. "It doesn't really matter. At the end of the day, it all comes down to what we choose to do. That's the part you're going to have to answer to yourself over years down the road each night when you're trying to get to sleep."

She looked at him. He was looking back at the Golden soldier being taken away by the scout back to camp. His brow was furrowed, heavy with haunting memories. He spoke from experience, she knew.

"Captain Malay," one of the haltia called, coming over to her. "We thought you had fallen."

Fin left her to handle her men as he returned to his.

She looked over what was left of the haltia bowmen that she had led into battle. Only twenty or so remained up and able in the surrounding area. She was sure a few more were out past the treeline, providing a going-away present to the retreating enemy force, but the sheer number of haltia that lay dead on the forest floor all about them was a blow to her spirits. Half of the men that she led would be buried in Rediron country.

She could understand the haltia's unfavorable tone as he gave his report.

The morning light was fittingly a rusty hue, the smoke and fires obscuring most of the carnage along miles of the highway from view. The smoke did little to muffle the cries of the many wounded still on the battlefield yet to be tended to, and to the injured that had already been transported into camp.

Reza had left Hazel, the senior remaining haltia officer, in charge of rounding up the haltia crew while she checked on the situation back at camp. They had won the battle, but she needed to check with Reid on the state of things. Likely all reports were funneling to him.

She entered camp and simply stood there for a moment, taking in the sight. The barricades had been blasted and burned down. Horse and man flesh lay heaped in piles at the chokepoint. Redironers were carrying on with hauling the wounded back into camp, shoving their way past Reza as she caught her bearings.

How am I going to find anyone in this mess, she wondered, looking at the smoky, bloody scene.

"Reza," a woman called from up the rise.

She looked towards the voice. After a moment she spotted Freya through a parting cloud of smoke.

"Come with me," Freya said, turning to trudge up the hill to the command tent. "Your friend Cavok needs some sense talked into him."

Reza paused, fearing the worst. Something about Freya's demeanor unsettled her.

She stumbled up the slope, sloppily making her way around and over wreckage and the dead to catch up to her saren counterpart.

Freya lifted the flap to the commander's tent as Reza arrived. She slowed her step as she saw two field medics working on Cavok's multiple wounds. Revna stood over him with a scowl more severe than her usual.

From the shadows, Reid, Morgan, and a shrouded, frail figure stepped out of the tent. Reid met eyes with Reza. Reid looked frayed, but with an urgency and purpose that refused to tire.

"I received word of your arrival and support last night," he said, taking a swig from a canteen, wiping his mustache dry. The drink smelled strong. "We need to talk later today. Come and find me when you are able."

She nodded, and he and Morgan were off, descending into the massacre that was his own camp.

The shrouded elder hobbled off into the woods, away from the encampment. Reza's curiosity over the hooded senior was piqued, but she knew that now was not the time to investigate. A king had his various attendants, and she figured him to be one of them.

Freya's hand rested firmly on Reza's shoulder, bringing her attention back to Cavok who was lying very still in the tent. She wasn't sure if he was resting, or unconscious, or....

She ducked her head and entered. Revna came to her side to explain as she took note of the deep gashes along his right side.

"He's refusing a healing from saren hands," Revna whispered disapprovingly. "Says he'll heal on his own strength. That no one else is going to be burdened with his pain."

Reza could understand Cavok's sentiments. He had traveled with her for years and had seen how close she had come to giving her life up for others through her healings. He had only become more stubborn about things like this over time—it was not a shock that he was refusing Revna now.

"How bad are his wounds?" she asked the field medics.

Their expressions were bleak. "Honestly, I don't know how he breathes now. His will is strong, it might pull him through. We're doing all we can to clean him and stop the bleeding, but his wounds are deep. He may fall ill to the warrior's fever at any time."

Reza knelt down next to his still body. His eyes were closed. She cleared her throat and spoke to him, hoping that he could hear her. "Cavok, Revna is a skilled healer—not like me. She can reserve herself from the worst of your wounds. Let her help at least stabilize you and repair the worst of it."

He remained still, his breathing calm, almost peaceful. She waited for a response a while longer.

"As far as I'm concerned, that's a yes," Reza told Revna. "Do you want me to aid in the healing?"

Revna shook her head, knowing first-hand how chaotic Reza's aether flow exchange was. Revna sat down next to the large man, and Reza asked the two medics to stand back.

The room was quiet as Revna placed her hands on his chest. She winced, a jolt of life instantly leaving her as she connected with Cavok. Revna let out a low groan. For a moment, Reza worried that she had taken more than she could handle.

Her posture straightened and she began to breathe deep and controlled. She attempted to stem the exchange of life energy. To Reza, it looked as though she had succeeded in finding a balance as her wince lightened and she sat back, a bit more at ease.

Cavok's hand shot up, gripping Revna's frail wrist firmly.

"Cavok!" Reza barked, warning him to ease up on the much smaller saren before he hurt her.

Her matronly reprimand triggered something in him, a primal warning voice that he was forced to yield to. He let go of Revna's wrist, glaring at the two.

"I said no healings," he growled.

"You were good as dead, Cavok. We weren't going to let you go if we could help it."

Though his demeanor refused to change, he at least did not argue the point.

"Revna, are you alright?" Reza asked, shifting her attention to her sister.

"I'm okay. I only just repaired the damage to his organs though. His flesh is unmended."

"I'll *mend* my own flesh," Cavok insisted, but Reza held up a warning hand, giving him a look that once again silenced him.

"Is he stabilized?" she asked, to which Revna nodded her head, still rubbing her wrist where Cavok had gripped her.

"Stay. Rest," Reza ordered the both of them and was about to leave when she thought to rest a hand on Cavok's good shoulder. "I'm glad to see you again, Cavok. Stay put, okay?"

"You think I'm going anywhere like this?" he gruffed, but she could see that he had softened a bit.

"Where's Alva and Lanereth?" Reza asked of Revna.

"They were sent off to Canopy Glen just before the battle. Lanereth was not feeling well."

That was a sensible move. Logging the information away, she headed out to find Freya again.

"Reza!" shouted someone towards the entrance of camp.

Through the smoke, she saw Kaia and Malagar trudging up what was left of the barricade. Malagar placed a hand on Kaia's shoulder and pointed up to the command tent where Reza stood. Reza walked over to the small grove of trees next to the command tent and waited for them to arrive, needing a respite from all the smoke and carnage of the campsite's center.

"Reza, the haltia soldiers have returned and regrouped. They're looking for you, awaiting your leadership," Kaia said, out of breath.

Reza looked away from the smoky camp, peering into the backwoods beyond any scar of the battle that had just taken place. The woods beyond looked so peaceful—so unnervingly normal. *How could a place so close to so much death and pain seem so unfazed?*

"Reza," Kaia urged, wondering if Reza had even been listening to her message.

"Malagar. Tell Hazel that I'm convening with the Rediron leadership to assess where we stand after that battle and to determine our next move. It might take the rest of this day to come back with firm answers. Until then, I want you to be my liaison. Instruct them to establish camp a half mile east up the hill from their current location. They'll breathe easier there. If anything urgent comes up, send word for me. I'll be back as soon as I can after I get some answers."

"And Kaia?" Malagar asked.

"She'll attend to me. I'll keep an eye on her," Reza gruffly assured him.

Malagar bowed slightly and sprinted off through the tumble of camp and out of sight.

As they watched Malagar disappear into the smoke, Reza asked in a calm voice, "Kaia, how many haltia made it back? There were only a scant few when I came to."

"Malagar took count," Kaia nodded, glad to be of help. "Fifty-two. They're still gathering wounded and the fallen, as well as recovering supplies and arrows, but that's the number that are up and able."

"Not as bad as I suspected, but worse than I had hoped," Reza mumbled to herself, considering briefly how dedicated her loaned soldiers would be to their cause after such a loss. She wouldn't blame them if they harbored nothing but resentment for her as their captain.

"Kaia, did you see where Freya's saren are gathered? I need to speak with her."

"Malagar said most Rediron forces are gathering on the southern side of camp. It looked like the Golden army didn't make it down there, so there's less destruction on that side of the road," Kaia explained, a tremble of nerves still in her voice.

Reza considered the young woman. She noticed a slight quiver and an unsure face. Kaia had not seen battle like this before. Had not seen death on this scale.

Reza put her arm around her, nuzzling heads for a moment. She didn't know if softness was the right answer for Kaia just then. Perhaps it would have been best to force her along with no reprieve to stop and think of how traumatic and chaotic the night had been. Either way, she tried not to overthink it for now. She simply hoped that Kaia knew that she was not alone.

"Stick with me today, okay?" Reza whispered into her hair, still looking over the untouched forest just behind them.

Kaia nodded. Her cheek was wet from tears when they pulled apart from each other, but she was controlling herself well otherwise.

"Come," Reza said, still struggling with her stripped throat.

They were off through the ruins of camp, slowly making their way to the southside where the carnage gave way to a bustling scene of hundreds of Redironers shouting orders and handling the wounded.

"Over there," Kaia pointed, spotting Freya speaking with King Reid, King Waldock, and his son.

Reza patted Kaia on the shoulder approvingly.

Reid took note of Reza's arrival and waved her into their conversation. "Good timing, Reza. Our troops are returning from chasing the Golden army off—what's left of them, at least. We did well, and I've heard much of that success is owed to the Rediron rangers, Fin and his scouts, and your fortunate arrival with haltia troops."

"We seem to have arrived not an hour too soon," she agreed, not sure if she herself could agree with King Reid's positive assessment.

Reid continued. "Can I assume you were able to convince the Silver Crowns to join our cause? When might we see more than a detachment? If there ever was a time we could use a haltia army by our side—"

Reza held up her hand to stop him. "They did hear us, at the highest level of government in fact. They did agree to go to war with Umbraz and all that align with him. However, the Black Steel kingdom has invaded their borders. They're dealing with that threat now. They could only offer a hundred haltia troop—which now is a fifty-two haltia troop. There will be no further direct support from Silver Crowns, other than the fact that they are occupying the majority of the Black Steels' army."

"That is no small gain," Reid mused, considering the news of the new ally. "Umbraz must fight on two fronts now. With the Golden Crowns army broken, and the Black Steel army preoccupied, Alumin is vulnerable."

"So is West Perch," Freya added.

"Aye, but the Black Steel are also exposed. With both Rediron and Silver Crowns, we could move to reinforce the haltia. Once we handle the Black Steels, it should be easy with our combined forces to sweep Alumin clean of the White Cloak influence."

Reza could see the divided motives amongst the group of leaders. Each had disparate goals, even though they wished for the same overall outcome. She wondered who else saw the issue for what it was.

She decided to attempt to shift the conference's focus. "First, King Reid, what of our losses? And what of the Golden Crowns' losses? I was not at the front line and did not see the battle unfold here. By the looks of the entrance of the camp, it was hell for our troops. Before we make any plans to move against the enemy, it would be prudent to know some general numbers. Have your commanders been able to give you casualty reports yet?"

"Most of our people are still recovering the wounded from the battlefield; we haven't sent for an exact count yet. Just based on my estimation, I'd say we lost anywhere between five hundred to a thousand Redironers in last night's battle," Reid answered, taking another swig from his canteen, mulling over the hard truth of the loss a moment longer before spitting out, "Not quite half our force, but close."

"We've lost at least fifty of my battle sisters last night. We're still searching for a few missing, that number could be a few less," Freya answered.

Johnathan also had preliminary reports, as their smaller force was easier to acquire accounts of. "We called all riders back early this morning. Most of our leaders have reported in. We're looking for those missing now, but I can confirm at least two hundred Lost Kingsmen still ride under our banner."

"We may have won the battle, but our people have suffered a costly loss," King Waldock noted.

"So have the Golden Crowns—much more so," Reid rebutted. "I know the early signs of warp poisoning. Many of their men and even commanders had the signs of it. It seems they fell for our trap. Even the thousand or less that retreated northwards may not truly have escaped their fate. The warp may finish them, or at least unhinge them enough to consider deserting."

"To resort to poisoning our enemy…" King Waldock lamented, slowly shaking his head.

"Those men would have ravaged and raped every town in Rediron and done so with pleasure. This is war, King Waldock. The consequences of losing are too great to hold to honorable sentiments," King Reid said vehemently.

Neither King Waldock nor anyone else had a rebuttal.

"So the Golden Crowns army has effectively been crippled at this point. We've won two decisive victories over them. They'd have to be fools to charge headlong at us again," Reza mused.

Johnathan nodded. "I believe their role in this war has been severely reduced. They may try to support Alumin, but I doubt they'll be used as an attack force from here on out."

"If Alumin is the Golden Crowns' fallback point, and the Black Steels' military is currently engaged with the Silver Crowns, then I believe our move is to go on the offensive. We already have a network in place to deal with a smaller invading force that the enemy might be hiding.

"We have a few options available to us. We could march west and invade Black Steel kingdom while their army is fighting the haltia. Once the Mad Queen is dethroned, we could reinstate King Waldock. From there, we could march on West Perch and reclaim Freya's home. We would then begin a siege of Alumin while defending both Rediron and Black Steels' borders from any returning Black Steels coming home from the war—"

"That would take weeks...months even," Kaia cut in.

The group looked at the young saren.

"War is a slow game," Johnathan remarked. "It's not won overnight."

"We won't have months or even weeks before Umbraz is born," Kaia explained, a tremble in her voice.

"What do you mean by that, girl?" Reid probed, a tension rising amongst the group that there was some major key element in play that none had been aware of.

"Umbraz is soon to be summoned into this world, and once he is, the fabric of reality as we know it, will change. *He* will change it."

"How? When?" Reid pressed. "Where did you hear of this?"

Kaia looked to Reza, partially for approval to speak, but also to ensure she had her back. She stepped forward next to Reza and took the father's scripture out of her bag. "When Reza, Nomad, and I investigated Rosewood, we learned many things of Umbraz's plans. We obtained a scripture there, written by one of

Umbraz's foremost followers. Terra and I have been studying his writings and are convinced Umbraz's coming is imminent. We're not long from when he is prophesied to enter our realm. A week, maybe days even at this point. The signs are already there."

"What signs?" Reid asked.

She took out a handful of stringed pearls and held them forward.

"What of this?" Johnathan inquired.

"They're...glowing slightly," Reza whispered, looking closer at the prayer beads. She dug into her pouch and retrieved the prayer beads that she had kept. "They've never done that before."

"They're resonating," Kaia explained. "This *substance* will become the flesh of Umbraz. I don't exactly know how or why, but the scripture says *upon his coming, his flesh shall attune to his will and shall shine like a star upon a hilltop, undeniable to all.*"

Reid, Johnathan, and the others seemed confused by it all.

"The heavens went dark, two nights ago, you saw it, didn't you? The stars seemed to go out. I didn't see them last night either," Kaia went on.

"It was just overcast, girl," King Waldock said.

"No. Well, last night, yes—it was overcast. But even so, I watched diligently for openings in the clouds. I even had Malagar watch with me. Haltia can see clearer through smoke and clouds than we can, and he agreed, it wasn't just clouds that darkened the stars in the sky. They truly seem to be obscured by something else, or not even there at all!"

"I did notice a darkness these last two nights that seemed unnatural. Besides the light of the moon, I saw not a single star. I thought it strange, but…" Reid admitted, thinking on her warnings.

Emboldened, Kaia went on. "The scripture says that the sky will go dark as the lord approaches as his arrival overturns our hold in this reality."

Freya spoke up. "You're saying that Umbraz's arrival will rewrite our reality?"

"If *these words* are true and not just the ramblings of a fanatic"—she emphasized this by holding the scripture up—"then *yes*. All things we have ever known will soon come to an end. What comes after that is anyone's guess. Not even the father knows what Umbraz intends to do at that point. Perhaps Umbraz himself doesn't even fully understand the possibilities of existence quite yet."

Reza could see that some in the leader's circle were still at odds with the inconvenient narrative. "I've seen evidence and have had experiences that align with Kaia's accounting. This is a real threat and I believe that this war we're fighting isn't just for the future of the Crowned Kingdoms, but ultimately will determine the fate of our realm."

Reid broached the subject after seeing that no one else planned to ask the obvious. "If this is true, how do we stop his coming?"

Reza patted Kaia reassuringly. Kaia held up the prayer beads. "All pearls are to be collected—brought to the icon of Umbraz for the ceremony to be completed. Terra and I believe this icon to be the obsidian statue Reza and Nomad saw in the Rosewood monastery."

A thought came to Reza. "Did you notice any White Cloaks in the battle last night? The only White Cloaks I saw were the ones on the other side of the bridge. I don't think they were moving to meet up with the Golden army. I think they were headed past them to Alumin. The call must be sounding for Umbraz's followers."

"It's true, there were no reports of White Cloaks in the army we fought last night," Reid agreed, scratching his scruff.

Reza continued. "We think they have moved that statue to Alumin, specifically, the Valiant synagogue dedicated to Elendium."

"This is just an assumption? And why there?" Reid asked.

"We haven't actually returned to Rosewood ourselves, but Seldrin says the Silver Crowns did perform an investigation into Rosewood after we were transported back to Alumin. They found the grounds abandoned and there were no reports of a black statue in the underground altar."

"Why Valiant synagogue?"

"The Elendium faith has been housing Umbraz's cult for years. They're merely a front for the cult at this point. The central-most monument for Elendium is the synagogue. If they chose to relocate the statue anywhere, that's where I believe they would put it. They tried to hide it in a remote place and that didn't work. They would be smart to hide it in the most defended place, and where does this war center around? Alumin. Nowhere else makes sense."

"Let's say we can storm the synagogue," Freya proposed, "and we find this statue before the pearls are gathered. What then? Do we simply destroy it? Even if it's that simple, can't some fanatic just make another at some point?"

"I'm not entirely sure," Kaia admitted. "The father was very vague about how Umbraz's maturation process works. There does seem to be a point of vulnerability—a climax point if you will—where the father stresses their god's protection during his formation. If Umbraz's protection during his development phase is of the utmost importance, then there's potential there for us to disrupt his summoning. Perhaps that is one of our best shots at stopping him."

"That is extremely vague," Reid sighed. Turning away from the group, he looked out over the busy, beaten camp.

"It's more than what we had before," Freya offered. "Suddenly, the White Cloaks' strange movement over the last year makes more sense. I wish I had known all this and was able to convince the Sisterhood before they moved on West Perch," she whispered to herself.

"We all wish for the gift of knowing," Johnathan remarked, placing an understanding hand on Freya's shoulder. "Each of us only had part of the puzzle—but we're together now, sharing, sacrificing, and fighting together. It's important to remember, we're stronger together than ever before apart. I…have faith in this alliance. We will find a way forward."

"So we need to infiltrate Valiant synagogue immediately," Reid said, dropping his fist in palm. "That's easier said than done. Last we had word, Alumin has many hundreds of soldiers stationed there, and with the beaten Golden Crowns army returning to lick their wounds, it'll have many hundreds more. We cannot hope to break through Alumin's front gates and burst through the chapel doors head on with force alone. We don't have the numbers or the battlefield advantage."

"True. It'd be a pointless massacre if we rushed the gates head on. Their walls are well fortified and manned," King Waldock agreed.

Freya spoke up. "We could move as though we were planning on a full-frontal attack. Move the bulk of our army just outside the reach of the city towers."

"What would that serve?" Johnathan asked. "That would only be effective in giving our enemy a clear view of our position and numbers."

"Are you hinting at a bait-and-switch?" Reza asked Freya.

Freya smiled. "I was getting there. If we wished to divert the enemy's focus for a coordinated attack, a full-frontal show of force would direct attention away from a smaller covert task force. There are many entrances into the city, after all."

"A simple enough tactic. How do we know Umbraz's force in Alumin will fall for such a rudimentary move?" Johnathan asked.

Reza jumped in. "Umbraz's force is made up of multiple kingdoms and fealties: Golden Crowns, Black Steels, Alumin governance and city guard, the White Cloaks and Elendium faithful. As far as we know, Umbraz doesn't have a reliable or clear line of communication open with even the top leaders in the organization. Their strategy as it stands seems to be *hold everyone off until Umbraz himself arrives and takes his throne*. If we're going to out-strategize anyone, it's this motley gang of thugs."

Freya nodded. "Apart from that, I don't see an operation like the one I'm thinking of as all that simple."

"Let's hear it," Reid prompted.

Freya bent down and drew a rough map in the dirt. "This smaller force would head west before crossing the river and split up—half crossing Alumin's west bridge to draw the attention of the occupying force at West Perch. If we can draw them out of the fort, the group lying in wait will storm the fort and liberate the sarens there. That would add another hundred saren priestesses to our force. We'll pincer the occupying force from there and then proceed to Alumin's west gate."

"By then, word will have made it to the gate. It'll be up and guarded," Johnathan pointed out.

"Sareth gives her knights strength but her priestesses her light. I believe with enough faith, our priestess sisters can manage to bring a gate down," Freya answered.

"We don't have siege weapons. How is the larger force going to enter the southern gate?" King Waldock asked of King Reid.

Reid hesitated. "I…might have an idea for that one."

Johnathan sighed and pinched the bridge of his nose. "This sounds very tenuous."

"Yes, it does," King Waldock agreed. "Are there any other options?"

"Any other plans I can think of would take more than a fortnight to accomplish," Reza argued. "If we are looking for the most direct route to access the synagogue, that very well may be our best shot."

"Now is the perfect time to attack the capital—we should not hesitate." Freya doubled down on Reza's argument. "When news of the Golden Crowns' defeat reaches their leadership, they may withdraw the Black Steel army back to bolster Alumin to bide time until

Umbraz's summoning. Now is the time to strike—hard and fast."

None could refute the women's points.

"Then who constitutes the larger and smaller groups?" Reid asked.

"Me and my sarens are an obvious choice for the liberator role at West Perch," said Freya.

Reid thought on the plan. "And who's going to be the bait?"

"My riders can outpace any tail," Johnathan boasted.

"Right, and I think the troops occupying West Perch will see that. We need a slower target, one not mounted and a reasonable target," Freya countered.

"My haltia," Reza offered. "They have excellent range with their longbows. There's only fifty left, though. Perhaps with a small contingent of scouts led by Fin and some heavies led by Cav—" She stopped herself, remembering his near-fatal wounds. "I almost forgot. He's in no condition to be leading a contingent, let alone fighting in a war. His injuries looked dire. He'll be laid up for weeks."

"That man…" Morgan sighed, everyone turning their attention to the silent bodyguard of the king. "He is likely the reason our northern flank held, even after it had been reduced to a handful of soldiers. He fought with the fury of a devil. I've never seen anything like what he did. I still can't believe it."

Reid validated the statement. "It's true, by the account of the survivors of the north flank, he held back scores of Golden Knights."

"He is strength incarnate," Reza agreed. "I hope to convince him to allow for further healing to recover his wounds quicker. I'd like to have him at my side in the upcoming operation."

"Yozo or Nomad could take his place if he can't join you. They are both experts in close combat," Kaia suggested.

"That their skill is unmatched with the sword, it's true, but that does not make them a leader of men. Perhaps Nomad, under different circumstances, but…his foreign blood…forgive me for saying this of your peoples, but the Crowned Kingdoms have not been so open to Nomad's lineage as it has to us from the Southern Sands. They would follow Cavok easier than they would Nomad. Cavok would be a better fit for that position. I will do my best to convince him of the need."

"Would you then be leading the other half of the covert unit?" Reid asked, seeing Reza nudging to that conclusion.

She agreed. "I have extensive experience with running unique operations like this, and so does my crew."

"Take whomever you need from my troops to field your company, Reza," Reid offered.

"That leaves my riders and your army to constitute the main force," King Waldock concluded.

"Indeed it does." Reid nodded heartily. "Having you and your son's experience at my side would mean a great deal. We'll make an assault upon those walls like Alumin has never seen."

"It's agreed upon, then? We'll split the force and move out as soon as we're able?" Reza asked.

Reid offered one final point. "We'll need communication between the two groups. Luck would have it, a few days back we had a falconer from

Tarrolaine volunteer his and his aviary's services to the war cause. I'll send him with you. We won't be more than a dozen or so leagues apart. We should have a responsive communication line open."

"It's agreed then," Freya concluded.

They realized that this could be the last time they talked with each other, at least as a leadership council before heading out on a mission likely more dangerous than any had ever seen, let alone led. The days ahead were heavy with risk and consequences if any one of them failed their part.

Everyone took in the image of each other in the golden light of the morning sun.

"Be careful out there. Trust in those that stand beside you," King Reid offered. "Now go. See to your men and women's needs. Send word when you're ready to move out."

Some began to head off to tend to their troops. Freya took Reza by the arm and walked off with her, Kaia following at their side.

"We'll need Cavok healthy and ready to lead," Freya explained. Reza saw now that she was leading her back to the command tent where Cavok was.

"It may not be as simple as you think to convince him to accept a blessing. He's very much against it," Reza replied.

"No offense, Reza, but perhaps he needs a firm touch this time. I'll make sure he accepts a healing. We need him."

"I'll...try and reason with him one more time. After that, we can try it your way," Reza said. It was clear to Freya and Kaia that Reza was uncomfortable over the subject. "He's not going to be happy with us."

"He doesn't need to be," Freya said. "As long as he's up and fighting on our side, our chances of saving this kingdom are better. We can't afford to lose this one."

Reza knew Freya was right. Cavok's sentiments, or anyone else's for that matter, be damned—they needed to defeat Umbraz at all costs. She hoped it would not come down to forcing the man to accept a healing against his will. He might not ever forgive her if she demanded his compliance.

They stormed up to the commander's tent and Freya flung open the tent flap, entering with Reza and Kaia close behind. Revna watched from Cavok's side as the three women approached.

Cavok, who had been quietly resting, squinted his eyes open to see them standing over him.

Freya looked to Reza.

Reza cleared her throat as best she could and spoke softly to him. "Cavok. I'm sorry to ask this of you, but I need you to lead a troop of knights into battle with me. We need to storm Alumin, and I need you to be my muscle."

Cavok looked at Reza for a moment before closing his eyes and laying his head back down.

Freya knelt over him and snatched his wrists up, clutching them in one firm hand. His eyes shot open, a baleful glare frightening Reza, Kaia, and Revna, but Freya was unfazed. She bound his hands with a cord and straddled his wide, slashed torso, putting her full weight on him.

"Priestess," Freya called to Revna, her eyes locked with Cavok's. "Heal him."

"Saren," Cavok said in a frighteningly calm tone, "untie me. I guarantee you will regret it if you do not."

"Save your threats for the enemy. I will not have mercy on you if you struggle while she performs a blessing."

Cavok's sides split, seeping fresh blood, and his arms began to bulge as he tested the strength of Freya's rope. His many gashes wept streams of crimson as he strained and clenched his teeth.

Her hand clenched around his throat and she squeezed firmly, clamping off blood flow.

"I'll put you to sleep if you can't behave," she hissed, struggling to handle Cavok's bound arms, mounted on his heaving chest.

Veins in his forehead and temples bulged and he began to turn purple. He stilled slightly, wound tight with tension but considering if he was willing to expend a dangerous amount of effort and tear his body apart to escape the saren's bonds.

He gave up his struggle completely. As Freya released her chokehold, color quickly began to clear up in Cavok's complexion.

He breathed deeply to clear his system of the dump of adrenalin, as did Freya.

"Priestess. He's ready," Freya said, holding Cavok's bound hands tight to her body to ensure that he was secured.

Revna looked to Reza, not sure of Freya's methodologies. Reza looked miserable, but she nodded for Revna to listen to Freya, then covered her face in a hand, turning away from the scene Cavok had insisted on making.

"What makes you think that when she's done healing me that I won't snap this string and grind you to a pulp with my bare hands?" Cavok asked, deadly serious, holding eye contact with Freya as Revna began placing her hands and speaking a quiet prayer to begin the healing process.

"You do that, and you'll be aiding Umbraz. I don't think you want that," Freya said, calming her breath now and smiling slightly. "Besides that, I'm the best wrestler I know. Muscles aren't everything in a tussle."

Revna worked fast. In the silence between Freya and Cavok, his lacerations rapidly stitched together, color and vitality coming back to his face.

He flexed, blood flowing through his swelling, mended muscles. His flex raised Freya up in a silent show of strength.

She waited a moment longer before unwrapping the binding.

He opened his hands, and for a moment Reza worried he was reaching for Freya's neck, but he clenched his fists, circulating blood back through his slightly purple hands from the tight cord.

She stood up and dismounted him, and walked to the tent door.

"Saren," Cavok said, not loudly, but with command in his tone that forced Freya to pause. "You will pay for what you just did."

"After we defeat Umbraz, feel free to collect your payment," she responded without looking back.

She lifted the tent flap and left the rest of the tent in silence.

Cavok, after some time, heaved a sigh and got up. His trousers were shredded, caked in blood, and barely covering him. He stripped the rest of the rags off of him and proceeded to dunk a rag in the wash basin, wipe himself down, and then rummage through King Reid's war chest where the royal garb was stashed. Picking out a new pair of smallclothes, slacks, and a tight sleeveless top, he dressed and finally faced the three saren who were all still stunned by the whole occurrence.

"Revna. You alright?" he asked.

"Weak, but I—I'll recover in a day or so," she said. By her tone, it was clear the healing had drained her greatly.

"I'll tend to you till you've recovered," he said, some softness returning to his voice.

Reza rested a hand on Cavok's forearm gently, tentatively.

"Reza, whatever it is you needed me for, go ahead. Once again, you've gotten your way with me," he said, exhausted with her at that point.

"Yes," she said. She thought of where to begin, slightly hollowed out over forcing her friend into something that he had been adamantly against from the start.

She had violated his trust—his free will. That would not be an easy thing for them to recover from. She might be dealing with the ramifications of that for years, possibly for the remainder of her days.

"Alright, Cavok," she started, clearing her head from the mounting guilt. She needed—*he* needed her to proceed with confidence now that he was on board. They could not afford hesitation. They'd have to save their personal issues for after the war.

Chapter Twenty-Two
Calm before the Mission

"You ever think about having kids, Reza?" Fin asked as the two trotted lazily along through another strip of light woods. The noonday sun cut through the forest canopy, bathing them in a warmth that had been rare over the last week.

Reza gave Fin a perturbed look, one that reminded him of her old self.

"You do know that sarens are barren, right?" she asked, slightly annoyed at his ignorance after knowing her for so long.

"Hmm. Guess the subject never came up. Have you ever thought about adoption?"

"Where the hell is this coming from, Fin?" Reza asked. "We're about to invade Alumin. Get your head cleared."

"That's what I'm doing." Fin leaned back in his saddle, looking up through the treeline. "After all, this might be our last casual conversation before things go sideways."

Fin's remark quieted her. She let the thought sink in for a few moments of silence.

Most of the troops marched at a slow but steady pace behind them. There hadn't been enough horses to spare for their whole troop, but the distance they needed to travel was not too terribly far. The slower pace had been intentional to allow Reid time to start moving his men north along the highway, following the retreating Golden Crowns army.

"You thinking about having kids someday?" Reza asked, her tone softer after giving Fin's comment some thought.

"Yeah, probably," he replied, scratching his scruff. "Could be a new adventure. Not sure how much longer I can hang with you and go to war every other year. My thoughts have often been lingering elsewhere lately—I think I'm going to start losing my edge at some point, and that's not a spot I want to put myself in, or my comrades."

"You think you're passing your peak?" Reza asked, a bit of worry in her voice.

"I think so," he freely admitted.

"I hardly think so," she scoffed. "Look at all you've managed to survive through this last year. You accomplished more than any of us, I'd argue."

"I *survived*, not *thrived*. I barely made it out of Rediron the first time I visited," he corrected, thinking back on his time with Malagar and Yozo in the hellish ordeal of the warp. "I was bested by a random hitman," he said, pinching his bluish gray cloak he had taken from Mr. White. "Until then, there wasn't anyone I didn't *know* I could beat in a duel. That shook me more than a little."

"You're alive," Reza stated. "Is he?"

"I'm only alive because Yozo was an even better swordsman than he was," Fin chuffed. "Imagine, thinking you're top dog one moment and then realizing you were sharing the room with two of your superiors. Who else out there are you then going to come across who's faster, stronger, has better technique, smarter, *hungrier*?"

Another silence set in.

"All fighters go through that humbling realization," Reza offered, having cursed herself endlessly through the years when her strength and skill had failed her.

"It's different this time," he put simply. "After this, it's time to take a break."

She rode her horse up next to his until their saddles rubbed together. He looked over as she grabbed his hand. Looking down at her thumb supportively rubbing along his knuckles, he smiled.

"As long as you don't leave me, I think I'll be able to come to terms with whatever decision you come to. You mean too much to me to even think of losing you—" she said, choking up at the end. She broke away from him to attempt to compose herself.

He smiled and patted her on the back. He was about to reassure her when Cavok approached.

Reza hurriedly wiped the moisture from her eyes, clearing her throat as Cavok settled in with their pace next to the pair.

She gave him a hard glare after composing herself. He glared back, still extremely displeased with her behavior back in camp two days earlier.

Fin broke the awkward silence. "The knights keeping up back there? Those haltia are looking antsy up ahead, bet they were wishing the men had horses just to match pace with their marching speed."

Cavok ignored the remark, choosing instead to get to the point of his intrusion.

"We need to discuss the details of this plan of yours, Reza—as a group. There're too many holes in it for me to feel comfortable risking other men's lives for," he stated, looking towards the next line of woods.

"As a group? Who do you mean?" Reza asked.

"Us three, Nomad, Terra, Malagar, and that damned saren knight," he spat.

"Freya," Reza corrected. Cavok remained quiet. "I think Kaia would be relevant to have in that discussion, as well as Yozo."

"Kaia, fine, but not Yozo. He's not needed."

"Cavok," Fin sighed, exasperated with the man's long-standing prejudices.

"Keep out of this, Fin," Cavok warned. "Reza, tonight 'round the campfire, we talk about fine-tuning this plan of yours."

"Fine," Reza gruffly agreed.

Without another word, Cavok drifted back to his knights at the back of the troop, leaving Reza and Fin once again relatively alone ahead of their units.

Reza shook off the tension she had been carrying in her shoulders and took a deep breath to reset herself.

"Stubborn fool," Fin said, more out of pity than spite.

Reza nodded, whispering, "I can't blame him for it. I'm just as bad. Stubborn as hell most of the time."

"No, you're different," Fin waved off.

"Uh huh," Reza remarked sarcastically.

"You are a bit more bull-headed than you need to be sometimes," Fin smiled as he corrected himself. "But you're actually trying to improve your hang-ups. Cavok…I don't know if he'll ever get better at letting go of grudges. Once you cross him, it's nothing but trouble."

Reza's shoulders started to get tight once more. Had *she* crossed him in the command tent days back when she had allowed Freya to manhandle him?

They leisurely trotted through the meadow clearing before Fin concluded. "Well, I'd better connect with my scouts. Out of anyone in our troop, they'd know this patch of trees we're coming up on. Don't want to come across any surprises today if we don't need to."

Reza was glad for a moment alone to reflect. She needed to collect her thoughts on the finer points of their invasion scheme. Though at its core it seemed simple enough, Cavok was right in questioning some of the details that had been purposefully left out when she had first given him the mission overview. She and Freya had not been able to agree on a few things. It would be helpful to get trusted feedback on strengthening their plan, but first, she needed to consolidate her own ideas on the matter.

"Reza," Malagar called, trotting up to her.

She rubbed her neck and waited for the haltia to approach.

"What is it?" she asked after his horse fell in step with hers.

She noticed he was holding prayer beads as he answered. "I've been collecting these Seam pearls from Kaia and any others in the company. I heard you had some?"

"Yes," she admitted. She dug out the satchel that held the string of pearls.

"What do you need them for?" she asked, waiting for an answer before handing over the dangerous items.

"I have a theory, though before I come to any conclusions, I need as much of this Seam-tainted substance as we have in our possession. It may help factor into whatever this Umbraz is attempting," Malagar answered as they approached the next section of woods.

"It may help us fight Umbraz?" Reza conjectured.

"It may," he replied. He saw now that she wasn't going to hand over the pearls without further explanation. "These pearls aren't pure Seam residue—they're diluted with a substance from our realm. That having been said, I'm wondering if I can tap into the Seam with a greater quantity of these pearls. If I can do that, I may be able to investigate Umbraz's nature further."

"You could gain access to Umbraz's realm?" Reza asked.

"Perhaps. It's not as simple as that. As I understand it in talking with Kaia and Terra, Umbraz intends to use these pearls to bridge the gap between dimensions somehow. There's a reason its construct is half material from this realm and half from the Seam. There are still unanswered questions. That's why I need those pearls you have, to further my study."

Reza slowly handed over the satchel, recalling, with dread, the time she had mutated a squirrel on a grassy cliff.

"Careful with those things, Malagar," she warned. "Apprise me of your findings."

He nodded, stashing them in a side bag.

"Hey," she called as he began to steer his horse away, "find me at the campfire tonight. Make sure you bring Terra, Kaia, and Nomad with you. We'll go over strategy for the upcoming operations."

"Yozo?" Malagar asked, turning back.

"No."

He nodded after a moment and headed off.

She sighed, once again feeling her shoulders locking up from the stress of non-stop decision making.

She did the best she could to steady her breathing, loosen up, and clear her mind.

As she crossed the treeline of the next stretch of woods, she closed her eyes and let the cool shadows of the forest canopy wash over her.

Yozo had finished brushing down his horse some time ago, but he had lingered, seeing to his gear and checking his equipment over. Typically, he traveled at Malagar's side. The haltia was a sensible sort with a calm nature that he had an affinity with. Fin was constantly occupied with the burdens of command, and so had not had time for Yozo.

He finished tinkering with his things and leaned against a tree in the dark of the woods, looking to the campfire that Reza and her crew sat around, talking heatedly.

He looked down and slid his sword a few inches out of its wooden scabbard to inspect the soft orange glint rippling along the hamon wave of the polished steel blade. His mind wandered aimlessly along the corridors of the past—the countless times he had owed his survival to that sword. It was one of the few remaining relics of his past life in Silmurannon. The same could be said of Nomad and *his* sword.

The two men were similar in many ways; birthed in the same motherland, raised under the same tutors, learned of the world through their journey across untold cultures and peoples—they had both traveled halfway around the world and had become experts of survival, both in civilizations and wildernesses. They had formed an almost sacred bond with that one ultimate tool that had borne them through endless trial and tribulation. They owed their very life to their blade.

He supposed that he could see why Reza had thought of Nomad's return to the bandit camp for his sword as lunacy, but he perfectly understood Nomad's insistence on the matter. In a way, it was all that tied him to his past self, and no matter how painful the past was to either of them, to forget their early life would disrespect the memory of those they had loved in their youth. Holding to this memory alone was enough to sacrifice greatly for—a risk even worthy of their life.

He slowly slid the blade back home to its scabbard, snapping it closed. He looked back to the campfire and noticed the group slowly disbanding. Curiosity and slight resentment lingered with him as he watched the associates he had traveled with in the past few years meander back to their solitary stations and duties. Why they had not invited him to their gathering, he could only guess at.

The large one, the one whom he had bad blood with, headed his direction, though it seemed not intentionally.

They had stayed separate enough on the trail whenever they were forced to travel together, but the times they had exchanged words with each other could be counted on one hand.

Yozo moved to fidget about his horse's bridle once more, making some noise to warn the man of his presence before he came upon him.

It worked. Cavok's keen senses immediately took note of him in the dark, and he slowed as he recognized Yozo's presence. Cavok sneered at the foreign man but ultimately changed his course, disappearing back into the tents of the Rediron knights at the back of camp.

Yozo patted his horse's strong jaw, moving for his camp pack at the base of the tree his horse was hitched to. He needed to get his bedroll out and turn in for the night. It was apparent now that Reza and the others would not be requiring his presence at least until the morning.

"I do not doubt Reza wished for your input, but I have a suspicion she did not want a scene between you and him," a familiar voice said as he approached.

"Hiro." Yozo acknowledged Nomad by his true name, more than a little surprised that he had not heard his brother-in-law coming.

"That name…" Nomad sighed and rubbed the flank of Yozo's horse soothingly. "Seems like a life ago that I went by that name, when we lived among our people."

"That it does," Yozo agreed.

Nomad struggled with something he wished to say.

"What is it, Nomad? Out with it," he urged.

Nomad looked up to the tree's canopy. There was no starlight beyond the leaf cover. His reflective voice split the quiet night. "Things are coming to an end."

"They will if we do not defeat Umbraz."

"Beyond that," Nomad waved off. "Things will be different for us—all of us—after this is over, I feel it."

"Perhaps, for the others," Yozo grunted.

"For you as well, I think."

Yozo remained quietly in his thoughts.

Nomad met eyes with his estranged counterpart. "If we both remain among the living on the other side of this war, I have a personal request of you, brother."

"Bold of you to request anything of me," Yozo said, venom entering his voice. "Need I remind you that I hunted you halfway across the globe to spill your blood."

"If you refuse my request, so be it, but at least allow me the privilege of asking it."

"Fine," he chuffed. "On the morrow, find me bright and early. I'll hear your request before we get moving for the day, but do not expect me to accept it."

Nomad smiled and leaned back with an arm resting on the horse's flank. Yozo frowned and snapped, "Is that all you came here for?"

Nomad folded his arms. "I requested for us to serve together in the coming operation. I wanted your approval to fight side by side against the enemy."

"That depends," Yozo said, softening his tone. "What's our mission?"

"A small, covert operation. To see Malagar to the synagogue." Nomad smiled once more. He appreciated the man's pension for risky missions as much as his own. "Reza and her crew will be doing the same, but they'll take a separate route. They think Malagar may be uniquely qualified with his connection to the Seam to play an important role in disrupting Umbraz's summoning. If that is true, we need to see him safely into position for him to perform his part."

"That would be…acceptable," Yozo said after some thought. "I will ensure Malagar's safety."

Nomad nodded his approval. "We'll connect with Malagar in the morning over the details. For now, get some sleep. I have a feeling we'll not be privileged many more restful moments before the end."

Yozo hefted his sleeping roll. "What do you think I was doing before you showed up?"

Nomad smiled and strolled off back towards the campfire where Reza still sat speaking with Freya.

He watched Nomad for a bit longer before rolling out his mat along the ground, brushing off the stray leaves and twigs on its surface. He looked back to the fire circle one last time, considering his feelings for the man that he had once called his brother—the man that he had later called his worst enemy. What he thought of Hiro Kasaru now was a subject still in debate in his tormented mind.

Shutting it all out, he laid down and closed his eyes and began his meditative routine to quiet his mind and still his body. There was one thing Nomad had been correct about—rest would be in short supply in the coming days.

Chapter Twenty-Three

Logistics and Coordination

The night before had settled Reza's mind on many points. For once, she had been able to rest soundly and so felt more prepared for their upcoming mission than ever before. The campfire talk had unified her leaders, even Cavok and Freya had talked cooperatively over the points of their units' interconnecting roles in laying out logistics and routes.

The one member of their inner circle purposely omitted was Yozo, and though she had regretted not including him in the planning meeting, Cavok's cooperation likely would not have been possible with his presence. Nomad had brought him up to speed with their decisions that night and following morning though, and she hoped he wouldn't harbor too much resentment in his heart over the arrangement.

"Reza," Freya nudged, drawing her from her thoughts, "I should be breaking off soon. We're nearing the borders of the Greenwood."

She looked back and noticed that Freya's saren knights were mounted and in formation, ready to move out at her command.

"I'll make sure that Kaia and Terra are well protected. They're with Jaunt, one of my finest knights," Freya assured her.

Clasping her hand, Reza smiled and nodded to her kinswoman. "May Sareth guide your way."

"May she guide us all." Freya returned the smile before heading off, waving for her troops to follow her lead.

Reza watched the troop ride off through the woods for a moment longer. She liked Freya. She wondered if she would have connected more naturally with her faith and her people if she had had even *just one* friend growing up. She had been alone and excluded in her childhood. Lanereth, though good at heart, had been ill-equipped to raise such a stubborn child as Reza. Perhaps companionship would have rounded her sharp edges a bit more.

She sighed, banishing the thought for now, and determined to spend time getting to know Freya after the war if they both were lucky enough to survive it.

She pulled back on her reins and trotted over to Cavok and his knights.

"We'll be relying on the strength of your men, Cavok," Reza said, falling in step next to him. "We don't know how many we'll face at the bridge castle. It's a small hold, but a hold with walls and a gate nonetheless."

"As long as Fin's men can keep the gate open for us, we'll handle anyone inside."

"Your tattoos—" Reza said, noticing his many scars cutting through his exotic designs.

She knew they were more than just decorative. They were hexweaved with enchanting effects that he had utilized in the past—sparingly—but when he had used them, his spells had been indispensable. Now his patterns were ruined, and even some of the color had seemed to seep from them overnight.

"Yes," he acknowledged. "Some of the spells have broken."

"You know this for certain?" she asked.

"I have tested most of them. Only a few remain viable. That is why I'm carrying a sword at my hip."

"I see," was all Reza could muster. She had heard of his great stand against a whole unit of Golden Knights on the northern flank of camp. She had no doubt that part of that impressive feat could be accredited to his access to the arcane. But it had obviously taken a toll on him.

"It matters not. War is in my blood, and I can fight just as ruthlessly with or without channeling hexweave."

"I don't doubt that," she offered, but couldn't help but wonder if he was overcompensating to keep his confidence high for the upcoming mission.

Reza looked overhead, noting the sun hanging low through the rustling leaves. "Well, I had better go and send Fin off. The evening is coming on."

"See you on the battlefield, then, Reza Malay," Cavok offered, smacking her horse's rump, starting it off prematurely.

After shooting a foul glance back at Cavok, Reza soothed and settled her horse's nerves. She rode over to Fin's unit and found him riding in the lead.

"Milady," Fin greeted as she rode up next to him, warranting him an immediate smack on the arm.

"Stop that," she scolded. "Now's not the time for jokes."

"No swords are clashing, no spears hurtling through the air. Lighten up a bit. Doesn't do your men any good to see you a ball of nerves before battle. If you're confident in our odds, you wouldn't be so worried, would you?"

"I don't need a lesson in leadership right now, Fin."

"Fine," he gave in. "What's on your mind?"

"Are your men ready to move out?"

"At your command."

"Then I command it," she said somewhat awkwardly, eyeing Fin afterwards to warn him not to return with a quip. "It's about that time. Start heading out."

"I can do that," he said, smiling. Turning in his saddle, he whistled to his company.

"We'll stay hidden along the banks and wait for first sight of you before we make our move," he said, sending a signal for his men to begin their new course. "See you at the castle, Reza."

She saluted and headed back to her own company. Calling out orders to the haltia and the Rediron knights, she led the group onwards through the increasingly sparse forest, the terrain becoming rockier as they neared the foothills of West Perch.

Just before sunset, once they were well out of the forest with West Perch in view a few miles off across the rocky rise, Hazel trotted up alongside Reza and said in a discreet voice, "Black Steel watchmen ahead, far off on the overlook to the left. Looks like they have eyes on us."

"Good," Reza replied, and called back down the line a new marching order to head from north to northeast, pointing them away from West Perch and straight to the bridge castle along the highway leading to Alumin.

"They've sent runners back to the keep now," Hazel informed Reza. "Only a matter of minutes before they make it back to the West Perch walls."

"Then we'll need to hurry. Lead the troop towards the highway. When you see the enemy give chase, open fire if they get too close. We need to ward them off until we reach the bridge castle walls," Reza ordered, looking back to Cavok's knights at the end of the haltia ranks. "I'll see that the knights protect your bowmen."

Reza snapped her horse's reins and trotted off to Cavok as Hazel issued the new orders to the haltia archers, everyone now picking up their pace.

"Cavok," Reza called as she rode up to him. "Double-time. We'll need to keep up with the haltia. When the enemy approaches, defend them at all costs."

"Double-time!" Cavok's voice boomed down the line.

"Have the back row light torches. It'll soon be dark. Let's give the enemy a point to focus on."

"Rear guard, light your torches!" he relayed.

The haltia were exiting the rocky foothills onto the open grassy plains, making quick time towards the highway. Looking back to the saren fort high above at the base of the mountain, Reza could see torches light up and a bustle of activity along the wall as news had made it back to the inhabitants of their bands' arrival.

The game was afoot now; they were committed to their plan. Her horse skipped along nervously, no doubt feeling the trembling tension in Reza's thighs.

She snapped the reins hard, giving the horse a firm heel, and spurred it into a canter over the remaining mounds of loose rock onto the grassy field.

The gate of West Perch fort opened with a shout from high up the foothills.

The enemy made ready to give chase.

Chapter Twenty-Four

The Battle for West Perch

Freya held her hand high, waiting for the signal from the five Rediron rangers that Fin had sent with her to run the stealth work of handling the fort's exterior lookouts. She had to admit, they had disappeared from her sight within moments of being sent out into the dying light of the evening along the fort's rocky sprawl.

She was just about to call for a few paces back of the frontline of knights on horseback when her eye caught a spark down past a few small ledges. She held for a moment longer until she could clearly see the brief shower of sparks before throwing her hand ahead.

That was the signal. The fort lookouts had been dispatched.

Her lead mounted knights were slow at first, crossing the cliffside terrain with a warranted degree of caution, but they traversed the backside of the fort's wall much quicker than the saren knights that were navigating the terrain on foot.

She once again held up a hand, stopping the advancing knights in their tracks as she listened to the sound of thundering hooves just around the next bend. Men along the wall shouted and whooped as Black Steel and White Cloak riders alike charged out of the open gate rushing headlong down the highway to intercept the small line of torches in the grassy depression below.

The commotion died down slightly, only a few stragglers charging out through the gate now. She knew it was time to make their move.

She threw her hand forward once more, signaling for all to follow. She snapped her reins and spurred her horse on and around the bend.

Her horse jumped onto the side path along the front wall, allowing her ride to charge forward on sure footing. Her mounted frontline knights were right behind her.

Just as she was about to the gate, another Black Steel soldier rode out. The rider caught a glance at the approaching saren troop and attempted to turn around, yelling back to the gatekeepers: "*Close the gate! Close the gate!*"

Freya ignored him, riding straight past him—the following saren did not. The saren knight plunged her sword straight through the half-armored man, spilling him over the other side of his horse.

Though the soldier had been silenced quickly, the word was out, and the gatekeepers along the wall scrambled to get to the winch.

With their presence announced, Freya yelled back to her knights, "Handle the operators!"

A few bolts flew down into the courtyard from along the wall, one thudding into the belly of Freya's horse. It bucked her off weakly as it tumbled to the stone floor. Another frontline saren went down, not as lucky as Freya had been. A bolt stuck out of her side as she crashed to the ground.

More saren riders rushed in through the gate before it began to lower. They dismounted quickly and the saren knights rushed up the steep gate side stairway, making short work of the ill-armored gate guards that were frantic at protecting the two men cranking the winch as fast as they were able.

The last gate guard standing between the lead saren and the winch operators handled his sword well, and after a flourish of quick circles around the saren's blade and a flash of a cut to her hand, he knocked her sword free of her grip.

He wore a grim grin as he thrust at his disarmed foe, but the smirk turned to a mask of doom as she batted his blade aside with the backside of her gauntlet to get closer in, barreling into him. The two tumbled over the edge of the walkway.

The next knight in line rushed into the winch alcove, hacking up the two Black Steel operators with all the ferocity of a starving wolf upon defenseless prey.

Another saren entered the alcove, kicked the dead men out of the way, and cranked the winch in reverse. The gate began to rise back up.

"Crossbowmen on the wall!" Freya pointed and yelled to the saren just arriving.

Men rushed out from the keep's main door, half dressed in their armor, some with nothing but their fatigues on. Their swords were raised and battlecries ferocious as any, Freya knew not to underestimate their charge.

"Get ready to receive them," she shouted to the last few riders entering through the gate.

She readied her mace and shield and dug herself in. The leading man leapt into her shield, smashing into her with all his momentum, and knocked her back.

She had no time to take a swing as a spearpoint thrust viciously in at her, glancing off the edge of her shield and helm. She staggered back again, jostled as the spear cut back in, sticking her in the side. Thankfully, the tip got caught up on her chainmail as she recovered her step.

She swung her shield back forcefully, knocking the spear wide and taking a blind step in, swinging her mace in the man's direction. The crenelated ridged head of the mace smashed into his shoulder, freezing him up in pain. She squared up and slammed into him with her shield, spilling him onto the ground.

Two mounted saren charged in, slashing and trampling those men unfortunate enough to be in their path. Freya dove into the center of the gang, taking advantage of the chaos. She let her mace fly freely, bashing in the heads of those who had been bowled over by the stampede.

Along the wall, saren were handling the crossbowmen easily, blocking the few remaining bolts with their wide shields, then moving in for an easy kill.

More saren rushed in to support and clean up the remaining resistance group Freya had engaged. She disentangled herself and returned to command the saren on foot who were finally catching up, rushing into the courtyard.

"Sweep the halls—squads of five! If you meet resistance, do not engage alone—report to me in the audience hall," Freya boomed, then grabbed a few passing sarens and the five Rediron scouts and stormed in with her task force at her back through the central building's large double doors.

Chapter Twenty-Five

Outrunning the Enemy

Another of Cavok's torchbearers fell, his armor all but splitting at the seams as a warp of flesh burst forth from within. More agonizing screams issued from the back line as the White Cloak riders began to catch up and chant their unholy prayers.

"Keep those riders at bay!" Reza yelled to her haltia bowmen. Bows twanged with an immediate renewed effort as the screams from the back lines began to multiply.

Though she couldn't see their enemy directly, the dark of the night fallen by that point, she knew they were there, and close. She could only hope that the haltia arrows would be able to silence the zealots' twisted utterances.

"Cavok, move! We need to get to that castle!" she shouted over the chaos.

"We need covering fire, damn it!" Cavok bellowed back, calling for her to get her archers to focus on covering his men rather than telling his already sprinting men in full plate to simply *run faster*.

"Focus fire on the nearest White Cloaks," Reza ordered her troop as they stumbled onto the road close to the river castle.

Reza could see the castle's ten-foot-high, rough shale wall up ahead. The main gate was unlit, making it hard to see how far out they still were. Her horse stumbled a bit on the cobblestone road, exhausted from the lengthy, muddy run through the field. Her only hope was that Fin's crew had beaten them to the castle and had been successful in securing the gate.

A few more screams from the back of Cavok's knights sounded as another knight clattered to the ground. They redoubled their pace, trying hopelessly to outrun the mounted zealots.

"There!" Reza called out, close enough to the gate now to see it wide open. "Cavok, just a few paces further!"

The announcement was the spark that Cavok's knights needed, now seeing hope in sight. They all rushed on, spending whatever remaining energy they had to make it safely out of the reach of the insidious chanting of the foul voices that had followed them the last hour like vultures.

Reza rushed in through the dark archway into the small bailey to chaotic alarm calls from within the donjon, torches and voices buzzing from the windows upon their arrival.

Cavok moved in behind Reza just as Fin shouted "Fire!" from the dark walls above. Arrows from Fin's hidden scouts shot down into the White Cloak ranks that had reached the men at the gate.

White Cloaks began falling from horseback as the rest of Cavok's crew made it through the gate. More riders were approaching, however, and not just White Cloaks, but armed Black Steel soldiers. Though none were well armored, there were enough arriving to warrant the urgency in Fin's voice as he called for his men to raise the gate.

The gate was mostly up by the time the approaching riders were there en masse at the walls.

With arrow fire wreaking havoc to the warband that was now shut off from their quarry, the remaining enemy unit began to call for a retreat to regroup out of archery range.

"They're headed back up the road," Fin called down to Reza as the *twang* of bowstrings grew less frequent.

Reza acknowledged Fin's report and trotted over to her haltia squad. "Hazel, take your crew and head across the bridge to the gatehouse post haste. Don't let anyone escape to send word to Alumin."

Hazel was off, relaying the message to her crew even as Reza turned to address Cavok nearby.

"I need you and your knights to storm the donjon. If they offer resistance, kill them. If they surrender, see that they're tied up and made not to follow us."

"Aye," Cavok returned, waving an arm forward to the tall tower before them.

She dismounted and ran up the steps of the interior wall to find Fin with eyes still on the road. Though the dark night hid from sight the retreating band that had pursued them, she could still hear the distant clop of hooves along the cobblestone road.

"Fin, can you see where they're headed?" she asked, attempting to peer into the dark countryside only illuminated by a sliver of moonlight.

"They're headed back to West Perch. At least, that's what my ears tell me," he said, his attention westwards. "Malagar?" he prompted the sharp-eyed haltia that had accompanied his troop, along with Nomad and Yozo.

"You would be correct," Malagar offered. "They're headed west along the highway leading back to West Perch."

"Good." Reza was happy to have the White Cloak force off her list of responsibilities.

"Fin, I'll need your scouts to head out soon to Alumin's western gate. We're going to try the same maneuver there as you did here. If you succeed in taking control of the gate block, light a torch and place it in the center of the road at the gate to let us know when it's safe for us to mount a charge into the city. If no signal is given in the next few hours, we'll head north and attempt an entrance at the northwestern postern. It'd force us to dismount and proceed without horses, and will also be guarded, but it'll at least give us a backup plan if things don't go well on your end."

"I'll get the men gathered immediately. Those White Cloaks won't be coming back anytime soon," Fin said, clapping Reza on the shoulder and returned to his men to deliver the update.

"Nomad," she said, gathering him, Yozo, and Malagar into a huddle on the wall. "I'll need you three to mount up and head out for that north western postern gate. Find a way into the city and make your way to Valiant Synagogue. We'll all be converging there as well, but we're counting on you three to find a discreet route in.

"See if you can disrupt the ceremony to summon Umbraz. You'll be looking for an obsidian statue. Careful of the prophet and his worshipers. As Nomad and I found out the hard way, they're hellbent on their master's coming and capable of dark magics."

"Understood." Nomad nodded. Both Yozo and Malagar were stoic but agreeable in their resolution.

She continued. "I don't need to tell you that this is a perilous but crucial mission we're entrusting you with. If our brawn ultimately fails and neither we nor the Rediron force are successful in reaching the synagogue, you are our only hope."

No additional assurances came from the three men as Nomad pointed for the other two to retrieve their steeds, which they were swiftly off to do. Nomad and Reza were the last ones on the dark wall.

Looking up, they just caught the light from the crescent moon fade swiftly, then disappear, leaving them in an unnatural darkness. The only light that now shown or gave radiance was from torchfire speckled throughout the bridge castle grounds.

"The signs…" Reza breathed in disbelief. "Umbraz comes."

Nomad pulled her in, gently forcing her to meet eyes with him instead.

He kissed her. She could feel no tension in his features—no worry about what was happening to the realm around them or what was soon to come. He was only in that moment—in that kiss.

Her lips ceased quivering, and she focused on him, forgetting, for a brief time, their world's plight and reality-changing night ahead of them. If all was soon to come to an end, she knew that she needed to savor their reality now.

He held her there a few moments longer, then let her go. She wanted more—more of his calming presence, more of their love—but time was short, and the disappearance of their moon's light was a stark reminder of that fact.

Without a word, they separated. Nomad gathered his things and mounted his horse alongside Yozo and Malagar. The three rushed off into the yard, leaving Reza there alone in the dark with the world falling into the shadow of Umbraz's coming.

Chapter Twenty-Six
A Black Night

"Before we worry about sending word to Alumin, we need to ensure that West Perch is defended first, damn it!" the Black Steel captain shouted to the White Cloak priest who had been verbally sparring with him the whole ride back from the defeat at the river castle.

"If we lose Alumin, West Perch won't matter!" the robed man spat back.

"We return to West Perch first," the captain insisted, ending the argument as he spurred his horse on, outpacing the zealot.

The priest was about to give chase when the moon's light waned, then disappeared completely, leaving the whole company of White Cloaks and Black Steel soldiers completely in the dark.

There was a stillness afterwards as the company came to a halt, confusion suppressing all.

"The master comes!" the priest hissed, the other White Cloak clergy rousing to the news.

"Silence!" the Black Steel captain barked, quailing the rabble momentarily.

Looking around, the captain caught the faintest flicker of torch fire upon the hill. "West Perch is just ahead. There, see the lights?"

There were murmurs in the dark: fearful, excited, hopeful. The captain knew he needed to get his company moving.

"Follow my voice!" he yelled. "We need to return to West Perch. Forward, ho!"

The captain took them at a swift trot up the cobblestone path leading back to their fort. What he was going to do from there, he had no idea. The pitch blackness that had fallen upon them on the trail had been so sudden and unnatural, he worried that his White Cloak counterpart was speaking the truth of the matter—that it was a sign of Umbraz's coming. He and most every other Black Steel enlisted in the Queen's army were under the impression that, though the cult had the means of placing them and their kingdom in a position of power, they ultimately lacked access to this Umbraz deity that they worshiped. If they were a misguided cult, the Black Steel kingdom would still gain from the cult's path of conquest and conversion—*but* if the cult were genuine in their rantings....

He shook off the possible doomed outcome, seeing the fort's gates open and lit before them.

Passing through the gate and into the courtyard, the captain waved his men onwards, relieved that he was able to see their faces again after the half hour of darkness they had just ridden through.

Most were in through the gate by the time he noticed the emptiness in the court besides themselves. The walls were bare where there should have been sentries. No one came out from the main hall to greet their return. Something was *off*.

"Hannus," he called to his second. "Take a few men and check the walls."

Even as he spoke, the chains of the gate began to softly clink, and the portcullis began to lower.

He looked back to the entrance just as the last few riders hastened to make it in before the gate lowered on them.

The large doors to the main hall opened and a volley of arrow fire peppered the nearest riders.

Some crossbow fire from above on the wall now shot down in their ranks. The screams from the confused crowd were drowned out only by the frantic clanging of the gate as it slammed down into place.

"Form a line!" the captain shouted. "I want men up on the walls and in that hallway!"

The men were panicked and only a few soldiers obeyed his order. They attempted to make headway up the steps and into the hall, but everyone's nerves were already strung tight as a drum from the ill omen that had befallen them earlier.

The captain grabbed hold of a soldier hiding behind his shield, refusing to rush towards the foe.

"Damn you, rat," he spat. "Get up those stairs now or I'll—"

A bolt split through his jaw as he spoke.

He fell to the ground, dizzier than he'd ever been in his life. He looked up to the heavens and only saw a void where the night sky should be.

Chapter Twenty-Seven
The Dark Approach

It was impossible to miss Alumin, a city now surrounded by darkness. Charting their heading was not the issue—guiding their horses through the pitch-black terrain was.

Nomad and his company were moving slower than they would have liked across the plains of brush with only the aid of a lit sappy stick to light the way.

Malagar led the group, getting the most out of the small light source than either Nomad or Yozo. They had purposefully gone off trail to cut a straight path to the location explained to them of the northwest side gate, but now that they were committed to the off-road route, they wondered if they should have simply stuck to the main road and then traveled north along the wall, even at the risk of being detected by the wall watch and traveling in complete darkness. At least if they had stuck to the highway, they would have had even footing for their mounts.

"What's the chance of us finding that postern in reasonable time?" Yozo asked from the back of the line.

It was Nomad who answered. "They may have that section of wall lit up at night. Rarely are entrances obscured in darkness, even low-profile ones. It makes it harder for the guard to see activity and easier for the skulkers to work their scheme."

"Never thought I'd have fallen in with skulkers working schemes," Malagar said with a bemused smirk.

Nomad shared his lighthearted observation—Yozo did not.

"Malagar," Yozo said after some time trotting through the dark, "what do you plan to do once we're in the synagogue? How do you intend to halt Umbraz's summoning?"

"I have an idea of what to do. Call it intuition or a gut feeling. I'll admit, though, until we're there at the foot of his statue tethering his aura to this realm, I can't say what exactly the plan is."

The three trotted along through the dark, then Yozo prodded the subject once more. "This is a suicide mission. With such stakes on the line, we deserve more details than *we'll see when we get there.* If there's more to the plan than either of you are not sharing, let's hear it."

Malagar took a moment to consider the thought and slowly nodded. "The Seam is a subject that is more difficult to explain than any other. It's a state of mind more than a science. For me to describe to you how I intend to contact or interact with Umbraz and try to steer him away from his intended course would be conjecture at best." The haltia paused to consider his next words. "All I can say is I *know* there is a path to intercept him at the focal point of his influence and power in this realm."

"So," Yozo chuffed, "your only assurance to us is to ask us to *trust your gut?*"

"I suppose that's the short of it," Malagar offered thoughtfully.

"Well...*I suppose* it's not much different than the usual with this group."

"I'm sorry, Yozo. I wish I could be more exact about the plan—"

"No, no," Yozo sighed. "I have trust in you, and your understanding of the Seam. It's just…"

"That this all seems tentative?" Nomad suggested.

"That is to put it kindly, yes."

"If there's one thing I know about this group," Nomad said, and the others got the sense that he was speaking of not just them, but Reza and the others, "it's that everyone will give this mission their all, and in the past, that has been enough."

"Perhaps," Yozo admitted with some hesitation.

"Watch your step. There's a ditch here," Malagar said, maneuvering his horse down a dip between property lines.

"Looks like we're getting close if we're already on the outskirts of the farmland wards," Nomad offered.

It was an hour more before they found a country road, and another hour before streetlamps allowed them to ditch their guiding flame. Soon, they were on the path that hugged the city wall.

"Not a single soul out this night," Nomad whispered to his companions.

"Not true," Malagar countered. "Oh, not officials or soldiers of the city," he reassured, seeing their worried looks. "Villagers to be sure. Watching us from yards and windows."

"Poor folk," Nomad murmured. "This war has upended thousands of lives."

"We may need to kill a few *poor folk* if they get in the way of our mission. Don't get needlessly attached," Yozo warned in a quiet, but deadly serious voice.

"*Ahead*," Malagar whispered, pointing to a side street leading down a hedged path that hugged the city wall. "That may be our postern."

"I see no guard on duty along the wall," Nomad offered.

"Nor are there any in the embrasures—that I can see at least."

The three slowed to a stop in the shadows between the long gap of streetlamps.

"Strange, is it not?" Yozo skeptically questioned.

"Perhaps..." Malagar replied. "Though..."

"Though what?"

"Well, the heavens are shrouded like no one has ever seen. If that is not an omen of our time, I don't know what would be," Malagar wondered aloud.

"Yes. So?"

"So...I wonder if all but the true believers, the White Cloaks themselves, are completely committed to seeing this through."

"I think I gather your meaning," Nomad cut in. "City guardsmen may fight a war for whomever at the top tells them to; after all, wars over territory are no uncommon thing for these parts. But at the sight of a world-ending sign—loyalties only go so far, even at the sword point of coercion. The sky going dark could be many men's tipping point."

They idled there a few moments longer, quietly considering the possibility that some, if not many, had abandoned their posts after the moon had gone dark.

"We should not count on that being true," Yozo said, breaking the silence, then dismounted, gathered his things, and started off on foot towards the hedged path. "But we do need to get moving. Stay close."

The others followed, making their way down into the ivy-covered alcove leading to a small, fortified door.

Chapter Twenty-Eight
The Charge

The torch below on the road was just about spent when Fin heard a clamor of hooves approaching.

Running past the cold bodies of what was left of the gate guard, he practically leapt down the steep wall stairway and ran through the gateway to meet Reza.

She was at the front of the line of her haltia, and he waved her in as they trotted through the structure.

"Report," she said impatiently.

"We were met with some resistance. A few scouts were killed in the scuffle with the gate guard, but thankfully, there were no more than a dozen or so city guardsmen stationed at this gate. They've all been put down," Fin answered.

"A dozen to guard a main gate? Why so few? Have we overestimated our enemy's numbers to such an extent?"

"Not sure, but those that were on guard already seemed uneasy before they even knew we were here. Perhaps word of our presence at the bridge castle had already arrived?"

"Doubtful," she dismissed. "In this darkness, it's a wonder we even made it here this fast, and we were led by haltia eyes."

Fin was about to speculate further, when an explosion at the south end of the city lit up the night. For a moment, they could see the whole sprawling expanse of town, the white glow of a massive phosphorescent fireball blooming at the city's border.

A deafening crack like thunder sounded a moment later, echoing through the streets of Alumin.

"What the blazes was that?" Fin let out. Everyone looked to the southside of town as the flame diminished, though refused to go all the way out.

"King Reid's wizard," Reza whispered.

Fin stared at the low, unnaturally white glow across town in wonder before returning to Reza.

"That old crow that's accompanied him in the command tent?" he asked incredulously. "I half figured he'd croak simply from being on the open road. How could he be responsible for anything that explosive?"

"It doesn't matter." Reza gave the pyre flames across town one final look before turning back. "We need to head to the synagogue at once."

"What about Cavok and the knights, or the saren, for that matter?" Fin asked.

"The light of Phosen and Kale have left us, Fin," Reza said, speaking of their moons. "Umbraz is upon our doorstep, there is no time to wait. *Someone* needs to get to that church and disrupt the summoning, *if* that's even possible at this point."

"I'll leave a man here to point them our way then," Fin said, accepting Reza's judgment.

"Captain!" Hazel called, riding back to them from down the main street. "A block of city guards headed this way!"

"We'll have to face them. We need this gate to remain open. Ready the troops to make a stand," Reza called back to her second in command. She was worried about getting bogged down at their current location but saw no alternative. She knew that they couldn't leave the checkpoint wide open for the enemy to retake, which would close off entrance to the city for Cavok and Freya's forces.

"Take your riders and cut through side streets and get to the synagogue," Fin suggested. "Me and my scouts will hold the gate till Cavok makes it here with his knights."

She wanted to turn down his offer. She didn't know how many were on their way down those streets and Fin didn't have many scouts left at his side. Splitting up would increase their efficiency, though—both of them knew that.

"May Sareth watch over you, Fin," she said, bending down to rest her hand on his shoulder and touch her foreheads to his in parting. She rode to a wide side street and called her haltia to follow her.

The haltia were quick to ship out, leaving the courtyard at the gate woefully empty. The few remaining Rediron scouts scrambled up stairs and rooftops to get a vantage point on the incoming soldiers. The enemy rushed in through the streets, answering the call of intruders at the west gate.

"Ready yourselves," Fin shouted to his men. Most were already hidden from even his sight in the nooks of the surrounding buildings.

He took out two throwing daggers, holding one in each hand, alone at the top of the gatehouse. City guardsmen came around the corner, charging confidently forward with twoscore in their ranks.

"This is going to be a bloody night," Fin grumbled, and waited for the first arrow to let fly.

———•◎•———

The white fire across town still burned at the south gate, which was the only reason Reza had been able to confidently charge so swiftly through town.

She worried for Fin. She hadn't stayed to see how many guardsmen had been dispatched to reclaim the gate and Fin's scouts had definitely diminished in count since they had set out that morning.

As she turned the corner, the brilliant white spires of the synagogue came into view. It was a stark scene—the sky was a void of darkness offset by the heaven-reaching spires of the church that she now knew was corrupt to its core.

The synagogue's tall, wrought iron gate was up ahead now. She flinched as a bolt whizzed past her, thudding into the haltia riding close behind her.

She saw a formation in front of the gate and heard more crossbow clicks. Neither she nor her haltia had time to avoid the assault. She lay tight to her steed's neck as the horse jolted in pain. Bolts sank shaft deep into the creature's front, pitching it over flinging her from her saddle. She tumbled roughly to a stop in the street as the rest of the haltia charged past, jumping over her and their downed countrymen.

Reza rose with a start. Hooves of a passing rider nearly missed clipping her head as she came to. She scuttled back to her felled horse and waited for the remaining haltia to jump past her.

As she waited, laying low to the ground up against the side of the horse's back, she watched the clash of the two forces. The haltia had drawn their swords and were ramming through the front line of guardsmen which had abandoned their crossbows and drawn their sidearms. It was not the guardsmen that Reza worried about, however. A rank of White Cloaks was behind the barred gates, chanting loudly, and she could see that many held high in the air signs of their faith.

Front and center of the zealots was a bald, spectacled man, one that she had seen before serving on the grounds—a Torchbearer. He shouted orders, which Reza knew would spell the doom of her allies.

"Disengage!" she yelled, jumping to her feet, running for the haltia. "Fall back! Bows out! Fire upon those White Cloaks!"

She ran towards the skirmish line, but even as she shouted commands to her men, the White Cloaks were deep in fervent prayer, eyes locked on her troops.

The haltia began to slow their attack upon the guardsmen at first, but very quickly they began to fall from their horses, smacking to the ground in anguish.

Screams erupted from the battlefield as their bodies began to mutate, and even the city guard halted their attack in the face of such brutality.

She stood there, frozen. There was nothing she could do to stop the grotesque process from proceeding. Her conscience would not allow her to abandon her men, but she also feared attracting the attention of the zealots to share in her men's gruesome end.

The spectacled man at the head of White Cloaks turned his gaze, ceased chanting, and met eyes with her. He smirked with recognition.

She saw his lips begin to move and realized that he was beginning a chant to his twisted god. She knew she only had seconds left to make a move.

She sprinted forward, retrieving her dagger from her hip. She already began to feel uncomfortably itchy as the man's eyes drilled into her.

It was a long shot, through a gate, but as the penetrating effect of the warp lashed out and began connecting with her, she knew she had to take it. It was all or nothing at that point—her life balanced on the point of her dagger.

She gripped the blade tight, cocked her arm, and flung it with all her might.

The blade flew end over end towards the zealot, his eyes going wide as he saw what flew speedily towards him.

There was a loud clang of metal as the dagger deflected off one of the bars of the wrought-iron gate. A split second later, the knife was on the ground.

She jerked sharply, clutching her side as the itch spiked into an awful pain. The zealot's chanting grew louder, more confident now that he knew he had her. She grimaced, knowing now that the end was nigh.

She crumpled to the ground, feeling her whole body beginning to burn up. All her senses were crowded out from the twitching flesh sensation that flooded her nervous system.

It rose in intensity for a few moments—and then…it receded enough for her to control her thoughts once more.

Her eyes shot open, the pain abating.

What happened? she wondered, attempting to crawl to her knees and gain her bearings.

She heard metal screeching, stone crumbling—men screaming.

Her vision began to come back into focus, and she looked to where the gate had been. The iron barred gate had been ripped from its hinges and saren and knights on horseback were riding into the courtyard, making quick work of the remaining city guard and White Cloaks, giving them no time to finish their prayers.

She saw Cavok at the gate, the heavy gate chain in hand as he lashed out at the White Cloaks with the makeshift whip, flogging all within range.

She rushed to him, recovering her dagger from the ground as she went. Running past the slaughtered haltia and guardsmen, she entered the courtyard. She wished desperately that she could give aid to the fallen, still hearing lingering gasps for air and cries of pain from the tangled mass of flesh behind her. She knew there was no time for it, though.

She stayed behind Cavok's swinging chain for a moment, looking for Freya and hoping to see anyone else in her company that she knew she could count on.

"Cavok! We need to get inside!" Reza yelled to the enraged man who was flailing and slashing the remaining White Cloaks in their path until they stopped moving on the ground.

Surprisingly enough, he seemed to have heard her. With the lash of a chain to the head of the nearest White Cloak, he ran forward, through rank of saren and White Cloaks alike. She followed his path.

Ahead, she could see the spectacled man scrambling up the synagogue's main steps and entering the ajar main door. Once inside, he began to close the tall, heavy door. By the time they had reached it, it was shut and locked.

Cavok pushed the door forcefully a few times. It was clear it was well fortified and solid enough to resist a brute-force entrance, even by Cavok.

"Any luck?" came a voice from the courtyard.

Reza turned to see Freya, Fin, and Terra ride up to the steps.

"They've barred the door, and nothing short of some siege equipment is going to open it," Reza said. "Can you open it, Fin?"

"If it's barred, which this kind of door likely is, no," he replied.

"Let's search for a ground level window then," Terra suggested.

Reza looked out over the ongoing battle in the courtyard. The sarens, Rediron knights, and what was left of the haltia were handling the remaining guardsmen and White Cloaks. They would soon be the victors on the battlefield.

"Very well," Reza nodded, taking Freya's hand to mount up behind her.

They trotted around the grounds, looking for anything accessible at ground level. The only windows they could find were higher up and deliberately difficult to get to from the ground. The grand building, though a house of worship, was well designed in the case of attack.

They raced past pillared buttresses after another until Fin called out from ahead of the group. "A back door, and it's open."

He was off his horse and to the door in a flash. By the time the others had dismounted and approached, he had already come to a determined speculation over the oddly ajar door.

"A hinge is off, looks like they broke their way in," he whispered, pointing for the others to see.

"Think this is Nomad's work?" Fin asked Reza.

"Who else would be breaking into this place?" she mused. She stepped inside the dark corridor, the others filing in behind her.

Chapter Twenty-Nine
The Eleventh Hour

Malagar snuck ahead, listening for activity in the halls for a moment before waving Yozo and Nomad up to his location.

The three came to an open grand stairwell leading up high into the synagogue's upper floors. They looked through the massive crystal chandelier that hung at the center of the tall domed room, listening for a moment. The group moved to hide behind the banister's base as they heard footsteps approaching.

They watched from the shadows as a group of White Cloaks ran through the halls in the direction they had come from.

"Where should we check first?" Nomad asked.

Nomad and Yozo looked at Malagar. He had been the one Reza had put in charge of the mission. They both knew that he had some sort of unquantifiable connection to the source that Umbraz was made of—the Seam.

Malagar was about to speak when everything around them went dim—an inversion of light and color. Pressure bore down on them and a ringing in their ears threatened to burst their eardrums—like they were deep underwater. Everything around them seemed to warp, flex, and mold into odd shapes.

The ringing shifted suddenly into a roaring torrent, and gravity shifted diagonally, throwing them to the ground. And then, in a blink, everything returned to normal.

Yozo let out a tumble of words as the others gasped for air. "What the devils was that?"

"It's beginning," Malagar said between breaths. "He's phasing into our reality."

Both Yozo and Nomad were at a loss for words. Neither knew, nor could know, the full impact of Malagar's ill tidings.

"We need to hurry. We're going to go through a lot worse if we don't stop Umbraz's singularity point," Malagar warned. "I know where he's going to end up now."

"Lead on," Yozo offered, the two swordsmen waiting for Malagar to guide their path.

Listening for footsteps, Malagar started up the golden banistered stairwell, heading to the top floor.

The halls, white and gold with elaborately framed paintings of saints of the faith hanging all along it, was otherwise empty. The soft, warm candlelight of the candelabras were mostly washed out from the brilliant white phosphorescent fire burning on the other side of town, shining through the windows.

Malagar stopped at a large set of double doors for a moment, looking to the others to ensure they were ready for what lay beyond.

"It's somewhere ahead. It's close," he whispered.

Through the door the three could hear a commotion. A chant, wailing, crying—an awful service being held on the other side of those doors.

In unison, Nomad and Yozo unsheathed their blades. Nomad's glowed with the faintest sheen of white. Seeing the two poised, Malagar placed a hand on the doorknob and cracked the door open just enough to slip through with Nomad and Yozo following close behind.

A great, black void of a statue loomed in the vaulted heights of the spire room they entered. At first, that was all they could look at, as though they were being hypnotized by its soft vibrations.

The chanting and racket that had persisted since they had arrived at the door ceased—they did not know how long for. All eyes were on the three intruders at the door—all watching in complete silence.

A blinding flash and a wave of bubbling nausea slammed into them. They pitched forward, gravity shifting as it had at the base of the stairwell. They slammed to the floor as a roar of force blew through them, stripping flecks of their consciousness from them.

Straining against the pull and push of the unseen force, Malagar looked up, and for a moment thought he saw a presence. Not a figure, necessarily, but a unique consciousness, appearing to him as a dark outline amidst the blinding brightness.

He was vaguely aware of something in his hand. The Seam pearls were warm, and as he gripped them, the noise of the mind-bending fracture in reality began to calm and the entity above him came into focus for the briefest of moments.

And then…the surroundings of the room came snapping back into view, and where the entity had been, now stood the massive black statue.

"I need to reach that statue before the next phase shift," Malagar slurred to his companions, sensation still coming back to his flesh.

Nomad and Yozo were up first, running into the zealots that were still twitching, attempting to regain the use of their faculties.

The mark of the white robe was their death warrant. Both Nomad and Yozo had seen the handiwork of Umbraz's faithful. They gave their temporarily debilitated foes no time to raise their voice in unholy prayer this time. Only in agony did they cry.

Their sword blows were crude and inefficient, their limbs still numbed from the reality shift they all had been exposed to, but white robes were quickly turning red, and Malagar stumbled forward, wholly focused on the giant, black silhouette ahead of him.

"Reverend father," the prophet Yunus called from the top of the steps leading to the base of the statue, garnering everyone's attention. "They wish to delay our savior's coming. End them with haste."

The mutated giant of a man that had been prostrated before the dark statue arose now. It stood no less than ten feet tall, turning to set its eyeless, featureless face in the direction of the advancing group upon the long stairway up to the risen precipice. Its mass was grotesque, making little anatomical sense.

To Nomad, the sight of the abomination reminded him of the giant in the basement of Rosewood, only this creation seemed sculpted out of human-*like* parts— sections of the creation only resembled body parts of a living creature, but never quite hitting the mark.

It moved. Neither Yozo nor Nomad could explain *how* it moved, but it was rushing towards them with stuttering swiftness.

Yozo slashed out at it first, just in time to slice into the fleshy arm that swung for his head. The cut bungled the extremity, but it was quick to flail another as Yozo tumbled to the side, out of the thing's reach.

Nomad brought his sword up to deflect the sickle-like bone limb, but just before connecting with his sword, the thing seemed to sense something off about the blade. Retracting its sharp arm, it clubbed at Nomad's legs with a meaty appendage, off-balancing him enough to slam him from the side and send him flying back down the stairs into Malagar.

The two tumbled down the stairs in a tangled heap. Nomad was quick to get off Malagar, but as he did, blood began spreading quickly across his friend's garment.

"Mal!" Nomad gasped, shocked to realize that he had skewered Malagar through the side as the two collided.

Malagar removed his hand from around the blade and looked down to inspect the damage.

"Clean through," he hissed, then gripped the blade and yanked it sharply out. He gave out a short, painful yell and dropped the blade to the ground. His hands, covered in blood, were trembling terribly.

Nomad pressed hands to his wound which was seeping blood. He was wordless in disbelief at their misfortune.

Malagar's slick, red hand reached up for Nomad.

"Nomad..." he grunted, trying to hold his focus on his comrade long enough to get his message delivered. "I need to get to that statue. It's imperative—"

He winced in pain, his breath coming in short gasps.

"We need to get you to a saren—" Nomad started, looking back at the abomination attempting to chase Yozo down.

"No," Malagar said with as much force as he could, shaking Nomad's shoulder weakly. "Get me to that statue, Nomad. It's the *only* path now."

Nomad could see the absolute determination in Malagar's pale expression. He was asking Nomad to trust him. He didn't see how anything but a saren's blessing could bring him back from the grave, but Malagar's conviction was absolute. Against his own instinct, Nomad took a silken sash from his waist and tied it tightly around Malagar's middle. He hefted the man's arm over his shoulder. After a steadying breath, the two started back up the steps together.

Yozo hacked deeply into another limb, but the gummy-like substance that resembled flesh, resisted the impeccable sharpness of his blade, refusing to sever completely.

It's sickle arm swept low, hooking his ankle. When it jerked its arm in, Yozo was yanked off his feet and onto the steps.

The point of the abomination's scythe arm clanged down to the ground next to Yozo as it righted itself. Yozo rolled to the side as the thing's thick club arm smashed into the steps where he had been a split second earlier.

He thrust his sword point up into the creature, which sank in with some sluggish resistance. The blow didn't even register with the brute. The sickle clanked down again, this time stabbing Yozo right through the shoulder, pinning him in place.

Its bludgeoning arm came down repeatedly on Yozo's chest and head, smashing him over and over again.

He did his best to put up his guard, his good arm framed to take the bulk of the thing's club arm, but the slams were only increasing in intensity, and the sickle was ripping his arm to shreds.

He kicked the thing's leg sideways—barely succeeding in moving its mass, but it was enough to roll the direction of the tilt of the bone hook, allowing him to dislodge the spike.

Another bludgeon from the father's arm knocked him across the steps one last time before it turned its attention back to Nomad.

Nomad hoisted Malagar to his side, standing between him and the abomination. He held his slightly glowing sword up, the one thing the father seemed to consider cautiously.

A slash from Yozo's blade to the back of the father's legs staggered the hulk for a moment and it flailed back at Yozo blindly. Twisting its torso completely around, it swung out angrily at the persistent swordsman.

Yozo had bought them a little more time—and he was paying in flesh. Nomad turned back to the statue and trudged on with Malagar barely conscious at his side.

"You come to deliver yourselves to Umbraz?" Prophet Yunus asked, watching the two struggle up the stairs.

"Yes…I do," Malagar replied in a weak voice, clutching the Seam pearls tight in his hand. "He comes, there is no denying or stopping that at this point. I wish to greet him."

Nomad could see that the reply was unexpected to the prophet as the two continued to make their way to the base of the statue.

The prophet's mood changed from smug assurance to calculating suspicion.

Prophet Yunus slowly raised his hand, which began to distort before Nomad's eyes.

Nomad snatched his camp hatchet from his belt clip, chucking the impromptu weapon head-over-shaft at the older man.

Yunus waved his hand and the hatchet blurred, disappearing and reappearing some feet away from him, flying harmlessly in another direction. Unfazed by Nomad's attack, he began to raise his hand once more, ready to strike the infidel with Umbraz's terrible power.

A cosmic pulsation erupted in their heads, and everyone, including the prophet, staggered to stop the room from spinning.

Malagar looked up. He could see a figure before him where the statue had been. He looked to his left and could see the blurry fiery outline of the prophet. He was transfixed, watching Umbraz in awe.

He looked down to his stomach. Gore seeped through his bandage over his gut as he released pressure—but the pain was completely gone.

Looking back up to Umbraz, he took a disorienting step onwards, and then another. He stretched his hand forward, reaching towards the giant figure of brilliantly fluctuating light.

The prophet's features contorted, shifting from awe to horror and disbelief. The haltia was moving through the Seam—an all but impossibility for mortals, so he had thought.

The spirit of Umbraz, which had been static until that point, slowly looked down, taking note of Malagar. It was a look of curiosity, devoid of any other motive or emotion. It watched as Malagar came tantalizingly close to touching its ghostly robes….

Then reality came snapping back to everyone in the room with Malagar only inches away from the statue's robed feet, the pain from his gut wound keeling him over on the spot.

Yunus gasped, panic deep set in his features as he looked to where Malagar had managed to advance.

"How," Yunus said, catching his breath, as did everyone from the phase shift, "can you move in the vision?"

The prophet raised his hand, pointing at Malagar, and once again his hand began to distort and shimmer.

Malagar slumped, accepting the inevitable. He had no strength to evade whatever assault the prophet aimed at him.

Nomad snatched the prophet's hand away from Malagar. No sooner had he done so than the prophet's hand shone brightly, blinding them.

Nomad grunted, a hot, wriggling pressure in his clenched hand demanding his attention. He opened his eyes and extended his arm further from him in horror. His fingers had elongated, turning into fleshy tentacles wrapped boneless around the prophet's hand.

Yunus was in Nomad's wriggling grip. He attempted to yank his hand free, but the ever-growing knot of tentacles coiled tighter over Yunus' wrist.

Yunus panicked. As he began to chant, his arm started to vibrate and shimmer once more.

There was something else that began to glow with power. Nomad held his sword tight in his good hand, and before Yunus could finish his spell, Nomad brought his shining blade down, slicing easily through both his and the prophet's forearm.

Both his and Yunus' hands thudded to the ground, the finger tentacles still wriggling frantically as if controlled by some other mind. Nomad retracted his stump arm which had been cauterized by the holy flame of his blade, but Yunus reeled back, his mutilated arm flickering in and out of existence, flashing brilliantly as the prophet's bisected bone and flesh shot out in strings, winding in erratic circles, stretching out further and began to bifurcate into fractions of itself.

Yunus continued his chant—and it seemed to Nomad he now chanted against his own will. Yunus wore a mask of doom, completely opposite from the supreme confidence he had shown upon their entrance into the ceremony. Things were unraveling swiftly for the man of faith, and as he chanted faster and more frantically, the visual shivering around the prophet's figure began to increase.

Nomad slashed into the expanding stringy tendrils, slicing through them like vines, but more sprouted quickly from their endpoints.

The prophet's chanting stopped, and he let out a cry of pain as the unraveling of his arm traveled into his torso.

"Umbraz!" he cried out, almost as a lost child for their parent.

If his cry for help was heard, it was not heeded. The prophet's chest split open in strands, his flesh curling up in ropes of tissue. His body shimmered a dull silver, and Nomad had to step back to give space to the expanding, unraveling man.

Nomad held his shining sword towards the deconstructing figure, watching in disbelief as what was once the prophet morphed into a new creature—one of horror and nightmares.

His robes had shredded apart by the fleshy growth. Sleek braided knots of skinless muscle stretched across the majority of the man's torso, up into his neck and face. The prophet's eyes were hollow, and his mouth hung agape. Though the prophet twitched and moved, Nomad doubted the man was still alive, at least of his own volition.

Nomad clenched his sword tight, snapping out of his momentary daze at the mere sight of the sudden and violent mutation. He cut in at the reborn prophet. His shining blade lopped off a thick veiny appendage, the rope of meat thudding sickeningly to the ground.

A sharp pressure jolted into his core, causing him pause as he attempted to understand what had just happened. Looking down, he saw a spear of writhing fleshy cords punched directly through his stomach.

Light began to fade from his blade. He attempted to cut through the root of flesh, but his slashes were not slicing cleanly through as before. Each cut was followed by regrowth, like a network of worms stitching back together the area where Nomad had just opened up.

His gaze drifted sluggishly to what was left of the prophet's head. Something bulged behind the man's eyes as though the worm-like tendrils had infiltrated deep within his skull, looking for a way out. The man was a husk—a vehicle of flesh for his god.

His head lolled, his strength failing him. He looked to Malagar, slumped over at the base of the devil's statue. Nomad couldn't tell if he was alive or dead. He hadn't heard or seen Yozo for a time either.

He turned his attention back to the horror that had gored him, and a sudden, surreal realization hit him. If their world—their universe—had a hope now, it would be left to Reza and her crew. His attempt…was through.

Chapter Thirty

To the Cathedral

They clutched their heads as a debilitating effect wracked their frames and threw them to the ground. None knew what was transpiring or for how long they had been in the time warp.

The next thing they knew, they were gasping for breath in a dark hall in the synagogue on their hands and knees.

"What the hells—" Freya gasped.

"Umbraz," Terra said, struggling to arise. "I thought that was it—the moment of his birth. But…perhaps we still have time to make a difference."

"We need to get to wherever they're performing the rite," Reza said, getting back to her feet.

The group started off again. Though the temple halls were dark, Fin easily led them in the direction of the muted voices, into the chapel area at the front of the building.

He held up a warning hand to Reza and the others as he peeked around a corner. They obeyed his silent command, and only after a short wait did he retreat to them to explain what had held his attention.

"That White Cloak with glasses—he ran off down a hallway up ahead."

"We need to follow him," Reza whispered back. "He might be running to the prophet to warn of the defeat in the courtyard."

Fin nodded and looked around the corner once more.

Freya spoke up from the back of the group. "I need to unbar the chapel doors. Our troops need guidance and orders. You lot go on ahead, I'll catch up with enough support to cleanse this whole synagogue."

"You can't go alone," Fin contended. "What if you run into other White Cloaks?"

"I'll handle them," she simply stated.

"They'll not come after you with weapons, Freya. If one begins a chant on you, you're through."

"Then I won't let them start a chant."

Fin shook his head, not convinced with Freya's plan. He offered an alternative route of action. "Reza, follow that zealot to the ritual room. I'll accompany Freya and gather what troops we have remaining. Wait for us before breaking any doors down, okay?"

Reza gave a quick pat on his shoulder and asked which direction the spectacled devotee had gone. Fin pointed to the large hallway to the right in the open room before them, and then sprinted to catch up with Freya who was already rushing off to the left where she assumed the chapel doors to be.

Reza came to the hallway Fin had indicated and saw no sign of the spectacled man. She let out an exasperated sigh, wondering if they had lost their chance by deliberating too long over tactics. She waved Terra and Cavok to follow her lead and started down the faintly lit hallway, illuminated only by a ghostly light washing through the stained-glass windows on their left.

She saw no obvious turn offs to take as they rushed down the hall, and soon, they were at the end. A grand staircase lay before them. It was one that she remembered from her time in the synagogue months ago. It was a sight hard to forget.

The light inverted and everything melted around them as their reality warped once more. The floor was no longer solid; they scrambled for purchase on anything to keep them from falling through it. Someone let out a distorted cry, and Reza could hear her gasps for air reverberating deafeningly in her head.

Everything was turning on its head when in an instant, reality snapped right back into focus.

Reza traded worried glances with Terra and Cavok. They all knew there was precious little time left.

Feeling eyes on her, Reza looked up the long stairwell. At the very top floor, the robed man looked down at them. Seeing that he had been spotted, he dashed off towards the synagogue's tower wing.

"After him," Reza ordered. Cavok was charging up the stairwell before Reza even finished.

By the time Reza and Terra had made it halfway up the stairs, Cavok had sprinted ahead to the top floor and was running all out for the man at the end of the long hallway.

"Careful, Cavok!" Reza yelled up the stairwell, but he and the zealot were well out of their sight.

Cavok hefted his sword in hand as he bounded down the hallway towards the dark figure at the end.

"You cannot stop his divine coming," the zealot quivered, perhaps to try and ward off the approaching hulk, or to confirm the fact to himself.

He began a chant, frail and meek at first, but as he held up his prayer beads, his voice strengthened in conviction and his god's powers began to flow freely through his incantation.

He was still three doors down when Cavok's steady clip wavered as a sharp pain entered his skull. It took all he had to keep charging forward, to push the blinding pain out of the way and to focus on his charge.

The zealot's voice boomed louder now, his confidence growing, seeing that his god was close. He had never felt such a surge of his divinity as he did at that moment.

Another wave of crippling pressure and pain slammed into the side of Cavok's head, and this time, he began to feel a wriggling sensation erupting from within his skull. Something fundamental had changed. He was aware of at least that. His mind was unraveling, as though parts of his brain were coming undone quite literally.

Memories of his life, of his time with loved ones, of friends he had lost, flooded suddenly down a drain, never to return.

Thump, thump, thump went the rhythm of his heavy feet, still clipping along down the dark hallway. He was close to the dark figure now. Why that mattered…was becoming increasingly fuzzy for him.

The robed man sang out in chorus, and Cavok's vision quickly degraded. Something squirmed along the side of his face by his eye socket.

Something he had been gripping dropped to the floor, and his hands raised as he came closer to the robed man. He forced himself onwards. The man's voice grew tentative, then panicked.

Cavok smashed into the zealot at full speed, slamming him through the stained-glass window at the end of the corridor. Cavok couldn't see or comprehend the fear on the man's face as he flew out into the night's sky, many stories over the stone courtyard below, silently falling, spending his last moments of life in terror with the wind knocked out of him.

"Cavok!" Reza yelled from down the hall.

Even in the dark of the night and at a distance, Reza could tell something was wrong.

They slowed as they approached Cavok, who was standing very still, facing the shattered window.

"Cavok," Reza said softly as she rested a hand on his shoulder, her voice tight with worry over her friend.

Terra covered her mouth in horror as Reza turned Cavok around. Wormy shoots had flowered from his eye socket and out his ear on one side of his face, and as she looked into his good eye, she could tell that he was adrift in thought, hardly recognizing her as his glance passed over her.

"Oh, Cavok," Reza groaned, witnessing the damage the zealot had done to her friend.

Abruptly, another shift in the fabric of reality jostled them violently—this one more forcefully than before. A bright light shone through the door they had stopped at, and they could feel the approach of a strong presence within.

Reza tried holding her head to force the world around her to stop undulating, but even raising her hands proved to be near impossible.

"*Calm,*" a thought intruded into her mind. "*Be at ease.*"

The implanted thought had some strange numbing effect upon her subconscious, but the juxtaposed cacophony of the moment made it all the more confusing as she tumbled to the floor, attempting to remain upright against the ever-shifting pull of gravity.

She looked at the double doors, towards the force she sensed from within. She wondered if this was Umbraz. Though the thought sickened her, his presence felt different than what she had expected. Warped and confusing it all was, but aside from that, there was a sense of—what she could only interpret as—otherworldly curiosity.

Barely had she time to consider her thoughts of the entity before the phase shift abruptly ceased and she was once again in the dark hallway. She remembered where she was suddenly and could hear Terra weeping over Cavok's irrevocable misfortune, holding onto his arm.

The double doors to the chapel tower burst open and Reza scrambled back. She dodged the man that came tumbling out into the hallway just in time.

"Yozo!" she called, both relieved and confused at the sight of the man before them.

"Watch out," he warned. Jumping back to his feet, sword in hand, he readied himself for whatever was following him. Reza did the same, unsheathing her sword and pointing it at the room Yozo had just come from.

The doors slammed open with such force that both doors had all but come off of their hinges. Across the threshold came a figure Reza struggled to identify. Its movements, its proportions, its smooth face, all were alien to her. It gave her no further time to analyze it or for her to ask Yozo questions. It swung its sickle-like arm out at her with blinding speed.

She jumped back once more, slamming into the wall just out of reach of the thing. She was in trouble, she knew. She didn't know where to even start with an attack. She wondered where its vitals were. There was hardly anywhere to retreat to in the small hallway, and the thing's multiple weapon arms were extending before her, spelling her doom.

"At me!" Yozo screamed, desperately trying to grab the thing's attention, seeing Reza's dire placement.

He swung in at its strong arm, hacking into it, but Reza could see that Yozo's swings were weak, and now she saw why. He was covered in blood, and judging by his shaky swings, she guessed the blood was his own.

Yozo's attack did distract it for a moment, and Reza took advantage of the confusion, thrusting directly at the center of its mass—what she believed to be its torso. The blade sank in, but the substance didn't pierce quite like flesh. It was almost sticky, as though its blood was sap, and the tip of her blade did not penetrate more than a few inches.

"Damn," she cursed, watching the thing easily bat Yozo away down the hall.

It looked back at the sword in its chest. She yanked her sword out of the creature and brought her blade up just in time to deflect another arc of the sickle arm. The blow sent her tumbling to the side next to Terra and Cavok.

Reza scrambled to get to her feet and face the thing. She had both seen and felt its speed and strength and knew she could not match it. One look at Yozo's condition had all but confirmed that she was not equipped to tangle with the creature.

Its huge club arm swung at her. She tensed and balled up in the corner, hoping to survive the blow or at least remain conscious so that she could then attempt to scramble past it.

The blow never came. She looked back to the creature but saw Cavok's large frame in her path instead.

A white flame burst forth from Terra's amulet as she chanted hymnals to her god which flared into the creature's side. Cavok held firm the bludgeoning hand that had been intended for Reza.

The creature hesitated—reacted—for the first time since bursting into the hallway. Their rally was giving it pause.

Chapter Thirty-One

One Last Spark

There was a feeling of completion—an end—as though some great task would soon be over. The feeling put him at ease.

But…there was one final thing he needed to do. Perhaps it was the task that would allow him to rest in peace.

The dark figure before him—it needed to end with him. It, like him, no longer belonged here.

A dull impact to his gut shook him—a momentary ringing in the ears. There was a sharp pinch in his arm, then leg, then a rip in his chest. He was vaguely aware that he was losing function.

End it! something within the depths of his mind shouted, and he spurred onwards, blindly wrestling with a figure that he only occasionally could process flashes of. In those flashes, he could tell that the creature had been wounded. It was being shut down just as he was.

Finish it! he heard, and he wasn't sure if it was his voice, or someone else's—somewhere, out there.

He gripped the writhing thing, clutched it to what was left of him, and squeezed harder and harder until there was a cascade of snapping sensations—his or the beast's, he wasn't sure, nor did it matter. The fight of the creature was dying.

He gnashed his teeth into something gooey, clenching around the thing with all his might—with every last ounce of strength he could give.

And then…he had given everything. With one great sigh, he released and fell.

He was tired; more so than he could ever remember being. Though his sight had flickered out some time ago in the final press, somehow the darkness became darker then. A void rushed up to take him, and he plunged into its icy grasp.

Chapter Thirty-Two

One Last Breath

His vision was slipping. He could see a familiar sight, a place he had been twice before—the hallway of ancestors. The ghostly image was blurry, and he struggled to see the faces of the dead—to make sense of it all.

Then the vision faded. A shaft of tendrils had spiked out of the prophet's mouth, lancing its way at Nomad's face.

A reactionary slash with his sword caused the cord to go limp. He surged energy into his blade—his last reserves—and slashed a large arc that blazed white, hacking the tentacles goring him cleanly at the root.

With every ounce of concentration and will, with all his years of sword study and practice leading to this moment, his final signature in the art, he guided his sword steady and true. His blade sliced across the prophet's neck, peeling back layers of mass; then, he brought his sword high and down with everything he had, chopping straight through the tangle of flesh. His cut bisected the whole abomination.

The mass of flesh collapsed, the prophet's head severed and split in two.

He held his stance unwavering for a moment, and then, someone yelled out his true name.

"Hiro!" Reza shouted.

He collapsed to the ground. The corridor of death began to blur into focus once more.

He could vaguely hear footfall approach, but sounds were quickly starting to muddle, just as vision had.

"Hiro, stay with me," Reza said, close now. He was jostled, and then: "Terra, call to your god in aid, I'm going to attempt a healing."

"No!" he said, grabbing her hand that was holding his head. "No, Rez—ha—" He struggled, blood seeping out of his mouth.

A vision engulfed him once more. He was beginning the walk of the great transition. He saw faces of the past. Ones that were lifetimes ago. Ones that he had known deeply.

He was drifting to a familiar soul—one that had meant the world to him once. His early wife had departed their realm much too soon. He had thought about her every day since. She spoke to him now and he strained to hear her.

"…going to heal…" he heard a distant voice say. One that did not belong upon the steps he now walked.

"Let…" he struggled, being torn between the two places, "...me go…to them, Reza."

He could hear Reza crying, and for one last time, he witnessed the world she dwelled in, only to behold her sweet face. Tears were pouring from her eyes, and he struggled to brush her hair aside.

"It is my time," he whispered, his vision dropping out completely from her world and into the next. "We will meet again." He did not know if the message reached her, for he was now walking with the one he had been separated for far too long from.

This time when she spoke, he heard her perfectly.

Chapter Thirty-Three
Rapture

His hand slapped the cold obsidian statue, the life all but bled out of him. Malagar was in a stupor, but he knew he needed to make contact with that stone—with the one it represented.

Behind him he could hear distant weeping. *Is that Reza?* he wondered. In the end, it wouldn't matter, he now knew. It only mattered that he found Umbraz in time.

As if his touch enacted another rift in space, the two realms once again chaotically merged, neither pleased with sharing one time or place, disagreeing violently with each other's physical laws.

He looked up, and within the tearing fabric of the Seam, he saw that his hand rested upon the hem of Umbraz's shroud. The face of a god looked down upon him, and his whole being was filled with awe at the overwhelming presence that he lay prostrate before.

There were muted screams behind him that made him look back. Warbled images of Reza, Terra, and Yozo stood some ways down. He turned his attention back to Umbraz, the only entity that mattered now.

Umbraz slowly looked down to the lone figure at its feet. Malagar stood, clutching the Seam pearls and extended his hand.

The god paused for a moment, curiously considering the being that seemed to move freely within its realm. It reached down, engulfing Malagar completely in its brilliant light.

Malagar had beheld not but a few oddities and wonders in his short life, but as he was bathed with the infinitely spectrumed light of Umbraz, all other experiences paled. His mind expanded all at once, taking in the consciousness of a complete alien entity.

He could feel an apex of monumental significance. It was touching down on a new realm, a new dimension of being, and Malagar was its very first contact.

Within the blink of an eye, a galaxy of information had been dumped upon him, and for a time, his mind remained broken and floating adrift, lost in the mountains of knowledge and thought that had struck him like a million bolts of lightning all trained upon his head.

Blissful silence reigned for some time…and then a scream rent the fabric of the Seam. He was shocked to realize that the scream was his own.

His vision had gone blank; that, or his mind simply didn't have the capacity to allow him vision due to the overwhelming flow of information that Umbraz had shared with him. His sight was only now beginning to return to the surreal colors and brightness of the Seam.

He was on his back, lying still at the foot of Umbraz's looming figure. It had seemed as though a millennium had passed, but as he looked over and down the steps, Reza, Terra, and Yozo still remained blurry figures in the same position as they had before contact with Umbraz. He briefly wondered where Nomad was.

He sat up and noticed how freely he had performed the motion. Moving in the Seam realm always came with difficulty for denizens from his world.

Visitors there were either bound up completely, like Reza and the others, or if they could move, it was as though moving through a torrent of viscous liquid. Now, he moved freely, as though he were back on Una—no, more easily than that even. It was as though simply by willing himself to sit up, the action was taken for him.

He wished to stand.

A moment later, he was standing.

What had Umbraz done to him? Thinking through the billions of thoughts that had been poured into his mind was futile. He couldn't pinpoint a single thing that may have explained what he had learned or how he had been adapted to traverse the Seam so effortlessly, but something within the flood of information had bestowed upon him a fundamental understanding of the mysterious and dangerous realm that so few had accessed.

He had come here for a reason, he reminded himself: to stop Umbraz from collapsing their realm. It was almost an afterthought to him now after what he had seen and learned just by coming in contact with Umbraz.

He looked back to Reza. She and the others gave him a renewed purpose—determination to finish what they had worked so hard to accomplish. It was possible that he could provide them resolution on the matter.

He looked up to Umbraz. Umbraz returned his gaze, smiling knowingly.

Malagar wished to converse with the god—to plea for the plight of his kind's world and existence.

No sooner than he wished it did Umbraz reach out to Malagar, offering him its hand.

Malagar raised his hand, but hesitated. Somehow he knew accepting that hand of energy and thought would change his existence forever. He would no longer be Malagar. He would no longer be a haltia, or mortal for that matter. To accept this union would mean absorbing all that Umbraz was, and vice versa, he himself would be absorbed into *the everything* that was this entity.

He looked back to Yozo, then Terra, then finally to Reza. He wondered if they'd ever understand. He knew they wouldn't. Regardless, it was what he knew he had to do.

He placed his hand in Umbraz's.

His mind opened, and Umbraz embraced him, the two melding every fiber and thought until they were one.

Chapter Thirty-Four
Final Light

The chaos of the Seam tear ended, and Reza fell forward, kneeling on the steps to catch her breath.

She looked back at Terra and Yozo, who seemed to be recovering from the same jarring event just as she was. Then...she saw Nomad lying lifeless on the steps beside her.

It hadn't been just a bad dream. Nomad was gone. With how dire his condition had been when she had arrived, she wasn't even sure if a healing would have saved him. Both him and her could have died in the attempt—but she had been willing to *make that attempt!*

He had refused her blessing, and for some reason...she had honored his request. Now she was torn up inside, the moment having slipped through her fingers so quickly. She knew that she'd forever be second guessing her decision.

"Reza," Yozo said, a bloodied hand raising to point her attention towards the brazen dishes filled with Seam pearls. They had begun to shake and rattle in the brass pan. Then, one by one, they shot up and smashed against the looming obsidian statue, liquifying and coating its surface.

Shimmering liquid rushed in through doors, windows, and cracks in the stonework, blasting in to cling to the statue. The spray of pearlescence swirled all about them, pelting them like a torrential rain.

The three huddled and shielded themselves from the thunderous and painful assault which continued for some time. Like a gravitational well that only attracted Seam residue, the statue had been completely transformed from black obsidian to a living surface of swirling pearlescence.

"We're...too late," Reza breathed, getting to her feet, completely defeated by the sight. "We've failed."

She felt a hand rest on her shoulder, then an arm squeezed tight around her waist.

"We did all we could," Terra whispered in her ear.

The clang of steel on stone startled them, and they looked back just in time to see Yozo collapse upon the steps.

"Yozo!" Reza called. The man was completely covered in blood and his chest wound gaping now that he no longer held it tight.

"Can you save him?" Terra asked as Reza gathered the man in her arms.

She looked over his condition and answered uneasily, "He's in bad shape. I'm not sure..."

She looked to Terra, hoping for help, but she knew Terra had no training in healings.

Her eyes slipped to Nomad's empty body. Gods how badly she had wished she could have saved him. If he had only allowed her to help....

She wouldn't let that chance slip again, not for a friend that still lived. She was terrible at healings, but she was his only shot at life now.

"I don't know what comes next," Reza said to Terra, "but be on your guard with whatever comes out of that statue, Terra. I may not be conscious to protect you. You'll have to rely on Elendium for that."

Terra nodded and knelt next to Reza for support as she began her blessing.

She placed her hand upon his chest and closed her eyes, beginning a prayer to Sareth.

Reza shook violently. A sudden jolt of pain from Yozo to her lit up her system. She began to worry that she had jumped into a healing that she was not adequate enough to handle on her own.

Though her eyes were closed, she could tell that something in the room was lighting up, brighter and brighter. A wind whipped all about her and a horrible howling sounded from what seemed like all directions.

None of that mattered to her, however. She was numb to sight and sound, her healing absorbing her attention and consuming her energy.

Terra held her arm in front of her face to protect herself from the swirling cyclone in the room. She yelled Reza's name and huddled next to her and Yozo, but both were unconscious and did not respond. She lay over them to try and protect them from the braziers and candle stands rolling then crashing to the ground and flying down the steps.

The wind blew itself out all at once. The strobing light from the statue blinked one last time before going out, leaving her in darkness as the braziers rattled and clanged down the steps.

And then…all was silent, and all was still. A solitary candle was lit by someone at the top of the stairs.

A face, illuminated softly by the candle, smiled down at Terra. She stood, looking up to see that the statue of Umbraz that had been behind the figure, had vanished. The figure was bathed in a sheen of colorful oils, which even in the dim light of the candle, Terra could tell were exotically disparate. Its face appeared to be carved out of marble—perfect, inviting, enigmatic...otherworldly. She was entranced by its gaze that seemed deeper than all the forgotten seas.

It stepped down, making its way to her with something beyond grace. The flow of light reflecting from its countenance ran like a stream out into the tower chamber. Any surface the reflected light splashed on left a soft, permanent light. Soon, most of the room had been lit aglow, and the nude figure stood before Terra who was the only one conscious to behold the glory of the luminous visitor.

It stood there in front of her for some time. She dared not look away. Her every thought was pulled towards it. She was hypnotized by its presence—its skin, curves and angles, its slow movements, its eyes...everything about it identified it as something hewn from the eternities.

"Beautiful—" Terra finally breathed out, trembling slightly as she wiped tears away from her cheek.

It reached out for her, touching its pastel-toned hand gently to Terra's cheek. The contact flooded foreign sensations through her. Like an ocean invading an inlet, Terra had no control over the waves of feelings and thoughts that the being was drowning her in. Images flashed through her mind. Only once she had fallen to the ground, away from the eternal's touch, did she come back to reality.

"Too much—" she stuttered, holding a warding hand up to the being.

It recognized Terra's distress and waited for her to recover, gazing at her with candle in hand.

She was reeling, her head spinning with all sorts of unprocessed—and likely un-processable—information from the contact. She attempted to catch her breath, but the strange feelings that had entered her still crawled beneath her skin.

She rocked herself, eyes closed, and mumbled a prayer to Elendium. At first, she was unconscious of the child's prayer that she frantically recited. After a moment, she recognized the rhythm of the hymn that she hummed, and she began to speak the words more clearly and with deliberate intent.

Elendium had been distant from her in recent times—ever since the war with Sha'oul and his arisen army. He had not come to her in comfort often, and when he had heard her prayers and graced her with his spirit, it was faint and quite muted from times in the past.

As she raised her voice heavenwards, she began to feel a warmth, contrasting with the cold presence of the other dimensional figure standing before her.

A soft ray of light filtered down through the vaulted windows high above, ever so gently illuminating her in prayer upon the chapel steps. Tears fell down her face once more—different tears—tears solely formed out of an overflowing of love.

The being gazed curiously upon the scene, patiently watching as the hymn came to a close, and the light from the heavens slowly dimmed and finally departed.

Terra opened her eyes, a new calmness and assurance in her features. She knew what Elendium needed of her now, and she knew he would be with her through the worst of it.

The being extended its hand once more, its smile never changing. Terra reached up, grasping its pale blue hand.

Her eyes squinted shut as a fresh flood of foreign emotions and experiences rushed through her soul, weaving through every fiber of her being. All the while, she could see the entity's visage as clear as day. She could more than see it, she *became* it. Every contour melded with her own visage, swirling together in a beyond intimate cycle.

Its eyes were galaxies deep and were the last thing to inhabit her psyche. They blazed with intense breadth and reach of infinite potential existences. They burned through her until they were sharing eyes.

Umbraz, Terra knew now, was not *Umbraz*, or anything any of them, the prophet and White Cloaks included, thought it was. She wasn't even sure if one could describe its presence as a singular entity. It was a conglomeration of many things, she could sense, though how to define those *things* escaped her.

The words of her hymnal came to her again, and she sang for the being. Elendium's presence washed through her very essence. The two soaked in the song's context and melody as the spirit lifted their souls.

The heavenly light of Elendium shone through the melding beings, and Terra could tell the entity had been excited by the new divine presence. Their souls mingled in the bath of radiance for some time before the song concluded.

The tides of Umbraz washed away, and slowly, Terra returned to herself.

"I see," Umbraz spoke, its first words in this new dimension. Its voice was lyrical—colorful in nature. "A new perspective you and your friend Malagar have given me."

Terra looked around the dimly lit room. "You have spoken with him? Where is he?"

Umbraz's smile almost seemed maternal as it placed a hand over its chest. "With me."

Terra wondered at the implications of Umbraz's words.

"He joined of his own free will." Umbraz held up a calming hand, and a warm sedative effect fell over Terra at the gesture. "All his life, he had been drawn to the place you call the Seam. He wishes to explore it further with me, together as one."

"So…you plan to return to the Seam? You will leave Una?"

"I will. I was drawn here by the many desires that had conjured me into being. At first, I only gravitated towards your realm out of a law of thought attraction. At first, I was a reflection of those that called for me. Coming closer to your people—as more came to *think* of me, however, things became clearer. Communing with Malagar and now you has shown me the delicate nature of your existence, and the wonder of it. Your pocket of life in the expanse may be small, but it is vibrant and unique. I do not wish to disrupt its song now that I understand its melody."

Terra couldn't hold back tears at the declaration. Of all the results of their efforts, of all the things Umbraz could have manifested as in their realm, she could have thought of much worse outcomes.

"I know your thoughts," Umbraz admitted. "You wonder what would have transpired without your intervention—without Malagar's intervention."

"Yes, I do," Terra admitted, still fearing the all-powerful being that stood before her.

"Your fears of what I might have been are not unfounded. I am, to this realm, what you and others *think* I am. I am made up of *your* sensibilities, *your* thoughts, *your* focus. Until Malagar tipped the scale of influence, perhaps Prophet Yunus and his followers would have determined my demeanor upon arrival."

Terra thought on Umbraz's words. She could only imagine what worldview it had inherited from Yunus and his cult.

"Prophet Yunus once held belief in my own faith. I hope you do not have the wrong impression of Elendium from him. Elendium is a good god, I know it."

"You have shown me his beauty, child." Umbraz smiled. "He is a worthy father, rest assured, and he will return to your realm in strength soon, in part owing to you."

Terra returned Umbraz's smile, feeling a warmth not just from Umbraz's presence, but from her heavenly father.

"Change has come to your world on my account," Umbraz admitted, a tinge of sorrow on its brow. "Before more alteration takes place, I need to return to the Seam." It gazed into her soul a final time. "Farewell, Terra, daughter of Elendium. May you and your kin continue to sing your hymn for all to hear."

Fresh tears came to her as Umbraz turned and walked back up the steps. The light upon its skin fluttered off, like butterflies taking silent flight, leaving nothing behind as they slowly dematerialized before Terra's eyes.

The room grew dim, the solitary candle on the ground the only light. She looked up through the arched windows and saw pale light from the moon and stars in the night sky and smiled.

"Terra," a soft voice came from behind her. She looked back to find Reza squinting and rubbing her eyes, sitting up weakly. "What was that light?"

"It was…" she said, considering where to start. "…the departure of a friend."

Chapter Thirty-Five
The Morning After

"I don't understand…" Fin whispered in the dark of the chapel room but left the thought unfinished.

Reza, sitting next to him, closed her eyes and bowed her head, knowing exactly how he felt and knew there to be no fulfilling answer for either of them—not then and there at least.

Fin and Freya had shown up in the tower chapel room with their troops soon after Reza had come around. Freya had helped Terra and Yozo down from the synagogue and had overseen to the recovery of Nomad and Cavok's bodies. The loss of both men was a terrible blow for all present, none more so than for their closest mates, Fin and Reza.

They had asked for privacy to have a moment to mourn, which Freya readily allowed. Reza knew there would be plenty more to do that night. Someone would need to convince the remaining military and government that the fight was over. They needed to begin to install a temporary leadership for Alumin and begin its reconstruction. She, however, was handing *that* duty over to others, as was Fin. That day, they came to terms with their friends' sacrifices and prepared themselves to walk out of that building alone, never to be graced with their partners' presences again.

"Ya know, I always thought those two would outlast us all. They had both been through more than most of us and still came through the other side in the end." Fin smiled, thinking warmly of the strength and resilience both showed in life. "I hadn't even given thought to the chance that our chats earlier today would have been our last…"

"I know," Reza comforted, rubbing Fin's back as it was his turn to dip his head to deal with the forthcoming tears.

"I've never known anyone like those two," Reza sighed. "There are few people you can ever feel completely comfortable with—people you can trust to let your guard down for. They both were that for me. The bond that tied us together…no one will ever replace what we had."

Fin sniffed, looking off to the walls of the tower that still faintly glowed from Umbraz's presence like flickering fireflies. He chuckled suddenly as the image of Nomad in the desert ruins the first day they had met came to mind.

"Nomad came into our lives out of nowhere. You were so against him tagging along those first few days," Fin reminisced, looking back to Reza, who smiled as she recalled the time. "He sure found his way into our hearts quick."

"Aye, that he did," Reza agreed.

"So loyal and selfless," Fin added, thinking on the memory of the man for a few moments more. "I always felt that he must have been shown a great deal of love and then lost it before he met us. Only reason I could see him sticking with us through thick and thin like he had. He knew the value of such a connection, or perhaps, the possibilities of being meaningful to someone in their lives."

Reza's throat hurt too much to offer words in return.

"And Cavok. He was my brother for all intents and purposes. Growing up on the streets of Rochata-Ung. Much of that time we only had each other to rely on. He saved my life more times than I can count. Never been apart for any real amount of time, me and him.

"Going to miss that man," Fin said, his voice wavering as sorrow started to overcome him. "Not really sure what I'm going to do without him—"

Reza had lost her voice long before, and she leaned into Fin as the two sat huddled on the stairs, comforting each other in silence as the morning sun began to rise once more across the Crowned Kingdoms.

Chapter Thirty-Six
The End of a Chapter

"May their souls find safe harbor in whatever may come next," Yozo said, placing a puck of Ko on Nomad's monument. Presenting Nomad's sword before him, he bowed, said a silent prayer, and tucked the sword beside his own in his sturdy cloth belt.

Fin and Reza had paid their respects to Cavok, Malagar, and finally to Nomad's monument. Now, the three friends took a seat in the crowded graveyard, reflecting upon their lost loved ones.

Leaders of the resistance had set aside that day to honor and lay to rest the many fallen soldiers in the war against Umbraz and his followers. Chief among the fallen heroes being acknowledged was Cavok of the Southern Sands, and the one known as Nomad, or Kazuhiro Kasaru to his own people far to the East. Though none but Terra had a good understanding of the haltia Malagar Zaval's ultimate sacrifice or fate, he was also included amongst the deceased. Terra supposed, in a practical sense, he had departed their realm, and in that way, had moved on like all the other's that had lost their lives in the war for liberation.

Many from Alumin, Rediron, and even haltia from the Silver Crowns, had attended the service. It was a much needed somber and restful day in the inevitable string of hectic and charged following weeks for the leadership of the various kingdoms since Umbraz's coming. For that one day, talk of the continuing fires of war, though greatly diminished after the grave defeat for the northern kingdoms in Alumin, was kept to a minimum, and the victorious kingdoms of Rediron and Silver Crowns took a moment to appreciate their victory against such great odds.

"I suppose it's time," Fin finally said, breaking the silence.

Terra, having split off from the group earlier to pay her respects to Cavok alone, finally returned just as they were about to begin navigating the crowd to the graveyard exit.

"You put in a good word with your god on Cavok's behalf?" Fin asked good-naturedly.

"I did, in fact," Terra admitted, smiling while wiping away some lingering moisture at her eyes.

"Wouldn't hurt for him to have an advocate," Fin smiled, remembering the trouble the two had gotten in throughout their lives together.

Terra shook her head in disagreement. "He's a brave and noble spirit. He'll be taken care of in the hereafter, be it with Elendium or some other shepherd of souls."

"Speaking of Elendium, what do you plan to do now? Your church has been decimated and dragged through the worst of scandals. I don't see how any followers would remain after Prophet Yunus' heretical reign," Reza asked as they began meandering along the green path.

Terra thought a moment on the question, finally coming to a decision on the matter. "I believe I'll stay here in Alumin for some time to fix Prophet Yunus' influence upon the land. There are faithful followers of Elendium, I know that without a doubt. They just need to hear a true servant's voice to come out and worship him once more."

"A monumental task," Reza warned, worried for her friend.

"One that Elendium will assist me with and ensure that I succeed in," Terra answered, completely confident in her abilities. "It has been many generations since we've had a prophetess lead the church. I intend to organize the remaining faithful members and lead them back to the truth of the father."

"Bede would be proud." Fin smiled, placing his arm over her shoulder.

"I agree," Reza nodded. She saw a new strength and sureness about the young woman she had not noticed before.

"Where will you start?" Yozo asked. "To preach to former Umbraz followers would be a dangerous task."

"Yes, but one that must be done. They deserve a chance at repentance and redemption," Terra said. Giving the question more thought, she added, "I suppose I will begin with visiting the synagogue. The Rediron army reportedly cleared the grounds of all remaining personnel. Perhaps I'll see about calling a town meeting there, open to any who wish to support and help repair the sacred grounds. We could also hold a few sermons dedicated to Elendium. I have no doubt the true believers will be quick to return to his house of worship now that the apostates have been driven from his house."

"This is a big task. You may need protection," Yozo said. He knew that not all zealots had been apprehended in the chaos of the night of their assault.

"Elendium will be my protection," Terra replied.

The group seemed torn. They were happy for her new determined vision of her faith's future, but also pragmatically worried for her safety.

"All the same, if you would allow, I will accompany you as you survey the synagogue." She was weary at first, but Yozo added, "Perhaps I can lend a hand with repairs as well. I am handy with that sort of thing."

"I was headed over there next," Terra finally acquiesced. "Would you be ready to visit the grounds now, or shall I wait for you there?"

"We'll head over now," Yozo agreed, bowing his head, then gave a casual salute to Fin and Reza as he walked off with Terra.

"Come and see us when you can," Terra called back to the couple, waving goodbye.

"We'll catch up with you both later," Fin agreed, figuring it best for Yozo to have a duty to keep him occupied and useful.

"Well that was unexpected," Fin whispered once Terra and Yozo were headed off down the street to the synagogue.

Reza shook her head. "She's grown up on us, Fin. I knew she was ready to head out on her own this last time we traveled together. She's a girl no longer."

Fin reluctantly nodded. "I'm glad Yozo decided to go with her. Maybe they can keep each other out of trouble for a while."

"Reza, Fin," a deep voice called over the crowd. The two looked back to see Johnathan and his father, King Waldock, making their way towards them.

"Ah." Fin bowed. "King Waldock—"

"Up, up. No need to bow to us here," King Waldock exclaimed, then gave the statement a second thought. "Though, if it were before dignitaries within my kingdom, then yes, I would expect you to follow the standard—"

This time, Johnathan was the one to cut his father off mid-sentence. "Father. They were headed out. Let's not keep them over-long."

"Yes, I suppose you're right, son," the king acknowledged, placing a hand upon his son's shoulder. "We wished to thank you two. We would have perished to the black and golden blade soon after our first meeting if you had not advised us to seek refuge within Rediron country. You helped us to save what was left of my people. And that…means more to me than you may ever know."

Seeing the uncharacteristic display of emotion, Johnathan attempted to cover for his father's broken voice and continued for him. "You both shall be commended with the highest honor our nation bestows upon servants of the state—the black star."

Johnathan handed them two unassuming pin medallions. Fin and Reza were speechless and accepted the gifts.

"Show these to any form of governance in our kingdom and you will be tended to. Any audience you wish will be granted at any state level. Only true war heroes and selfless servants who have served and saved the very fabric of the kingdom itself are ever rewarded this badge. Wear it proudly and see that you come visit Castle Blackrock once this war has died down and my father has returned to his rightful seat at the throne. We may not be in a state to properly reward you for a few years to come, but you have our word, you will be handsomely rewarded for coming to our king's aid, even when it was not required of you."

"My King, we are honored." Fin bowed with Reza following suit, both shocked to see such a different side to the Waldocks. They were genuinely touched.

"I didn't want to interrupt the ceremony," came a voice from behind them. General Seldrin stepped out and bowed his head as he entered the circle. "But I couldn't resist the chance to catch you all before I headed back to Lancasteal."

"Seldrin!" Reza exclaimed, and all but Fin were quite glad of the intrusion.

"General, I dare say my son and I were just discussing you as well," King Waldock was quick to say.

"What of, dear king?" he asked, a bit caught off guard.

"We understand that without you petitioning your government to involve themselves in this war, we may have not had the support of the Silver Crowns to help fend off the enemy. Your work at the front lines was exemplary. We wished to offer the black star to you as well, but we only have two to give out at this time. Though, perhaps it is for the best so that we might offer it to you in a proper ceremony once we take back Castle Blackrock from my wretched wife."

Seldrin was wide eyed. "You mean to return to the Black Steel kingdom? That land is still hostile to you, you must know that. Without support you would surely be cut down."

Johnathan offered to explain. "Our people and our land are still in disarray. It's unfortunate, but our own people under the direction of Queen Sabat, have been a key player in the enemy's corner. We have word that if we march upon Castle Blackrock now, they are in no state to repel an assault. We'll be taking our Kingsmen and marching out on the morrow to do just that. We'll finally take back our lands and see that our people are provided with just direction and guidance. There is much to repair and a great work ahead of us."

"Still, though your Kingsmen are commendable fighters—exemplary in fact—even just a pocket of a few hundred reserve soldiers the Queen may be hiding deep in Black Steel borders could prove disastrous for your campaign."

"We must take that risk. Every moment she holds the crown and commands our people is a moment that tarnishes our people's name and livelihoods. We need to put an end to this war, once and for all."

Seldrin rubbed his chin, understanding of Johnathan's and the king's sentiments, but not sure that was the best move for the Waldocks. "I was to return home with my archers and riders. We've seven hundred strong in our ranks. Perhaps we shall divert and accompany your Kingsmen to Castle Blackrock instead. If it turns out that we are not needed, fine, but if we are, let us camp with your troops. Who knows, though Umbraz is said to have absconded this realm, his cult will threaten all the peoples of the Crowned Kingdoms for years to come. We need to pull together in the face of such a communal threat. Let us hope they have not seeded your countryside in your absence. If they have, they'll face both haltia arrows as well as Waldock spear tips."

"Your words hearten me," the king replied, his gruff voice once again threatening to break. "We would be honored to share camp once more with haltia."

"Thank you, King Waldock, for this honor," Reza said during the pause, wishing to allow the upperclassmen to talk out the details together. "We need to be departing. We will be sure to visit your kingdom once things settle down."

"See that you do," Johnathan replied heartily.

"It was an honor fighting shoulder to shoulder with you," Fin offered.

"Safe travels," Seldrin said, torn between wishing to say more to Reza but still having details to go over with the king. "Visit me in Lancasteal someday, will you?"

"I'll be sure to do that." Reza waved to the group and led Fin by the hand to the cemetery's rose archway exit.

"Just so you know," Fin whispered in Reza's ear as they walked out onto the street, "if you ever do visit Lancasteal, I'm coming with you."

Reza swatted him away, still not approving of Fin's overprotectiveness towards the haltia General.

"Fin," another familiar voice called from the other side of the cemetery hedges.

The couple halted, sighing at another hold up.

Reid, along with the ever-present Morgan at his side, walked through the rose archway. Morgan had the trained eyes of a veteran bodyguard, watching everyone and no one all at once. Reid wore a brimmed hat today, with no regal garb, but Fin noticed his old marshal trench and outfit. He held a thin cigar between his lips, and took a puff once before approaching.

His drag of smoke cost him as Freya, with Revna and Kaia following close behind, made their way past him, not recognizing the king in his commoner's clothes.

"Ah, Reza. There you are," Freya greeted, stepping up to her. She patted her and took her in for a brief embrace.

Reid, behind the group of women now, caught eyes with Fin and motioned to speak with him alone off to the side.

"Oh, King Reid! Sorry, did we interrupt?" Revna said, noticing the mix-up.

"No, no. You're fine. I'll grab Fin's ear though if you don't need him. I'll catch up with Reza later, perhaps at Donovin's?" he said, referring to the famous Alumin pub.

"Perhaps we should join you. They have a rather dark, rich stout there, and an amber that I am fond of," Freya said, happy for the opportunity to have a drink with the king.

Reid held Freya's eyes for a moment, taking a drag of his cigar before replying, "That does sound appealing. Why don't we head over there now as a group?"

"There's no time like the present," Freya said, making eyes at the soft-spoken king as he tipped his hat to her, then started off down the street, leading the way.

"Reza, Fin, you're joining us, aren't you?" Kaia asked as Reid and Freya made their way to the pub, the two seeming to have forgotten about everything but each other for the moment.

"We'll meet you there," Reza said, smiling at the group of disparate friends getting to know each other outside of the battle zone for the first time.

"Go on. Save us a seat," Fin urged Kaia and shooed her along to catch up with Morgan, Freya, and Revna.

"Almost like a dream, seeing them all together." Reza sighed as they watched Kaia running to catch up to the puff of smoke down the busy street.

"Aye," Fin agreed. "I know you've known Revna longer than I, but I remember a time in Dolinger Crags in the Southern Sands where she and I were giving Sha'oul what for. Brave woman, that one. Seems like a lifetime ago."

Reza could tell Fin was having a moment, strolling through old memories. She found his hand and held it comfortingly.

"And Reid..." he continued, lost in thought. "When we first met, we were playing a game of whits. For a good while there, I was wondering if I'd have to *off* the man. Mind you, he was likely thinking of doing the same to me."

Reza squeezed his hand.

"I don't know," he said at length. "Like you said, it all seems like a dream now, all these different lives coming together so naturally."

The sobering moment struck them both as they held hands in silence, taking in the view of the city.

"Reid and Freya are definitely going home to the same bed tonight," Reza said, trying her best to keep a straight face.

"Yeah, I think you're right about that one." Fin gave a genuine chuckle at her irreverent observation.

He put an arm around her and pulled her close and the two slowly made their way to the pub, reminiscing on their adventures with their comrades, especially those that they would not be sharing a drink with until their walk on Una had ended.

Chapter Thirty-Seven

Farewell to an Old Friend

Though only a few weeks had passed since Umbraz's defeat, the Crowned Kingdoms had been a busy place alight with news, mostly positive from Reza's perspective. The fires of war had been mostly doused by the victory in Alumin, and now, even the embers were dying out.

King Waldock, with the aid of both Silver Crowns and Rediron support, had returned to the heart of Black Steel country, deposing the Mad Queen Sabat and sending her into exile across the border to the Ishari Republic. The people of Black Steel welcomed the change, and life in the northern kingdom began to turn towards licking their wounds and recovering from the ravages of war. A time of mourning and renewal had begun.

Alumin reestablished a city council, with the military leaders of each nation determining those council members who would oversee the restructuring and administrative duties for the interim period of transition.

Kaia had been appointed as the representative between West Perch and Alumin city office and was given a senior position among the board.

Terra had also been recognized by the state as the leading figure of the Elendium religious organization, which was publicly dissociated from the cult of Umbraz.

The two, with their new positions of influence, had been able to make real headway in seeing that the synagogue dedicated to Elendium had undergone repairs and that faithful worshipers were given sanctuary and respite in the house of prayer.

Though the Golden Crowns army had retreated after the defeat at Alumin, the kingdom had sent word of their official withdrawal from the Crowned Kingdoms alliance. None knew if their secession would remain permanent or the lasting effects it would have upon the people, but none on either side had pressed the point as the wounds from the war were still tender and none were interested in further conflict.

West Perch was reestablished, and the damage done to Freya's people—*Reza's people*—was being addressed. Freya's strong spirit had lifted the hearts of her sisters in arms and Revna had chosen to stay on during the period of healing, a presence Freya greatly appreciated. So valued was her talent and heart that she was ordained High Priestess and was asked to remain as delegate to help rebuild and renew relationships between both West Perch and High Cliffs Monastery.

Reza, Fin, and Yozo had spent a great many days with Terra and Kaia in Alumin. Reza had finally worked up the courage to tell the two women how proud she was of them, having seen such remarkable growth from both in taking the first steps down their own path so courageously.

With promises of reunions, Reza, Fin, and Yozo had set out to Castle Sauvignon in Rediron upon Reid's request, who wished to formally recognize and reward their war efforts.

Upon entering Canopy Glen, Fin had suggested they pay a visit to the farmer James, who had hosted them several months earlier. They had stayed the night and caught up with the older gentleman and his son, with Yozo giving another swordplay lesson to the youth in return for their board for the night.

On the morrow, a whisper in town had made the rounds that the famed heroes of the war were visiting, and the group received a visit from a familiar face.

Her saren-white tabard stood out on the backdrop of green rolling hills the farm village was known for as she made her way towards the streambank where Fin, Reza, and Yozo were resting.

"Alva?" Reza was more than a little surprised to see her battlesister there.

"Reza, thank Sareth the town guards spoke true," Alva said, coming down the grassy bank to the group by the brook.

"What are you doing here?" Reza asked, meeting her halfway. "I thought for sure you would have accompanied Lanereth back to Jeenyre by now."

"Surely I would have if her health hadn't dropped off like it did."

"She's not faring well? She's still here in Canopy Glen?"

"You need to come and visit her, Reza," Alva replied, tugging on Reza's hand to lead them back up the bank.

They wasted no time in returning to Lanereth's chamber. The mayor had known of her status and had insisted on providing Alva and Lanereth free stay at his own estate in the guest wing. He had even sent word to High Cliffs Monastery of lady Lanereth's condition; they had in turn sent a small caravan to transport her back as she was not well enough to ride horseback of her own power.

Alva explained all of this as they entered the guest wing of the mayor's estate, and that the caravan of three sisters had just arrived in town a night before Reza had. They were preparing to leave that day when she received word that Reza had just arrived.

They stopped outside Lanereth's door and Alva held Reza's hand as she explained. "I'll fetch Bethany and the others and give you some time to speak with Lanereth alone.

Fin, catching the hint, offered for him and Yozo to tag along to help the other sarens with packing.

"Fin," Reza said, catching him before he was off. "Make sure to send word to King Reid that our visit will be delayed."

He nodded and the three soon left Reza alone in the hallway as she gathered her courage and knocked on her matron's door.

"Come," came a frail voice from within.

Reza slowly turned the handle and opened the door.

Her matron was thinner than last she had seen her, and even then, she had been at an unhealthy weight.

"Oh, Reza." The senior saren smiled. "So good to see you safe. I had heard word after the war that you had survived. I made Alva check into it—"

Her thin voice trailed off into a series of weak coughs. Reza approached her bedside.

"What's wrong, Lanereth?" Reza asked, holding onto the woman's gaunt hand. "You've been getting worse each time I've seen you since…"

Reza struggled with putting a finger on when it had all begun to go downhill for the woman. The last few years had been so chaotic.

"Since I escaped the Planes of Ash," Lanereth filled in for her.

"What happened to you there?" Reza asked, realizing that even though it had been such a turning point for her mentor, it was the one subject she had refused to speak of with her or anyone else that she knew of.

"That place…aged me, Reza," Lanereth said, looking blankly at the wood ceiling. "I may have contracted some disease—some…*filth* from that hellish pit. My body…it wishes to give up, no matter how willful my spirit remains. I don't have that much longer."

The room was silent. Reza was speechless.

Lanereth struggled through a coughing fit once more. After catching her breath, she announced, "Perhaps what I wish for is to see Jeenyre one last time. If I can last that long, that would be enough."

"We can do that. I'll come with you," Reza was quick to offer.

For once in her life, Lanereth didn't contest Reza. Instead, she placed her hand on Reza's and patted it. "I was hoping for one last trip with you, Reza Malay. Here. We'll have time to talk on the ride," she said, grunting as she sat up in bed. "Help me up. I need to get dressed for the road. Alva and the others have been waiting on you to get headed out."

Fin and Yozo helped the other sarens with preparations. Before late afternoon, the caravan was gathered and on the road heading South to Green Cove, which would then lead them to Jeenyre.

The nights were still cold, and Reza slept with Lanereth in the fold-out cot of the coach to keep her warm. Even with the priestess Bethany's magic to warm the coach's interior, it was a struggle to keep the matron's spirit lively and the flesh responsive. Her health was flagging, and each day on the trail the group silently was coming to terms with the grim possibility that they might not be able to deliver their dear High Priestess to her destination.

One night, a little ways past Green Cove, they decided to break camp just before the river crossing as they knew fording the stream would take a good effort. They would save the hardship for the following morning.

Fin and Yozo had set up a campfire for the group, and Bethany and the others had prepared dinner and taken care of the team of horses for the evening. All were quiet as they heard Lanereth's barely audible coughs within the coach getting fainter and fainter as the evening wore on.

Reza finally came out of the coach as night came on. Approaching Alva, she whispered a few things into her ear. Alva nodded her understanding. Reza met eyes with Fin. No words were exchanged, but from her forlorn expression, words were not needed. They all knew Lanereth would soon see Mother Sareth.

Reza returned to the coach, and as she entered, she heard Alva's voice produce an angelic note. Bethany and the others joined in the hymn, singing into the cold, starry night to comfort their matron in her time of need.

"I remember the day you wandered into my life," Lanereth spoke, her voice merely a whisper.

Reza held her matron's hand in silence, allowing her time to catch her breath between sentences.

"I can recall, as clear as day, the look in your eyes—*a burning fierceness*." She smiled warmly and gave a laugh, thinking of the moment again. "I knew you were going to be trouble from the very first moment that we locked eyes."

Reza's grip tightened as Lanereth's laxed. She struggled to continue.

"But I also knew, Reza, that someday you were going to do great things in this world. That you were going to have the will and strength to make real change come to pass."

She reached her frail hand up and brushed Reza's hair to the side, gazing upon her daughter's face one last time.

"I am proud of you, dear," she said. Reza could hold her tears back no longer.

Lanereth's voice failed her now, completely spent. She mouthed "*I love you…*" before falling into slumber in Reza's arms.

Her soul left her body and mingled with the angelic voices that rose up past the firmament to their heavenly mother.

Chapter Thirty-Eight

Eulogy

"She was a mother to us all," Alva said at Lanereth's memorial in the Jeenyre Monastery chapel. "One we were each so fortunate to have been watched over by throughout the years. Now she goes to our mother Sareth. Into your arms, O mother, we commend her spirit."

Reza, Fin, and Yozo were seated at the front pew. Each knew the proud saren well in life, and each were struggling with their emotions having been so intimately present at her sorrowful passing.

The service was somber. Many of the sarens owed so much to the woman. Not a dry eye remained by the time the service had ended. Lanereth had lived a full life, and her influence as a High Priestess—as a mother to a whole monastery for several years—had endeared her presence in the annals of their people's history books, and in the tender memories of those still living.

After the service was over, some sarens stayed and sang hymns, others returned home, but Reza, Nomad, and Yozo walked the monastery grounds aimlessly and in silence, allowing their feelings to wander freely.

There was a heatwave that week, which had thawed a great deal of snow from the Jeenyre countryside. As Reza led Fin and Yozo through the orchard, the budding grass and flowers were a warm and welcomed sight to an otherwise heavy emotional day.

"I wonder what *really* became of Malagar," Reza said, taking a seat on the bench overlooking the Jeenyre mountain range. "Is he still alive out there in the Seam with Umbraz?"

Yozo propped himself against a tree while Fin came to sit on the low stone wall next to Reza.

"When it comes to the Seam, who can really say? The place is an enigma, even to our realm's gods," Fin replied, looking out over the whitecapped mountain spires of the vast countryside below.

"Terra may be the only one to have even the faintest understanding of the gist of it," Reza admitted after a quiet moment, reflecting on their lost friend.

"Good man, that one," Fin offered, paying his respects to the haltia. "His sacrifice likely saved us all from going down a very disastrous path."

"Malagar, Cavok, Nomad—they all paid the ultimate cost for us—" Reza said reverently, her voice trembling.

"I…" Yozo started. The others turned their attention to the quiet man. It was clear he struggled to find words for the subject. "I made a promise to Nomad—to Hiro—the morning of our last mission. He told me, if he should fall in battle, to retrieve his sword and see that it was returned to Silmurannon to rest with our ancestor's blades in the Hall of Forbearers."

"That's…halfway across the world," Fin noted. "You wouldn't be returning from that trip."

"I would not," Yozo agreed. He could tell the news had caught the two off guard. "I desire to reconnect with my people. My bones have yearned for the soil of my land for a long time now."

"When do you plan to make the journey?" Fin asked.

"I set out tonight. The moons are aligned. It is a good time to travel."

Both Reza and Fin were speechless. Neither had seen their friend's departure coming. In some ways, with the sudden news, they were feeling the emptiness of his presence already, even though he still stood before them in the orchard.

"I should gather my things," he finally said, breaking the silence. "The moon is already visible high in the sky. Fortune favors an early start."

"Yozo," Fin said, catching the man by the elbow as he turned to head to his quarters. Fin gave him a long look, each searching each other's eyes, remembering their strange and fate-filled exchanges. Both were from completely different backgrounds and cultures. Different mindsets and ideologies guided their internal compasses. Even so, their souls had found comfort and stability in each other's presence. They had helped each other through a pivotal time of each of their lives.

"I'll never forget you, mate," Fin said, a knot in his throat preventing him from saying anything more than "Stay safe out there."

Yozo smiled, holding the back of Fin's head, touching foreheads. "You righted my sails, Fin. No man has believed in me like you have." It was Yozo's turn for a well of emotion. "Never change, friend."

He released him, smiling and waving to Reza, and then he walked out of their lives, embarking on a path that would take years of his life. A path that would lead him home.

——•◎•——

Yozo had not misread the moons—the night sky was lit up brighter than Fin ever remembered it. He took to walking the grounds once more, alone this time, after all but the midnight guard had retired to their homes.

The air was crisp and chill, but with no breeze he walked the orchard without the need of his heavy coat.

Yozo had slipped away off down the mountain trail leading to Castle Sephentho and beyond earlier that afternoon. Their farewells in the garden had been their last exchange. Fin wished the best for the man who had so profoundly impacted his life. He seemed in a far better headspace upon his departure than upon their first meeting. Fin was glad he, Matt, and the others had been such a positive influence in the end.

He hiked a leg up on the low stone wall at the overlook he had come to favor. The view of the grandeur of Jeenyre was unmatched. He had never come across such a majestic sight in all his travels. It held his gaze for a long while as he sat in silence, the still night sky slowly drifting on its course.

He had spoken with Cavok there, months ago. Cavok had seemed lost then, without purpose or guidance. Fin suspected Matt's death had struck him deeper than he had let on. The world had changed throughout the war for the Southern Sands, and the strong man had not taken to that change well.

The world had changed once more after the war for the Crowned Kingdoms, Fin figured. They had again lost the companionship of dear friends…

He supposed that they had gained new friends though. Reid, Kaia, Freya, and others—he suspected that their lives would intersect many more times in the following years. He'd make sure to visit the gruff, honest king soon. He had already been through a lot with Reid, and he did enjoy the man's company.

Reza would likely wish to visit Terra, Kaia, and Freya later that year as well. They all seemed to get on together naturally, which was not all that common for Reza's occasionally sharp-edged personality—though she had softened greatly since he had known her.

"Time to start moving on, big guy," Fin said, his voice leaving trails of cold smoke as he whispered to the mountains beyond. "For both of us. Rest well, Cavok…my brother."

After a few moments of silence, he got up and walked away to see if Reza slept peacefully, or if she too struggled with the difficult loss they both bore.

The ephemeral clouds wisped over the snowcapped mountain range again that night as they had for time immemorial—a primordial dance of the fleeting with the everlasting.

Chapter Thirty-Nine
New Beginnings

Fin locked eyes with Reza and signaled to the thicket of trees ahead of them. The boar was close, he knew.

He watched Reza, bow and arrow at ready, lead to the right as he went left. They needed this kill. With nothing for dinner but rabbit and potatoes the last few nights, he did not wish for another grumpy night in the cabin, just the two of them and rumbling stomachs.

He stepped lightly along the game trail, hearing a snort not too far ahead through the thicket. He readied an arrow.

As the boar rustled its snout through loose soil at the base of a tree, Fin inched into view. He had a clean shot of the beast from his angle. He waited for the boar to still.

A snap of a twig in Reza's direction alerted both Fin and the boar. Fin hesitated for a split second. The boar bolted just as the bowstring twanged. The arrow thudded inches from the boar's head into the tree trunk as the boar bolted away through the brush, making quite a ruckus as it escaped.

"Damn it all," Fin cursed, just as Reza popped her head through the bushes on the other side of the brush.

She looked at the arrow stuck in the tree trunk. "You let it get away?"

He bit his tongue, thinking better than to start hurling insults at his hunting partner. "Not as good with a bow as I am a knife."

"Use a knife then next time," Reza mumbled as she went to retrieve the arrow from the tree's base.

"Well I can't start hurling knives at a beast like that, now can I? A skull that thick and a heart that deep? I'd end up out a lot of knives and us with a forest stocked with nothing but maimed and rotting boar," Fin shot back with a huff of frustration.

"I was just joking, Fin. I'm sorry," Reza was quick to correct. She knew that her playful tone was often just as dry as her serious voice.

He took a calming breath and approached her, giving her a forgiving rub on the back as she plucked the arrow from the bark and handed it up to him.

Many weeks had passed since Lanereth's memorial and Yozo's departure. Fin and Reza had become close after things had settled down at the monastery. They had even taken up residence in an old hunting cabin in the foothills. They had supported each other, emotionally—physically. Being among the few that could truly understand the impact from all the loss they had endured in the last few years, the two had bonded and had started to work through the trauma together in the simple solitude provided by the Jeenyre wilderness.

They knew they could not stay isolated there the rest of their days, but for now, it was soothing. They would stay for a time, until they were ready to return and visit their loved ones toiling away at rebuilding the Crowned Kingdoms.

He squatted next to her as something caught his eye. He unsheathed a knife from his belt.

"Fin, I didn't mean it. You're much better than me with a bow," she said, seeing his serious expression and the flash of the blade as he stuck it in the ground. She wondered what point he was trying to prove.

He began to dig around with the blade and turned up a few black knotty lumps. They both smiled as they appreciated the welcomed find. Truffles were a rare sight indeed.

"We'll have to make a trip back up to High Cliffs Monastery, but I bet we can trade this haul for a few weeks of supplies," Fin said, uncovering a few handfuls of the large, black nuggets.

"No more rabbits and potatoes," Reza sighed thankfully.

She stood up, sensing suddenly that they were not alone.

Fin momentarily stopped brushing dirt from the black gold to see what had caught Reza's attention. He had heard nothing, and he had the better ear by a longshot.

Her gaze darted around, trying to pinpoint what indeterminate sense had demanded her attention. She held a hand up to quiet Fin before he could start asking her questions as she saw concern in his face already. She had no answers for him yet.

She walked out of the patch of vegetation they were in and meandered towards a clearing, drawn to it for no other reason than ease of traversal.

Her eye caught a shimmer of white in the clearing—something moved ahead. Reza approached cautiously until it came into view. She stopped, taken off guard from what she saw.

A young girl looked around as if lost and confused. Barefoot and wearing only a pure white night gown, the child was woefully out of place in such deep wilderness, patches of snow still covering the ground in places.

"What in the—" Fin breathed as he saw what arrested her attention.

She held a hand up to quiet him. Fin might not have heard tale of such a sight, but she had. In fact, Lanereth had reminded her just before her passing of the story of her own arrival upon Una in a similar fashion.

She took a cautious step forward.

The child didn't seem fearful of Reza, merely in a daze.

"Where did you come from, child?" Reza asked in a gentle tone.

"Mmm…I was…" The girl struggled to answer, giving Reza a look as though she was thinking through fog.

Reza got closer, kneeling down to the girl's level. Suddenly a spark of recognition flitted across her features.

"I've seen you before," she proclaimed.

"You have?"

"Are you…my mother?" the girl asked innocently, moving close, studying Reza's face more intently. She brought a hand up and brushed Reza's hair aside, gazing upon Reza's features, trying to remember the significance of the woman before her.

Reza teared up.

"Lanereth?" she mouthed.

"What's your name, child?" Fin asked, kneeling down next to them.

"I don't remember," she admitted. "I just remember walking in a bright place with mother."

"I remember your face, though. You kind of look like her," the girl added, placing a hand on Reza's cheek.

"Well," Fin said with a warm smile, seeing how taken with the girl Reza seemed. "We have to call you something other than *child*. What shall we call you?"

The girl shrugged her shoulders.

"How about—" Fin started.

"Lannie," Reza decided, taking the small hand from her face and holding it in her grasp.

"Sure, that's a fine name," Fin offered, then addressed Lannie directly. "Well, little Lannie, how about we get you warmed up by a nice warm fire. We've got rabbit and potato stew we can cook up. I'll even give you a piggyback ride there."

"My feet are cold," Lannie admitted, not waiting another moment to start clambering onto Fin's back. "And a bit hungry."

Fin chuckled as he hefted the girl up. Tucking the truffle sack in his belt to the side, he began a conversation with the child like they were simply continuing an ongoing chat between the two.

"We'll take a trip up to the sarens tomorrow. Who knows, maybe someone at High Cliffs Monastery will know where your parents are. They're mysterious folk, those sarens. Might even have a priestess able to help you with your memory there."

Reza wiped the remaining moisture from her eyes as she watched the two head off to the cabin. Never in life had she felt the love of Sareth more so than now.

She knew Fin was oblivious to the fact that the girl was a saren herself and that she had just arrived from the arms of her goddess, or that he had known the girl, at least the past incarnation of her. For now, she was too emotional to explain the situation.

It was not only their tradition, but Sareth's will that the first of their kind to greet a newly delivered saren was destined to become their matron. It was Reza's charge to take care of the reincarnation of her former matron, Lanereth.

Her heart swelled with emotions as she walked behind the chatty pair. Fin would be a fine father—and partner—she knew. He had matured a great deal from the days of their exploits in the Southern Sands, and so had she.

They had planned to return soon to the Crowned Kingdoms, to see King Reid, Kaia, Terra, Freya, and the others—but perhaps, they'd wait a little longer. There was another, older friend that needed them now more than ever. One to whom she owed a great deal. She was glad to repay her in full.

The two most important people in her life were merrily chatting away, strolling along down the forest trail, back to the warmth of their humble home.

From the Author

Thank you to everyone who has joined me on this journey through the Lands of Wanderlust series. Your interest in this world and its characters means a great deal to me. If you enjoyed Seamwalker, please consider leaving a review on Amazon and Goodreads. Your support is greatly appreciated!

Thank you for reading with me. As I wrap up the publication of this novel, I've already begun work on the next series, and I hope you'll join me for what's to come.

Visit me online for launch dates and other news at:
authorpaulyoder.com
(sign up for the newsletter)

instagram.com/author_paul_yoder
tiktok.com/@authorpaulyoder
Paul Yoder on Goodreads
Paul Yoder on Amazon

Made in United States
North Haven, CT
31 October 2024

59672290R00186